That One Regret

CARRIE ELKS

CHAPTER
One

"TAXI!"

It was pouring with rain, and every part of her was soaked. Cars passed by too fast, kicking up spray from puddles so she had to jump out of the way, and of course that's when the only free cab in New York City turned around the corner.

And a tall, suited guy – with an umbrella, damn him – stepped forward and held out his hand.

"Shit on a brick," Grace muttered, because now that she was looking properly there was clearly a line. And she'd inadvertently skipped the whole thing.

Suit guy turned around, his brow raised. Then his eyes dipped, taking in her soaking clothes and her bedraggled hair. It had been almost twenty-four-hours since she'd left Paris, where the sun had been shining on the River Seine, regret filling her heart at leaving her favorite city in springtime and now here she was, stranded in a New York deluge.

"Did you say something?" the guy asked. He touched his bearded jaw with his free hand, his brows dipping as he looked at her.

"Nope."

"I swear I heard you say shit on a brick." His lips twitched. Damn, he was handsome, if you liked that sort of thing. Dark hair, perfectly clipped. Warm blue eyes. And lips that could do things to you.

If you wanted them to. Which she didn't. Not least because she'd sworn off men for life.

Thanks Pascal.

"I said that's the trick," she lied. "To getting a cab, I mean."

The yellow car pulled up at the curbside, causing a ruckus because three other people started running toward it.

"Are you trying to get a cab?" he asked.

"Nope, just enjoying the lovely New York weather." She blinked off the droplets of rain that clung to her eyelids.

Suit guy laughed. "Take it. It's yours."

"I can't. You have first dibs," she pointed out. And so did all the others waiting in line. Who were staring at her with daggers in their eyes.

His lips twitched again. They really were good lips. The kind you could kiss, if you liked that sort of thing. Which she didn't because she'd sworn off men.

Suit guy leaned forward to open the backdoor, and she was already beating herself up for not taking him up on his offer.

"Get in," he said. "Before somebody steals it."

Alarm bells rang in her head. Sure, he was pretty, if you were into older guys, but she still wasn't getting into a cab with him. She'd watched way too many Netflix documentaries to be taken in by a good-looking face.

"It's fine." She stepped back, waving her hand. "I can wait."

He rolled his eyes. "Get in."

Handsome *and* bossy. Which would be kind of dynamite if she wasn't standing in the middle of a rainstorm, shivering because she was stupid enough not to unpack her jacket from her suitcase.

"I don't know you," she told him, and his lips twitched again. Rivulets of water were running down her neck. "We're not sharing a cab."

"I'll share it with you," the next man in line shouted at suit guy. "I don't care if you're a mass murderer."

Suit guy lifted a brow at her. He wasn't smiling anymore. He looked kind of pissed, actually, which was the effect she seemed to have on most guys nowadays.

"I wasn't planning on getting in with you," he said, and Grace immediately blushed. Somebody pushed past her and took a lunge for the cab, but suit guy blocked them admirably.

"Can you get in, please?" he asked. His voice was low, like he'd already had enough.

"Okay." Grace nodded, finally resigned to breaking the standoff. "Thank you."

He reached for her case and slid it into the cab, then reached for her hand to help her follow it. His hand was warm, dry, strong. He made sure she was inside then slammed the door shut, leaving her alone on the back seat.

"Where to?" the driver asked, turning around to look at her. When he saw how wet she was, he grimaced.

She brushed her wet hair from her face and tried to put as little of her wet behind on the chair as she could. "The Solar Hotel. Do you know it?" She should be there now, warm and dry. Would have been if she hadn't left Ella's birthday gift in Paris and had to make a quick stop to buy a replacement.

"I know it." He nodded, pulling away from the sidewalk and from her knight with a shining umbrella, who was already looking for a second cab.

She stared at him through the droplet covered window, a pang of regret pulling at her chest. Maybe she should have offered to share with him. Maybe she should have flirted with him.

Maybe – if she was Ella and didn't give a damn – she could have invited him to her hotel room. But she wasn't Ella, and she did give a damn.

And you've sworn off men for good, remember?

The driver switched the radio on and she leaned her head back on the rest before remembering how wet she was and pulled it away again.

She was home. Well, in her home country at least. After almost four years away.

And the weather felt way too much like a bad omen.

———

Walking into the hotel bar later that evening, she took a deep breath and looked around for her friends. She was over-dressed, that much was clear. She was wearing a dress she'd bought in Paris last year – black and clingy with one of those plunging necklines that only work if you're not *that* endowed (thanks genetics). It had seemed the right choice when she pulled it out of her soaking suitcase.

The clothes inside had been dry, thank goodness. Mostly thanks to the fact that she'd put everything into vacuum bags. She had a limited luggage allowance and an entire closet to bring back to the States, so she had to be resourceful.

Her two friends and their boyfriends were in the corner booth. Ella stood and waved and Grace bit down a smile at the sash that fell over her jeans-and-dress top combo.

Birthday Bish was written in silver over the satin pink sash.

That was *so* Ella.

"You made it!" Ella pushed herself out of the booth and ran across the bar area, meeting Grace halfway there. Ella hugged her close, smelling of the Hugo Boss fragrance she'd always worn during college, then stepped back and held Grace at arm's length.

"Look at you! All French and chic."

"Hardly." Grace smiled. "You should have seen me an hour ago. I was a drowned rat." Ella led her back to the table as Grace regaled her with the story of the cab stand off with the suit guy.

"You *should* have brought him back with you," Ella said as the cocktail server came to take another order. "I wouldn't have minded if you were late for my party."

"Come on." Lucy, who'd roomed with them in freshman year, rolled her eyes as soon as Ella had filled her in. "When have you ever seen Grace have casual sex?"

Grace rolled her eyes. It had been four years since graduation. She'd moved to France shortly after, yet somehow their conversations still got back to her love life.

"Maybe now's her time to sow some wild oats," Ella said. "After Pascal."

Lucy grimaced. "I heard about you and him," she said to Grace. "I'm sorry."

"It's old history." Grace opened her purse and pulled out a small gift wrapped box. "This is for you," she said to Ella, pleased to change the subject. "Happy Birthday."

As she put her purse down on the seat beside her, she felt her skin prickle. Her Great Aunt Gina always said that meant a goose was walking over your grave.

Yeah, well, the goose could get out of there. Her neck was itching now.

"Hot guy at nine o'clock," Ella whispered.

"That's not nine o'clock. It's six o'clock, dufus." Lucy sighed. "And he's looking at Grace."

"Of course he's looking at Grace. Every man in the room is. Have you seen her dress?" Ella said.

Grace looked to her right – Ella's six o'clock – and the blush in her skin deepened.

Because it was *him*. Suit guy. Standing in the hotel bar, looking even hotter than he had in the rain.

"How old do you think he is?" Lucy asked. "Thirty something? Forty?" She shook her head. "Forty's too old, right?"

Grace's eyes connected with his. She waited for him to look away, but he didn't. She could feel her pulse throb in her neck.

"Forty's fine," Ella said. "I think. What's the equation again?"

"Half his age and add seven," Lucy said. "So if he's forty, you need to be twenty-seven."

"What's two years too young? It's fine," Ella said loudly. Grace grimaced, hoping he hadn't heard.

Luckily, her friends were distracted by the server carrying their tray of drinks over and their conversation paused. The three women took their cocktails, and the two guys took their drinks.

"It doesn't matter if he's sixty or sixteen," Grace said, taking a welcome sip of her cocktail. "I'm not interested. Remember?"

She glanced up at him again. Their gazes clashed, and he smiled before looking back down at his phone.

He'd taken his jacket and tie off and rolled his sleeves up. He was leaning on the bar, a half-drunk whiskey in front of him. She wondered what brand it was, mostly because growing up, whiskey had been her life.

The barman said something to him and Suit laughed.

He had crinkle lines around his eyes. How could wrinkles be attractive? And yet they were, if you were into that kind of thing.

"Of course you're interested. You can't stop looking at him," Ella said. "And no wonder, he's gorgeous."

"I wish he'd look at me," Lucy complained and her boyfriend chuckled.

"You're attached. And anyway he's probably married,"

Grace pointed out. What guy that age and with a body like that wouldn't be? "And I'm definitely not into that kind of thing."

"I can't see a ring," Lucy said, craning her head to look.

Could she stop already? This was getting embarrassing. "That means nothing. A lot of guys don't wear them."

"Then we should ask him," Ella suggested, giving Grace a grin.

"Don't you dare." Grace widened her eyes in horror.

"Did she say *dare*?" Ella asked Lucy.

"I think she did," Lucy confirmed, her eyes sparkling.

Ugh, not this. As freshman, Dare used to be their favorite game. There was one rule – if you got dared you had to do it.

"I didn't mean it like that." She was backtracking now. They were way too old for this game.

"A dare's a dare," Ella said. "Now come on, you're single and maybe he is too. I dare you to flirt with him. Ask him if he's married."

"She won't do it," Lucy said.

"If she doesn't, I'll go ask him." Ella looked like she meant it, too. She grinned at Grace. "Come on, it's my birthday. Give us some entertainment."

Taking a long sip from her cocktail glass, Grace let out a sigh. There was no way she wanted Ella to ask him about his marital status. She knew her friend too well. She'd embarrass Grace then pull her over.

And no. That wasn't happening.

She put her glass on the table. "I'll talk to him for five minutes," she said. "And then you two have to promise to shut up about him and any other guys for the rest of the night."

Ella and Lucy exchanged glances. "You're on."

Grace stood and took a deep breath. This was going to be fine. She was used to talking to sophisticated men. It had been her job for the last few years, after all. Talking about French wine to cultured merchants, explaining the grape and the vintage, persuading them to buy crates to sell.

"Your ass looks amazing in that dress," Ella whispered. "He'll never know what's hit him."

Ugh. Here went nothing. "After this, you guys owe me another drink," she told them.

Grace walked over to the bar, aware again of how over-dressed she was. Her light brown hair was curled in waves over her shoulders, and she shook it, hoping it could cover her too-obvious cleavage, too.

"Can I have a glass of water, please?" she asked the bartender.

"Still or sparkling?"

"Still, please."

She could feel Suit watching her. Her skin was tingling again, like she'd touched an electric fence and the pulses were washing through her body. Dammit, she needed to get this over with.

When the bartender brought her glass over, she turned to look at Suit, standing three feet away from her. "You're the cab guy, right?" she asked him.

He lifted a brow. "I thought I recognized you. You're the water rat."

Well, that wasn't exactly the compliment she was hoping for. Still, it was accurate.

She lifted a brow, because this needed to be done. "Listen, can I ask you for a favor?" she said, aware that Ella and Lucy were still watching her.

"You want me to call you another cab?" he asked.

She laughed. Damn, she liked him. "No. I need you to talk to me for five minutes."

He glanced over her shoulder, his brows scrunching. "Why? Is somebody bothering you?"

Oh. He thought she was trying to avoid a guy. "Not like

that. My friends…" She sighed. "They're being a pain. I just need to talk with you to shut them up."

He glanced over her shoulder again, presumably to where Ella and Lucy were sitting, because she heard them giggle.

Ugh.

"Actually, forget it. It's stupid and juvenile." She took her glass, ready to walk away and internally scream. "Have a good evening."

"Wait." He reached for her arm, his fingers brushing her skin. She felt herself flush. "I can talk to you," he murmured. "What is it, a bet?"

"Something like that," she admitted, feeling stupid.

He took a sip of his whiskey, eyeing her carefully. "What kind of bet?"

"They want me to flirt with you."

"And you don't want to?" he asked, looking interested.

"I don't know. I…" She looked at his left hand. "You're not married, are you?"

"No."

Oh.

"Let me buy you a drink," he suggested.

"I have some water." She pointed at her glass. She was pacing her alcohol intake – she had to be up early to meet her parents for breakfast in the morning. They were in New York for a completely different reason – her dad had booked Broadway tickets for her mom's birthday treat. And since they were in the city, they'd give her a ride back to their small hometown.

Where she'd be starting work next week.

"I can recommend the whiskey," he said, glancing at his own glass.

"What label is it?"

"G. Scott Carter. The international blend."

Her heart did a little leap. That was her parents' whiskey. Or at least it was made at the distillery they owned.

The place she'd be working at a week from Monday.

"I hear it's good," she murmured.

"It's the best. Can I buy you one?"

She nodded. Okay. One would be fine.

When the barman brought it over, Suit lifted his glass and clinked it to hers. "To bets and whiskey."

"Bets and whiskey." And steel-blue eyes I could get lost in if I let myself.

"What's your name?" he asked her.

"Ella." She had no idea why she lied. Maybe to protect herself. You couldn't be too careful in the big city. And maybe she was still a little tetchy about her best friend forcing her to do this. "How about you?"

He took another sip of his drink. "People call me Irish."

She smiled. "You don't look Irish."

"Nor does Bono."

"What part of Ireland is your family from?"

"Missouri."

She laughed. Then took a sip of whiskey and it made her feel like she was home. Sure, she loved the French wine she'd been working with for the past few years, but whiskey was in her blood.

"My father was half Irish," he said. "Which I guess makes me a quarter. Apparently enough for my team mates never to let me forget it."

"Team mates?" she asked him.

"College football. That's where I got the nickname and it stuck."

Oh, he was a football player. "Do you still play?" she asked. Her uncle used to be in the NFL. She could definitely have a conversation about football.

"No. Gave up after graduation. I wasn't that good." He shrugged.

"So, what do you do now?"

"I'm an agent," he said. "Sports management. How about you?"

She shifted her feet. "I'm between jobs. Just finished working at a vineyard in France. About to start working at a new place in my home town." She took another sip of the whiskey. "This is my first day in the US in almost four years."

"You picked a good day to come back," he joked.

"Right? Nobody told me about the biblical floods."

He laughed. Damn, he was attractive. She found herself moving a little closer to him. His gaze dipped to her lips, and she liked that a little too much.

"How long are you in the city for?" he asked her.

"Just for tonight. You?" For the first time, she was sad about that. Sad about going home tomorrow.

"Same." His lip curled. "I'm flying back to Europe tomorrow."

"Where in Europe are you flying to?" she asked.

"London. I have a business there. I spend most of my time on that side of the Atlantic."

"I love London. I used to go there a lot for the weekend, just jump on the Eurostar." She loved how the train from Paris to London went in a dark tunnel under the water between the two countries. Liked even more how fast the trip was.

"What did you do there?" he asked her.

"Mostly visited galleries." She smiled at the memory. "I love art. And the food. I know a lot of people say it's bad, but some of my favorite restaurants are in London."

"Shame you're not in Paris anymore," he murmured.

She wished she was.

"It's been five minutes," he told her.

"What?"

"Your bet. I think you've won it."

Did he want her to go? She'd barely drunk her whiskey. She looked over her shoulder at her friends. Ella lifted a brow at her and Grace rolled her eyes, bringing her gaze back to Irish.

"Oh. Okay." She tried to hide the disappointment in her voice.

"You want to tease them?" he asked her.

"How?"

"Like this." He trailed his finger along her cheek, tucking her hair behind her ear. A shiver snaked down her spine, making her thighs tingle.

Oh God, this man.

"We could do that," she whispered.

He leaned forward until his face was close to hers. "How old are you?"

"Twenty-five."

"That's what I was afraid of."

"How old are you?" she asked him.

"Too old. Way too old."

"Age is just a number," she whispered.

A smile ghosted across his lips. "That's what a dirty old man would say."

"There's nothing dirty about you."

His eyes narrowed. "You're wrong. I'm very dirty."

Her breath caught in her throat. He was too handsome, too easy to talk to. Just one touch from this man and she felt like she was on fire.

"Show me," she whispered.

"Show you what?"

"How dirty you are."

This wasn't like her. She wasn't sure who it was like, but for the first time in weeks she was having fun.

He blinked. "You're pretty, Ella. Really pretty. But you don't want this. Believe me, you want a guy your own age."

She'd had a guy her own age, but he'd hurt her. Maybe she wanted somebody to erase all that pain.

Just for one night.

"Don't you want to kiss me?" she asked him.

"I've been thinking about nothing else." His voice was low.

"Then why don't you?" she asked him.

"I'm trying to figure that one out myself," he said, and the thickness of his voice sent another shiver down her spine. She didn't have to look down to know that her nipples were hard against the fabric of her dress.

"Stop thinking and do it," she told him. "And then I'll walk away, I promise."

"That's what I'm afraid of," he murmured. But he curled his hand around her neck, his fingers feathering her hair, and her breath caught in her throat. His eyes were intense, dark. She slid her hands along his chest, touching him for the first time.

Instead of just being touched.

His chest was warm and hard. Either he worked out or he was wearing armor under there. She ran her tongue along her bottom lip and slid her hands around his neck.

"Kiss me, Irish," she whispered.

And he did.

CHAPTER
Two

THIS SHOULDN'T BE HAPPENING.

But it was, and her soft lips were driving him wild, her arms wrapped around his neck as her perfect body molded against his.

And yeah, certain parts of his body approved without reservation. Especially those that hadn't seen any action since his divorce last year. Ignoring the warning note sounding in his mind, he slid his hand down her back, her fingers lingering at the base of her spine.

Ella gasped into his mouth.

So she was sensitive. He stored that information away and kissed her harder, desperately trying to ignore the fact that he was too old and too jaded for her.

She didn't seem to care, though. Her fingers caressed the skin at the edge of his hairline, sending a pulse of need through him. It has been way too long, and he was too on edge and this needed to stop.

Not least because they were in a bar.

Reluctantly, he kissed her softly, then pulled back. Her eyes were trained on his, dark and sparkling. She let out a long breath and he could feel her breasts brush against his chest.

"Let me take you to dinner," he murmured, because he didn't just want to kiss her. He wanted to talk to her. Watch her eat. Hear more about France and wine and whatever else she had to talk about.

"I can't," she said, looking torn. "It's my friend's birthday."

"Tomorrow then?" He was supposed to fly back to London tomorrow night. But he could change his ticket. Flying back on Sunday would be fine. She was worth it.

"I leave tomorrow morning." She sounded sad about that. Her face was flushed, and the color looked good on her.

So that was that. Probably a good thing. When he woke up in the morning, maybe he'd think it was a lucky escape from making a fool out of himself. And making a fool of her, too. She was far too pretty and far too young to deal with his grumpy ass, anyway. She should go back to her friends, have a good time.

And he'd head up to his room and sleep, like he should be doing right now.

"I guess we'll always have New York."

"And Paris." She lifted a brow.

He was surprised she got the reference. Did twenty-some-things watch *Casablanca*? Grabbing his glass, he took a sip of whiskey, looking at her over the rim of his glass.

"Here's looking at you, kid."

She grinned. "Did you know Lauren Bacall was twenty-five years younger than Humphrey Bogart?"

He tried not to smile at her sudden change in direction, from *Casablanca* to Bogey's love life. "No, I didn't."

"They met when she was nineteen and he was forty-five." She shrugged.

"I guess he was a dirty old man, too."

She grinned again. Her lips were swollen from their kiss,

and he liked that too much. "I guess that's how she preferred them. They got married and stayed married until he died."

"You seem to know a lot about them," he said, and she nodded.

"I'm an old movie buff. If they made it in the nineteen thirties or forties, I'm there."

Yeah, he could see that. Like those old golden age movies, there was a timeless glamor to her. He wondered if she did that on purpose or if her style was just innate.

"You should go back to your friends now," he said, his voice low. "I think we convinced them." Because if she didn't…

She blinked, as though she'd forgotten about them. "Oh. Yeah. I guess."

"It's your friend's birthday," he reminded her, because he needed her to leave. He was already regretting kissing her. Regretting stopping more. If he walked away now, it would be fine. A funny little memory to think about when he next took the train to Paris and stepped out into the springtime sun. A girl who'd always stay pretty and young in his imagination, as he got old and cynical.

Who was he kidding? He was already cynical.

"Oh. You're right. I should." She looked almost reluctant. She touched her bottom lip with her fingertips, as though she were thinking the same thing he was.

That he wanted to kiss her one last time.

And then she turned to look over her shoulder and let out a little 'oh.'

"Everything okay?" he asked her, because she was looking back at him with a frown on her face.

"My friends have left." She sounded confused.

He glanced over her shoulder, seeing that she was right. The booth they'd been sitting at was empty. The server must have taken their glasses away and wiped the table clean. It was as though they'd never been there.

"Oh hey, your friend asked me to give you this," the server said, holding out a phone and a small purse. "She said to check your phone."

She was still frowning as she took them from the server, sliding her finger on the screen and reading whatever came up. Then she tapped furiously on the screen the way only somebody her age could. He smiled, because his thumbs were so damn big he could never text that fast.

"Where did they go?" he asked her.

"She didn't say. Just some club." She shook her head.

"Want me to get you a cab so you can join them?"

She looked up from her phone and her eyes caught his. They were both smiling at each other again, because that's what he did. He was her cab-caller.

"It's okay. I think I'll just finish my drink and crash. I have to be up early, anyway."

"Have you eaten?" he asked.

"No. Why?"

"At least let me buy you dinner. And then you can crash."

Her lips curled. "Okay. But only if you let me pay for it."

As if. He'd cut his dick off before he let her pay, but they could argue about that later. "Come on," he said, holding out his hand. "I know this great place right around the corner."

———

Two hours later, he was kissing her as he kicked his hotel room door shut, and she clung onto him like he was the only rock in a storm.

"We shouldn't be doing this," he murmured against her mouth. It didn't stop him from kissing her again, his lips trailing down her neck.

"I know." She tugged at his hair until his lips were on hers again, their tongues tangling as he pushed her against the wall of his hotel room, his body like a rock against hers.

They parted, breathless, and his dark eyes caught hers. She could see her face reflected in his dilated pupils. She looked ravaged, her hair a mess, her lips swollen.

"Tell me to stop." His voice was graveled.

"Do you want to?" she asked, her brow lifting.

"No."

Her lips curled. "Good, nor do I."

He chuckled, and she pulled at his tie, his head lowering to hers.

"But I need you to know I don't usually do this sort of thing," she whispered against his mouth.

Irish lifted a brow. "Neither do I."

"Sure." She rolled her eyes. He was too good at this. Too smooth and practiced. He had to do this all the time.

Grace didn't, though. But maybe she should have. She'd spent way too much time with guys who pretended not to be assholes. This one had no pretense. He made her feel good.

And she needed this. She deserved it. She really did.

They'd spend the last two hours laughing and flirting, their chairs getting closer and closer together as they ate the best French food she'd encountered outside of her favorite country.

He'd even chosen her favorite wine. And yes, it had loosened her inhibitions, but they'd only drank two glasses each. Enough to make her feel good, but not enough to make her choices seem suspect.

She was here because she wanted this. Wanted him. And she wasn't ashamed about that.

"Unzip my dress," she whispered.

And he did, his fingers deft as he reached behind her, finding the zipper without breaking their gaze. She felt the warmth of his hand against her skin, the smooth slide of her zip as he unfastened her.

And when it fell open, he pushed it down until she was in nothing but her bra and panties.

"You're beautiful."

Her lip quirked. "And you know how to make a woman feel good."

Irish winked at her. "It's my specialty."

And it was stupid, but it felt like more than just a one-night stand. There was this draw to him she couldn't ignore.

"These are beautiful too," he whispered, his lips reaching the swell of her breasts. He expertly unfastened her bra, then feathered his fingers lower, down her back, until he found the base of her spine and lit her nerve endings on fire as he caressed her.

She let out a gasp as his lips closed around her nipple. "Are you going to get undressed too?"

He released her nipple, and she immediately missed the teasing warmth of his mouth.

"I wasn't planning on wearing a suit for this, but whatever floats your boat."

She grinned again. Damn, he made this easy. She cupped his face, and he smiled back at her. This man needed to stop looking so gorgeous.

She watched as he unfastened his shirt, trying not to stare at the broadness of his shoulders and the perfect definition of his chest. There was a sprinkling of hair across his muscles and she traced the line of them with her fingers, stopping at his nipple, teasing it until he was the one looking hot and bothered.

His pants came next, revealing black shorts and thick muscles that made her mouth water. And then he was lifting her, carrying her to the bed, both of them almost naked.

But not quite.

Before she could point that out, he was kissing her, and she'd wrapped her hands around his neck because she couldn't get enough of him. He made her feel good. Wanted. Real.

After so much heartbreak, this was what she needed.

His mouth trailed down her chest, kissing her nipples until she was arching her back with pleasure. Then he slid further down the bed, his fingers strong against her thighs. He parted them and slid her panties down.

And now she was naked and his face was about two inches from *there*.

"Also beautiful."

"Shut up. I should have shaved."

And ugh, now she was embarrassed.

He looked up at her, his gaze penetrating hers. "Don't change a thing. You're perfect." And as if to drive the point home, he dipped his head and pressed his lips against her in a barely there kiss.

And then he did it again. Harder and longer this time. A long sweep of his tongue made her toes curl and her eyes roll up. She was right about him. This man knew what he was doing. Damn, he even looked like he was enjoying it.

God knew she was.

Her head fell back as he continued his onslaught, her whole body tensing and releasing, pleasure warming through her. Then he slid a finger inside of her and sucked at the same time.

Nobody had done that to her before. Why hadn't they? Because it felt like she was riding on a wave high above the bed. Then he curled his fingers, and it was explosive. Like dynamite exploding in her body.

"Irish!" she cried out. He didn't respond, just kept teasing her with his tongue and fingers until she was on the edge, her breath short, her body flushed, and still he continued his onslaught.

"I'm going to…" she told him, because her ex used to hate her coming on his face. But Irish didn't move. Didn't stop.

He just. Kept. Licking.

Pleasure exploded inside of her, making her back arch and her mouth fall open with a long, aching cry. Her legs clamped around his face, but he didn't try to fight it. Just kept licking and touching her until she came down from the edge.

His lips glistened with her when he finally lifted his head. His eyes were dark. As needy as hers.

"You okay?" he rasped.

"More than okay," she told him, breathless. "Now get inside of me."

"Shit."

"What?" She frowned.

"I don't have a condom. I wasn't kidding about not doing this often."

"There's some in my purse." Irish rolled over and grabbed it, removing the foil packet with a question on his face.

"There was a vending machine in the restroom," she told him. "I wasn't assuming. I just like to be prepared."

He kissed the tip of her nose. "Like a sexy girl scout."

"Whatever. Put it on. I need you."

He winked as he ripped the foil and rolled the condom on. And then he was kissing her again, and she could taste herself on him and it tasted good.

Like he was hers. Even just for one night.

She ran her hand down his back, her fingers digging into his ass. He groaned and caught her eye. "Are you sure this is okay?"

She liked that he asked. That he wanted her consent. "I want you," she told him. "I want this."

She wasn't lying. Her body was still pulsing with need for him. And when she felt the tip of him against her, right where she needed him, it felt like a tiny piece of heaven had fallen into a hotel room in New York City.

He kissed her again, tangling his fingers in her hair, and she kissed him back desperately. Her body opened up to him, welcoming him home as he slid inside, and he let out a low oath, his words making her shiver.

Almost immediately, she could feel the heat warming her

again. The build up, the buzz, the pleasure. With every stroke of him it was getting stronger. He kissed her softly but made love to her hard, and the combination was intoxicating. A man who knew what he was doing, who knew exactly how to drive her to oblivion.

"J'adore te baiser," he murmured against her lips, sliding his hand down her thigh to lift it higher, allowing him to go deeper.

Oh, she liked that. So much. The dirty French and the dirty fucking. She dug her nails into his ass. "Harder," she whispered. "Please."

He did as he was asked, lifting her other leg, rolling back on his haunches, fucking her until she tightened around him. Her breath was ragged as she called out his name, pleasure making her scrape her nails down his thighs.

He pushed one more time then groaned, his body stilling as he surged inside of her. He leaned forward, capturing her mouth with his, kissing her like she was the air he needed.

She moved her hands up, stroking his hair softly. He pulled back and gave her a lopsided grin.

Something pulled in her chest as she smiled back at him. Making it feel tight. Making her feel emotional. The man knew what he was doing. Maybe that was why women liked older guys so much.

She knew she did.

CHAPTER
Three

"SHIT." Her eyes widened as she looked at the clock beside Irish's bed early the next morning. "I have to go."

He rolled over, his eyelids heavy as he reached for her.

"What time is it?" he asked, kissing her brow. Oh, she liked that. Turned out he was a cuddler when he went to sleep. His chest had proved to be a surprisingly comfortable pillow.

"It's almost seven," she told him. "I really do need to leave now. I'm so sorry." She was having breakfast with her parents at nine. They'd arranged to meet in the hotel lobby and then they'd walk to a diner that her mom loved. After that, they'd start the drive home to West Virginia, to the little town she'd grown up in.

She was going home and now she didn't want to. She wanted to spend all day in bed with this adonis.

But he was leaving, too. And even though they'd done all the dirty things, she felt way too shy to ask if she could see him again.

"Can't I take you out for breakfast?" he asked. His voice was sleep-heavy and she found it sexy that he could still form words in that state.

"I'm already meeting somebody." She didn't want to tell him it was her parents that she was meeting because that made her sound too young. "And then I have to leave town."

He sat up, the sheet falling down around his waist. There was a bruise on his chest, mouth shaped, and she flushed, realizing she'd put it there.

She'd marked him. Dear Lord.

"I'll be back in New York in a few weeks," he told her. "Can we meet up, maybe?"

Her cheeks flushed, mostly because she was pleased he wanted to see her again. "Here?" she asked.

"Yeah. Let me give you my number. If you want to see me again, call me."

"Of course I want to see you again." She rolled her eyes, and he smiled.

"Call me tonight," he said, reading out his number as she tapped it into her phone.

"You could call me," she pointed out, sending her own number to his phone.

"Then I will. As soon as I'm back in London." He frowned. "Although, that will be your night time."

"I don't care." She was already looking forward to it. She wanted to talk to him. Wanted to laugh with him. Wanted to hear about his work and his flat in London and anything else he had to say.

"Come here," he said, reaching for her. His fingers curled into her hair as he gave her one last kiss. It tasted of hello and goodbye, and this could be something good.

It tasted perfect. And for now, it would have to be enough.

"Now go before I decide to tie you up to my bed," he said.

"Don't make offers you don't intend to keep."

He lifted a brow. "Next time," he said, and they both grinned like kids again.

"I'm really going now," she told him, grabbing her underwear and pulling them on.

"Okay." He rolled out of bed.

"You don't have to get up. I can see myself out."

"No, you won't," he said gruffly, and she couldn't help but take one last look at his body. Every part of him was masculine perfection, making her realize her previous love interests had been little more than boys.

Irish was all man. And she liked that too much.

Ignoring her scrutiny, he pulled on his shorts as she pulled on the dress she'd discarded last night. She didn't bother to make herself look presentable. Her room was on the floor below and it would take her no more than five minutes to get there.

And after that, operation *look respectable* would begin.

When she was dressed, he walked over to her, kissing her softly one more time. "Thank you," he said. "For the perfect night."

Oh, she really liked him. Way, way too much. "Thank you," she said, meaning it.

"Take care, beautiful," he said, pulling open his door. Reluctantly, she stepped out of it, giving him one last glance.

"Call me tonight," he told her.

"You'll be at the airport," she pointed out, but smiled anyway.

"I know." He winked. And she started walking.

———

A little over an hour later, Grace stepped into the hotel elevator, pressing the button for the lobby as she looked at her reflection in the mirrored interior.

She'd showered and washed her hair, then dried it carefully, before pulling on a pair of jeans and a shirt that she'd tucked into the waistband. Her lips were still swollen and her eyes were too bright, but hopefully her parents would think it was the after-effect of a night out with her friends, and not the result of a night tangled with a much older man.

The elevator doors pinged. She stepped out, looking around the high-ceilinged lobby to spot her parents. They were behind an oversized fern, and she had to step to the side to see them. Lifting her hand, she went to call out for them, but then she saw *him*.

Her Irish.

Standing with her parents, in a pair of dark tailored pants and another crisp, white shirt. Her mom laughed at something he said and then her dad said something that made Irish smile and it looked as though they knew each other.

Before any of them could catch sight of her, Grace turned on her heel and walked straight back into the still-open elevator. Her heart was hammering as she punched at her floor, turning away as the doors closed her view of the lobby.

How did her parents know Irish? She wracked her brain, trying to think of a connection. Her parents were older than him by at least fifteen years.

Did her dad know him through work? What was it he said he did again? Something to do with being an agent in London?

Her dad never visited London. Scotland, yes. Paris for sure, but London?

As soon as she reached her floor, she ran for her room, as though her parents had somehow worked out where she was. Pulling her room card from her phone case, she could see she had a message from her mom.

Hello darling! We're in the lobby. And guess who we bumped into? Michael Devlin. I don't know if you remember him, but he's Aunt Mia's son. Anyway, we invited him out to breakfast with us. Hope that's okay. Love you lots, Mom xx

• • •

The phone fell out of her hand, tumbling to the floor as cold blood rushed through her body.

Irish wasn't a friend of her parents. Or an old work acquaintance they'd bumped into.

He was her cousin. And she'd just spent the night with him.

———

"Technically speaking, he's only your step cousin," Ella pointed out. They were sitting in a diner in midtown, where Grace had arranged to meet her after *that* revelation. "I mean, you're not related by blood, are you?"

"We might as well be. You know what my family is like." Michael was actually her mom's brother's stepson, if you wanted to be correct about it. Which she didn't. Damn her oversize, complicated family. "His mom and Uncle Cam got married before I was born. Her boys are part of the family."

"He was hardly a boy when I saw him in the bar," Ella said dryly. "And he definitely wasn't acting like family."

Grace groaned, dropping her face into her hands. If anybody found out about last night, all hell would break loose. She was the apple of her family's eye. One of only two girls in a family full of testosterone-heavy boys.

A princess in their eyes.

"So what happened once you saw them?" Ella asked. She looked as though she was almost enjoying this, damn her. Not that Grace could blame her.

"I ran back to my room, messaged my mom, and told her I'd slept at yours. That I was completely hungover and I'd find my own way home." She let out a long breath. "What am I going to do?"

"I still don't get how you didn't recognize him," Ella said. She actually *was* hungover, and Grace felt bad for dragging her out of bed, but this was a crisis and she didn't want to go through it alone. Not when it was partly Ella's fault for making her talk to him.

Grace grimaced. She'd been asking herself the same question all morning. "He left town when I was young. I don't remember him," she told her. "And I don't think he's been back to visit for over a decade, or if he has, it was when I was in France and I didn't see him."

"What about photos? Your family must have photos of him."

Grace thought about her aunt and uncle's gorgeous ranch house, bought with Cam's NFL earnings. "All the pictures are of him as a teenager," she said. "Not with the beard and the…" She gestured at her body and Ella nodded knowingly.

He wasn't a man with a body built to make a woman go wild in those old pictures. In most of them, he was in his football gear, helmet on and helmet off. That part of her family lived, breathed, and died for football.

"It was good, wasn't it?" Ella asked, looking almost human now that she'd swallowed some coffee. "Tell me it was worth it."

Grace sighed. Because it was good. More than good. And yeah, it had helped put all those bad memories of Paris and Pascal out of her mind. He made her feel wanted. Alive. Like she was worth something.

He made her feel desirable, and it's been a while since that had happened.

"Yes," she said. "It was worth it."

"So what happens now?" Ella asked, gesturing at the server for a refill of her coffee.

Grace sipped at her Americano. She'd already thought this through. She couldn't leave now. She'd wait until later. Arrive in the middle of the night. That would have two benefits – firstly, it would seem more real that she had to wait until she was sobered up. And second, her mom would be too tired to ask questions. "I'll rent a car, drive home tonight, and then I'll get on with the rest of my life."

"I bet your mom was pissed that you weren't meeting up with them, wasn't she?"

"I spoke to her after I'd snuck out of the hotel and right into a cab." Which, funnily enough, were plentiful today. "I told her I was sick and in no state to join them." By that point, they'd all been at breakfast – her parents and Irish. So she'd asked the driver to take her to a diner twenty minutes away and messaged Ella to meet her here.

It had taken some persuading to get her mom and dad to leave New York and head home without her but somehow she managed. She was a grown up, after all. She'd lived in a different country since she was twenty-one. Renting a car and driving to West Virginia wasn't exactly brain surgery.

"And what if he's there?"

"In Hartson's Creek?" Grace clarified, then shook her head. "He won't be. He's flying to London tonight. He won't be back soon."

"He might if he knows you're there."

"He'll never know. He only lived in Hartson's Creek for a few years before he went off to college. When I asked him about home, he said it was Missouri." She was pretty sure that avoiding him wouldn't be a problem. It hadn't been for the last twenty-five years of her life.

"You'd better hope there are no weddings in your family for the foreseeable future," Ella said.

Grace rolled her eyes. "Have you met my cousins? Not a single one of them is anywhere close to a relationship, let alone getting married."

The server refilled her coffee and Ella sipped at it gratefully. "Actually, I have met one of your cousins," she pointed out. "And he's hot."

"Shut up and drink your coffee."

Ella smirked. "Yes, ma'am."

CHAPTER
Four

A YEAR LATER...

For as long as Grace could remember, in their little town of Hartson's Creek, Friday nights meant *Chairs*. It was the evening when residents would get together at the field beside the water, bringing their own chairs, along with food and drink, and settle down to gossip for the night. From April to September, if the weather was fine, that's where you'd find them.

And right now Grace was running late for it.

She'd been back home for a year. Had already gotten used to the old weather worn Victorian houses with their long lawns and wide roads. France seemed like a blip in her past.

And so did New York. When she allowed herself to think about it, which wasn't often.

She climbed out of her car and rapped on the door of a double story house with a cupola she used to adore as a kid.

Her Great Aunt Gina opened it right away, as though she'd been standing there waiting for a while.

Grace grimaced. "I'm sorry I'm late."

Gina was her mom's aunt, but really she'd been more of a mother to Grace's mom and her brothers growing up. And she was definitely a grandmotherly type to Grace. Which was why she'd volunteered to pick the older woman up on her way from work to the creek.

And why she felt so bad for being twenty minutes later than planned.

"No need to apologize," Aunt Gina said. She was looking smart in a pair of red slacks and a white sweater, her gray hair swept into its usual bun. She was almost ninety, but could still walk without help. Though Grace grabbed her chair and the cookies she'd made and carried them to the car.

It was a short drive from Gina's house – the house Grace's mom had grown up in – to the fields by the creek, and there were already people everywhere. The sun was setting, turning the water orange as kids played flag football and the old folk sat in circles, sharing gossip. Aunt Gina walked over to them and Grace followed, setting up Gina's chair and getting her settled, before greeting her aunt's friends and making small talk.

Taking her leave of the older women, Grace spotted a group of her cousins laughing and holding beers. There were a lot of them – Grace's mom was one of five siblings, and they all had children of their own. Her eldest cousin – Presley – beckoned her over, and she nodded, but before she could join him, she saw her mom approaching.

"Hey sweetheart." Her mom opened her arms to her, and Grace hugged her tight. "Were you working late again?"

"Something like that," Grace told her. They worked together at the G. Scott Carter distillery and the crisis Grace had solved could wait until Monday to discuss. Right now, she just wanted to relax and have fun.

God knew she needed that.

She'd thrown herself into work since her return from New York. She'd also changed her cell number – giving her family an excuse about not wanting to talk with Pascal – and promised herself that she wouldn't pine for the man who'd set her on fire.

Truth was, she *had* pined. A little. But she was feeling better now.

"Guess who's here?" Her mom leaned forward, her voice dropping into an excited whisper.

For a second, Grace's heart stopped. "Who?"

"Ethan." Her mom looked almost hopeful as she leaned in close. "He came back to town last week. I saw his mom at yoga and she said he might be here tonight."

Disappointment washed with relief. Ethan had been Grace's prom date senior year. She'd barely thought of him since then. "What's he doing back here?"

"He's come home to help his dad. And according to his mom, he's single."

Grace shook her head. "Please don't tell me you asked her if he was."

Her mom cupped Grace's face. "I know you've found it difficult since you came back from Paris. Pascal hurt you. But Ethan's a nice boy. Maybe it's a good thing he's back. You and he…" she trailed off.

Her mom wasn't wrong. She had found it a struggle since she came back to Hartson's Creek. The small town she'd grown up in hadn't changed in all those years she'd been in France. But she had.

She felt different. But she also felt wary. Despite her bravado, at first she'd been constantly worried she'd bump into Michael Devlin on the streets.

That he'd find out who she was.

It was convenient to let her mom think she was pining after Pascal, rather than constantly beating herself up for being reckless.

"Please don't go matchmaking," she told her mom. "I'm not ready."

"I don't need to. He's already asked about you."

Grace rolled her eyes. She loved her mom, but honestly, this was the problem with living in a small town. You knew everybody, and they all knew you. And maybe it was the lack of things to do, but their favorite pastime seemed to be to interfere. Her mom was cool, but she wasn't subtle.

"I'm going to talk to my cousins now," she told her mom, because at least she'd feel protected in their company. There were eleven of them in all – thirteen if you counted their step cousins, which no, she wasn't going to do right now. When she reached them, she hugged Presley and Marley, the oldest of their crowd, and then the others, including her younger brother who was home from college for spring break. He was talking with Sabrina, their only girl cousin.

She was also Michael's little sister. Or half-sister if she wanted to be precise. It felt strange knowing that. But that wasn't Sabrina's fault.

"Hey, long time no see," Sabrina said, smiling at her. "You look great."

Grace hadn't seen Sabrina since she'd been back from Paris. Her younger cousin had spent last summer as a camp counselor in Virginia, then headed straight to college on the West Coast.

"So do you," Grace told her. Despite the five-year age difference, she'd always had time for Sabrina growing up. "How's college?"

"A lot of hard work," Sabrina said. "Expensive. Fun." She shrugged. "How are you finding it back here?"

"A lot of hard work," Grace said, and they both laughed.

"I don't know how you do it," Sabrina told her. "I can't imagine myself living back here once I graduate. Especially after living somewhere like France. I'd die to move over there."

"No need to do that," Grace joked. "Just get a passport. It's easier."

"Whatever I do, I'm not going to end up back here," Sabrina said.

"What's wrong with here?" Presley asked. He was four years older than Grace, and the eldest of identical twins. The two of them ran a construction business, but their real calling was the band they played in.

Presley also had a little girl – Delilah, who was six years old. She was running in the grass with her friends, playing tag. Presley was a single dad since his wife had died. It was good to see them both looking happier.

Presley and Marley were in a band that had been doing well before the tragedy. They hadn't hit it big though they had a good local following. But Presley had taken a break from playing to concentrate on his business and raising Delilah.

"It's boring as hell," Sabrina said. "Nothing goes on here."

"It's not that bad," Marley said. Like his twin, he was talented and handsome, though he was the quieter of the two. The two of them were known for breaking hearts in Hartson's Creek and the surrounding towns.

Like their father and uncles before them, they had inherited the nickname of the Heartbreak Brothers.

Grace had even heard her own brother being referred to as an honorary heartbreak brother, and ew, she really didn't need that.

"Of course it is. Nothing goes on around here," Sabrina complained.

"Maybe that's how some of us like it." Grace winked at her.

There was a tap on her shoulder. She turned to see Ethan standing there. And though it had been at least four years since they'd both been in town, he automatically hugged her and she hugged him back.

"Your mom told me you were here," he said. "I didn't know you'd come back."

"Over a year ago." She nodded, smiling because it wasn't his fault her mom was interfering. And really, he was a good-looking guy. He'd filled out a little during his years since high school. His hair was shorter and darker, but his smile was the same. "How about you? Got used to being back home yet?"

He shook his head. "It's good to spend some time with dad. He's not doing so well."

Her smile melted. "I'm so sorry." Ethan's dad was a vet. He ran the only practice in town, having bought it out from the previous owner. Ethan had followed in his father's foot-steps, but for the last few years had been working out west, mostly with ranches and horses. "I didn't know."

"Not your fault," he said softly. "And it's nice to know at least one other person here in town."

"Give it five minutes and everybody will remember you."

"Yeah, I've noticed that. At least ten of my parents' friends have been trying to match make me with their daughters.

Her face heated. Please god, let her mom have not have been one. "If my Mom said anything…"

He laughed. "Oh no, she didn't."

She widened her eyes. "Good."

Leaning forward, he kissed her cheek. "I gotta go. Just wanted to say hi though."

"I'm glad you did." It was true. It was really nice to see him. To know that at least she wasn't the only loser back in town.

He lifted a hand in a wave and went to go, but then some-thing changed his mind. He turned back to her, his brows lifted. "Can I get your number?" he asked. "Maybe we could get together and catch up some time? You could fill me in on what's happened since I've been away."

Grace swallowed. It wasn't flirting. And it might be nice to have a friend in town that she wasn't related to. "Sure." She reeled off her number, and he put it in his phone.

"See you around, Grace."

"Yeah," she said, nodding. "See you around."

———

"I hear you went out on a date last night," Sabrina said two Fridays later when Grace joined her group of cousins by the creek.

"I went out for a drink with a friend," Grace told her, pulling out her chair. "It wasn't exactly a date." And it hadn't exactly lit her world on fire, either. Ethan was nice, but that was it.

She hadn't had to pick Aunt Gina up this week – it was Marley's turn – so she'd gotten here even later than usual, getting hung up at work. The sun was almost under the horizon and most of the families with kids were packing up their things to leave.

There were still a few younger kids around, their shouts from beside the creek wafting over in the breeze. The leaves in the trees were dancing with the wind, but it was still humid out here, enough for them all to be wearing shorts and t-shirts or tank tops.

Presley was strumming his guitar softly. He had the sweetest singing voice, and the dirtiest laugh. It was a lethal combination for most women. At least the ones who weren't related to him.

He and Marley had inherited their dad's musical talent. Gray Hartson was a rock singer, adored in his day, though long since retired. He'd spent most of the last thirty years producing records for other groups and raising his kids, Presley, Marley and their little brother, Hendrix.

And now there was Presley's daughter to keep them busy, too.

"And?" Sabrina prompted, pulling Grace out of her thoughts.

"And what?" She blinked.

"Will you be seeing Ethan again?" Sabrina asked.

Grace shrugged. "We live in the same town. Of course I'll see him again. Like I see everybody else."

"That's not what I meant and you know it," Sabrina huffed. Grace blew her a kiss because, as the only two girl cousins, they needed to stick together.

Marley picked up his guitar and joined in with his brother, and Grace could hear other people bringing their chairs over to listen. It wasn't often that her two oldest cousins sang at *Chairs*. As it was, it wasn't often that they were here.

But Grace was pleased to spend time with them anyway.

They started another song, one she hadn't heard before, when she heard somebody squeal.

"Oh my God," Sabrina said, looking over her shoulder. "No way."

"What?" Grace asked, annoyed because she was trying to listen to her cousins sing.

"It's my brother," Sabrina said breathlessly.

"Mason?"

"No." Sabrina shook her head, standing up so fast her chair fell over. "Not Mason. My big brother. Michael."

Grace couldn't help it. She turned around, the skin on her neck prickling as she came face to face with Michael Devlin.

And the sound of her blood rushing through her ears was almost deafening.

CHAPTER
Five

MICHAEL'S MOM was full-on sobbing into his chest. His plane had arrived two hours ago, and he'd messaged his stepdad to make sure it was still okay to surprise his mom.

Cam thought it was a great idea. Told him to come straight to *Chairs* where the family would be gathered.

And he'd done it, even though now he was regretting all this public PDA.

"I thought you were coming tomorrow," his mom said, sniffing into his shirt.

"I managed to catch an earlier flight." He hated that she was so emotional to see him. He didn't deserve it. It was his choice to live in London, his choice to never have time to visit Hartson's Creek when he was back in the US.

Until he got the phone call from his stepdad.

Mom didn't want me to tell anybody but she had a little lump removed from her breast a few weeks ago. It's non invasive, but the doctor wants her to have a course of treatment just to be safe. I thought you should know but please try not to worry.

Yeah, well, he was worried.

"How are you doing?" he asked her, worried he might be hurting her where she'd had surgery.

"I'm fine. I was in and out the same day." She sobbed a little more. "I'm just so happy my boy is home."

He smiled because she was getting those hiccups people got after too many tears. "You got a funny way of showing it."

His mom looked up at him, eyes shining in the moonlight. "You're my firstborn. I've missed you. Give me a break."

He kissed her head. She still used the same shampoo she always did, and it made him feel like he was fifteen years old again. A punk who hated the world. Who felt like nobody understood him.

And yeah, that wasn't happening again.

A slap on his back caused him to turn to see his stepfather, Cam, standing there. They shook hands, did that manly half-hug thing that was always awkward as hell, and then suddenly he was surrounded by Hartsons.

His sister threw herself into his arms. Sabrina looked so much older than he remembered - when the hell did she grow up? Then his aunts and his uncles were hugging him, telling him how pleased they were to see him, asking him about London and New York and his flight.

And then he felt it. The weird sensation that he was being watched. An itch on his neck that didn't go away from him rubbing it.

"You should come meet Grace. It's been a long time since you last saw her," Becca – his step-aunt, was telling him. "She came back from Paris last year. She can give you all the tips for getting used to a small town again.

He vaguely remembered that Grace was Becca's daughter. Becca and Daniel owned the G. Scott Whiskey distillery on the edge of town. When Michael, his mom, and his younger brother arrived penniless in Hartson's Creek so many years ago, it had been the distillery that had given his mom her job.

He always appreciated them for that. And he liked Becca a

lot. He'd seen her last year in New York by coincidence and as always she'd been so happy to see him.

But he couldn't remember Grace at all. She had to have been a little kid the last time he was here in town. Maybe Sabrina's age?

"Come over here, Grace," Becca shouted. He followed her line of sight and what the hell.

Her?

Here?

His blood turned cold. No, that couldn't be Grace. Maybe she was a friend? He opened his mouth to ask, but then the woman he'd slept with in New York was walking over, not meeting his eye and swallowing hard.

"Honey, do you remember Michael, Mia's son? Michael, this is Grace, my daughter."

What. The. Fuck?

He'd spent weeks trying to track her down after that night they spent together, convinced he'd somehow saved the wrong number, even though it was the one she'd called him from. Tried to get her last name from the reception desk, tried to find her LinkedIn profile, not wanting her to think he was ghosting her.

"Hi." Grace smiled at him, her eyes wary. And it pissed him off more because all he could think about were those lips. That long dinner. The way she'd softly sighed his name as he tasted every part of her.

"Hello." His voice was sharper than he intended, making her wince.

"Michael's here for a couple of months," Becca said, her brows dipping a little as though she were trying to communicate something to her daughter. "Spending some quality time with Mia and Cam."

"That's nice." Grace shifted her feet. She was wearing a pair of jeans and a white t-shirt, knotted at the waist, with a sweater slung over her shoulders. Still smiling like butter wouldn't melt in her mouth.

He wanted to grab her, pull her away, fire a million questions he needed answers to. Because she didn't look like she was as shocked as he was. Did she know who he was all along?

Did she have sex with him knowing that it would be such a mess later?

"We should get you home," Cam said to Michael's mom. "It's been a long day."

"You'll come over tomorrow, right?" Mia asked Becca and Grace. "Let's get the whole family together. It'll be my last chance to entertain for a while. We'll have a cookout to celebrate Michael's homecoming."

"Bringing out the fatted calf for the prodigal brother," Sabrina murmured. He barely registered it. He was still too busy looking at Grace.

"Stop it," Mia said, shaking her head. There was a smile in her voice, though. It mingled with her tears. If she'd been a sky, there'd be a rainbow now. "I'm just so happy he's home."

"I have a rental car," he told them. "I'll follow you there. I just need to go to the drugstore to pick up some razors."

"Cam has some you can borrow," his mom said, looking upset at the thought of being parted from him for even a minute.

"It's fine. I'll get my own." He lifted a brow. "I've just spent hours on a plane. I could do with burning off some energy."

"Don't be long," his mom said. "I'll be waiting up for you."

"I won't," he promised. His gaze moved to Ella again. No, *not Ella*, she was Grace.

His cousin. The apple of her parents' eye, from the way they talked about her.

She was such a pretty little liar, and he hated that he couldn't get that night out of his mind.

Yeah, well. He needed to do exactly that.

———

Breathe. She needed to breathe. After several missed attempts, Grace pushed the key into the lock, pushing open the front door to her house and stepping inside. She closed it behind her and leaned against it, tipping her head back and inhaling deeply.

She needed to focus. Think this through.

She knew this day was a possibility. He had family here, after all. Even if he hadn't spent any time with them in the last god-knew-how-long. Maybe if she'd known before tonight about her Aunt Mia's diagnosis she could have prepared herself. Her mom had only told her about the lump in Mia's breast tonight. Non-invasive with a good prognosis, but still, if only she'd known earlier. She'd have guessed he'd be coming home.

What kind of son would he be if he hadn't flown here to spend time with his mom?

She needed to get it together. Pulling her sneakers off, she shucked the sweater from her shoulders, putting it on the chair to put away later. She'd take a shower and head for bed, then maybe she could think of an excuse not to go to her Aunt Mia's cookout.

But then there was a knock on the door. More of a slam, really. The sound of a fist connecting with wood in a way that made her shiver.

"Who's there?"

"Me."

She would have laughed if there was any humor in it. Grace knew who 'me' was, just as she knew that when she opened the door, she'd have to finally face the music. She wasn't surprised he'd found out where she lived. Hartson's Creek was a small town and everybody knew everybody else.

"One moment." She looked at herself in her hall mirror. She loved this house. It belonged to another uncle – Tanner. A real estate mogul in Hartson Creek, he owned a lot of houses. This place had been free when she moved back, and she really hadn't been wanting to live with her parents.

So here she was. In her own little home, safe and sound.

Or maybe not.

Curling her fingers around the knob, she turned it fast, like ripping off a Band-Aid. He was standing on the doorstep, his dark hair illuminated by her porch light.

"Can I come in?" His voice was low.

For a moment she thought back to that *Lost Boys* rerun she saw years ago at the local drive-in movie theater. Vampires can only cross the threshold if you give them permission.

Her lips twitched because this was stupid. He wasn't a vampire. He was a man who rocked her world for one night.

"Sure." She held the door open, and he stepped inside. His arm brushed hers and it took everything she had not to jump. She'd forgotten how tall he was. How much space he took up.

How her body reacted to him.

This was a small, modern house. He looked out of place here. Too big. Too angry.

Exuding way too much masculinity.

"You didn't look surprised to find out who I was," he said, when she finally looked at him.

Grace shook her head. "I already knew who you were."

"How long have you known?" he asked.

So he was throwing himself right into this. He looked pissed, and she knew he had every right to be. The man wasn't exactly having the best evening of his life.

"The morning after we spent the night together," she told him. "I came down to the lobby and saw you talking to my parents. Then my mom messaged and told me you were joining them for breakfast."

"You didn't know the night before?" He didn't look like he believed her.

"No." She shook her head vehemently. "If I had, I wouldn't have… we wouldn't…" *Oh God.* "I didn't know."

"Is that why my calls didn't connect? Did you block me?" There was no emotion in his voice.

"No, I changed my number."

"Cute." He sounded even more pissed.

"I don't think there's anything cute about this."

He ran his hands through his hair. "You told me you were twenty-five."

"I was. I'm twenty-six now."

There was a flash of relief in his eyes. He ran his finger over his rough jaw. She tried not to remember how his beard felt against her thighs.

"Who knows about this?" he asked.

"My friend. Ella."

He laughed, but there was no humor in it. "Is she imaginary, too?"

She'd forgotten she'd used Ella's name instead of her own. "Look. I'm sorry. I was just protecting myself. You were a stranger. I didn't want to tell you my name."

"So you were okay with me fucking you until you saw goddamned stars, but not with me knowing your name?"

Her face flushed. "It was stupid. But it's not like I knew your name either." It all was stupid. That was the truth of it. She'd thought she'd been so empowered, pushing memories of France away.

But she'd brought a whole heap of pain down around them all.

"Your parents? Do they know?"

"No. Nobody here does."

There was that relief again. Softening his features.

"Okay," he muttered, more to himself than to her. "We can work with this."

"We can?" She frowned.

"You don't want anybody knowing, and nor do I. We keep it that way."

She nodded again. His eyes were soft when they met hers. Neither of them spoke, but her head was so noisy she couldn't think straight. Could only think of the way he'd kissed her a year earlier.

Soft and hard. Needy and teasing.

She exhaled raggedly.

He glanced at her lips. "I should go," he told her. "My mom thinks I'm at the drug store."

"You should probably go to the drug store then," she said.

"I don't need anything."

"But your mom will expect you to carry something in," she pointed out. "Wait a minute, I have a bag somewhere." She opened the hall closet and dropped to her knees, her t-shirt riding up her back. She grabbed an empty bag and stood.

"Here we go. Just put something in there and she'll be none the wiser."

"Sneaky." Yep. He was still annoyed with her.

"Just thinking things through," she said softly.

He folded the bag in his hands. "Thanks. I'll go now." He glanced at the door. "Are you coming to the cookout at my parents' place tomorrow?"

"I was trying to think up an excuse not to."

"Come. I promise not to speak to you."

Weird how she didn't like the sound of that. "Don't you think people will get suspicious if you avoid me?"

He tipped his head to the side. His lips parted as he exhaled. She felt like he was assessing her, reading all her thoughts.

"We have nothing in common," he said. "We're different generations. I don't think people will think anything of it."

Ouch. Why did that one hurt? "Okay then. Avoiding it is."

"Good." He nodded. "Good." He lifted the bag she'd given him. "Thank you for this."

"Any time."

He reached for the door, still looking at her. "Are you okay?"

Her heart clenched at those three little words. Like they were giving her a glimpse of that man she'd spent the night with. "Does it matter?"

"Yes, it matters," he murmured.

"Then I'm okay," she lied.

Michael nodded and walked out of her house, not bothering to look back.

CHAPTER
Six

SATURDAY MORNINGS WERE FOR RIDING. Grace
had been wild about horses ever since she was a little girl. At
first she'd just come to the farm to feed them, to listen to their
whinnies and pat their noses. And then, as she got older,
she'd climb on them, grip the reins and squeeze her legs to
get them to walk.

But right now, she was in no mood to walk. She was
galloping through the fields; the wind whipping her hair,
feeling like she was riding and flying and the same time. Her
thigh muscles were clenched as her body rose and fell with
Arcadia's movements, the two of them in sync as they rushed
across the plain.

She'd missed her horse while she was in France. Her mom
had mostly taken care of Arcadia, but every time she'd visited
home, his stable was the first thing she'd run to. She'd
thought about taking him to France with her, but was worried
he'd find the journey too much.

But she was home now, and he was here. And that made
her happy.

"Wait up!" The voice pulled her out of her reverie. The
owner was on a horse galloping toward her, and Grace recog-

nized it instantly – as well as the owner. Her mom's hair was flying out with the breeze, her face pink from a combination of air and exertion.

She slowed her horse down to a trot, and her mom caught up in less than thirty seconds, pulling on her horse's reins to come alongside Grace.

"I didn't know you were coming out today," her mom said, breathless. "You should have called me. I would have met you here."

Here was the farm her Uncle Logan and Aunt Courtney owned. Made up of sprawling fields with a mix of crops and livestock, plus a huge restaurant and inn that attracted locals and tourists alike. From *Field To Plate* was an award-winning eatery, with an ethos of only using locally sourced ingredients, mostly from the farm itself. They also stocked G. Scott Carter whiskey and wine from the vineyard Grace had worked in when she lived in France.

"I thought you enjoyed sleeping until noon on Saturdays," Grace teased. Even though she still had the energy of somebody much younger, her mom was slowing down now that she was in her fifties. She and Grace's dad were planning on slowly retiring over the next few years. Taking more trips abroad, handing the reins over to Grace and the team they'd built up.

Her mom was still beautiful, though, her dark hair tied up into a ponytail beneath her riding helmet, her skin smooth and warm as she smiled at Grace.

"I couldn't sleep," her mom confessed. "Your brother and Ethan were clattering about in the yard, tinkering with Scott's car."

Grace's brother was a motor head, crazy about cars. He had four of them – none of them driveable – at their parents' place. Most college holidays he could be found under one of them.

"Ethan's with Scott?" There was a big age discrepancy

between them. Scott was five years younger than she and Ethan were. It made her uncomfortable to think that Ethan was trying to ingratiate himself with her family.

"He offered to help. He's good with cars." Her mom's voice was even. "He asked about you."

Grace swallowed. "Did he?"

"Yeah. Wanted to know if you're going to the cookout at Cam and Mia's this afternoon. I told him you were."

"Why did you do that?" She looked at her mom from the corner of her eye.

"Because he asked, and I answered." Her mom shrugged. "He's a nice boy, honey."

"He's a man," Grace pointed out. "And anyway, since when did you like the nice ones?"

Her mom laughed. Mostly because Grace's dad had been an ass when he first started working with her mom. It took a lot of fighting for them to get where they were today.

"Since my daughter started dating," her mom said. "And got her heart broken."

"Pascal didn't break my heart," Grace told her. And it was true. Yes, he upset her. Mostly because she thought they were serious, but he was only using her for a bit of fun before he settled down with a French woman his parents approved of, but that was old history now.

"Of course he did. I remember when you came home, how sad you were. I used to watch you when you didn't know I was looking. You'd stare at your phone as though you hoped he'd call."

Grace blinked. Her mom had it all wrong. She'd stare at her phone, thinking about how stupid she'd been to sleep with Michael. Panicking that somebody might find out.

"Why not let me find my own nice guy?" Grace asked her. They were getting closer to the hills now. Where they'd need to turn back and return to the farm. She wanted to finish this conversation. To feel the wind in her hair once again.

To forget about French boyfriends and cousins who weren't cousins and prom dates who wouldn't get the message.

"You're no fun," her mom complained, and Grace rolled her eyes. "I just wanted to do a little matchmaking."

"Do it to somebody else," Grace said, giving her a warm smile. "Because I'm perfectly capable of organizing my own love life." Well, kind of.

"Okay then, I will." Her mom rolled her eyes at Grace. "Let's see. Michael's back in town. He's single now that his divorce was finalized, I guess I could matchmake him.."

"He's divorced? I didn't even know he was married." Grace frowned. Why hadn't she known this?

"Neither did Mia for a while. They eloped." Her mom laughed. "I think that happened while you were away. And then it all went to hell from what I can tell and then they got divorced last year. Mia doesn't really like to talk about it. You know how quiet she can be about her personal life."

Grace stared right ahead, her teeth clenched. That meant he was married when they'd spent the night together. A wave of fury washed over her. What right did he have to lie to her and then come storming into her house like a self righteous pig?

Oh, he had some answering to do.

"Come on, let's stop talking and ride," she said, because she needed to work this energy off.

"Okay." Her mom grinned, turning her horse around. "Race you back to the farm."

And that's what she needed. A race, a fast ride. Anything to push the thought of him – and his stupid marriage and their one night together – out of her head.

―――

"The team isn't playing ball. They're refusing to make an offer unless we agree to a one year extension."

"We said two. And a new contract." Michael shook his head at the laptop in front of him. He wasn't supposed to be working. Wasn't supposed to be in his room above the garage – the one his mom and Cam had built for him when he was still a teenager, but he'd barely stayed in. And yeah, he felt guilty because his mom really tried to make this place feel like his home.

There were photographs of all of them. Him, his mom, stepdad, and Josh, the younger brother he also shared a dad with.

Josh and Cam had always been close. He'd even taken Cam's surname when their mom had married him. But he'd been nine and Michael had been sixteen by that point, and there was a vast gulf between being an excited kid and a grumpy-ass teenager.

It was funny, really, because Michael was the reason Cam and his mom had met. He and Josh had been throwing a ball in the street and damaged the paintwork on an expensive sports car, only for the owner to climb out and chase after them.

The owner had been Cam, of course. And then he'd turned out to be Michael's football coach at high school, too.

And that's how Cam and Michael's mom had first started talking. And why he'd hated the thought of them together. It had been embarrassing, and at the time he still hadn't gotten over his parents' divorce.

As an adult, he was much more understanding. Shit happened. You found happiness where you could. And who was he to stop his mom from being happy?

"Let's do nothing until Monday afternoon," Michael said. "Make them sweat. Call the client, let him know the plan, and tell him to get out and get papped this weekend." Michael lifted his brow. "Not drinking. Just having a good time. Looking casual."

"Casual. Got it."

"We'll talk on Monday." He'd have to get up at a stupid hour to make sure they had a plan on Monday morning, but he'd do it. "Now go enjoy your evening. Or what's left of it." He said goodbye and hung up the call, slumping in his chair.

It was two o'clock in West Virginia. Which meant it was seven o'clock in London, and there was another layer of guilt, that the people he employed were working on a Saturday evening because he'd come back home.

He'd spent the morning catching up on all the emails he'd been sent yesterday while he'd been traveling. And there was a huge ass pile of shit to deal with before Monday. He knew it would be harder to do his job from across the Atlantic, but what choice did he have?

You could have stayed in London.

Yeah, he could. And then he'd be feeling guilty there, too. It was a lose-lose situation.

Even without the whole Grace debacle.

He'd thought about her last night, when the jetlag stopped him from sleeping. Remembered the way she'd looked at him in her hallway when he'd asked her if she was okay. All doe-eyed and soft. He'd wanted to taste those lips, feel her breath against him, make her sigh the way she'd sighed that night a year ago.

But she's not yours.

Yeah, and it needed to stay that way. She'd agreed to avoid him and that was good, wasn't it?

Because no one knew what type of shitshow would ensue if her parents found out about their night in New York. That he'd buried himself inside of her until they were both breathless and sweaty. That he'd held her all night and thought it was just the beginning.

This needed to stop. She was way too young and his life

was complicated enough. He was here for his mom, nothing else.

"Hey bro?"

His door opened and Josh was standing in the gap. His brother had arrived earlier that day and Michael had been so happy to see the kid – though he wasn't a kid anymore. He was grown up with a fiancé and a house in Charleston.

"Everybody's arriving," Josh told him. "Mom wanted me to get you."

He nodded. "Cool. I'll be down in just a minute." He'd been up since the ass of dawn helping Cam set everything up. Tenderizing steaks, making burgers, carrying in cases of beer.

"Everything okay?"

"Yeah." Michael gave him a wry smile. "Just work stuff."

Josh gave him an understanding look. He worked for a tech company in Charleston. "I know that feeling. Anything I can help with?"

It was still funny seeing how grown up his brother was. "No. It's all good."

"Excellent." Josh lifted a brow. "Mom's gone all gaga about having her 'babies in one place'. She wants a photo of us all later."

"Can't wait," Michael said dryly, his eyes catching Josh's. But they'd do it for her because she wasn't well and they wanted to make her happy.

"I'm glad you're home," Josh said.

"Yeah, me, too." Michael winked at him.

And it was only a bit of a lie.

———

"You get a beer," Hendrix said, passing a bottle to Grace. "And you get a beer," he said, giving the next one to her brother, Scott. She lifted a brow at him – he was too young and he knew it, but he just shrugged and took a mouthful before she could stop him.

"What the hell. EVERYBODY gets a beer!" Hendrix started throwing them out at all the cousins. And there were a lot of them.

So many she was losing count. Hendrix was as handsome as his older brothers, but according to gossip he was more dangerous with the ladies. Luckily, all the ladies here were related to him and rolled their eyes at his antics.

He threw another bottle, and Sabrina caught it, grinning.

"Your mom okay with you drinking?" he asked her. She still wasn't twenty-one.

"I don't know." Sabrina shrugged. "Anybody gonna tell her?"

Of course somebody was going to tell her, this town was too small and mouths were too big. Luckily, it wouldn't involve Grace.

And then Ethan walked over. He was wearing a pair of long shorts and a t-shirt, his hair mussed up the way it always was. "Hey." He smiled widely at Grace. "I tried to call you earlier. See if you wanted to come over together."

And she'd ignored his call because she didn't have the energy to deal with him. "Sorry, I didn't check my phone. How are you?" she asked politely, because now she felt bad. But she also didn't want to give him the wrong impression.

"I'm good now that I've seen you." He clinked his beer against hers. "I hear you went riding today."

And there it was. Proof positive that nothing remained a secret around here. Well, almost nothing. "Arcadia needed to stretch his legs. I haven't taken him out for a week," she told him.

"Next time tell me. I'll ride with you."

She smiled. "Sure." But she wouldn't. She rode to think, to be alone, to feel elated. And it was one thing having her mom there, but not Ethan.

It felt too weird.

From the corner of her eye, she could see her uncles and her dad by the grills, beers in their hands, all laughing. Then her heart did a little twist when she saw Michael there.

She looked away quickly, her cheeks burning.

"I mean, only if you want," Ethan said.

Grace took a deep breath. "I mostly ride alone," she told him. "But maybe sometime."

"Okay." He grinned at her. "By the way, I met Arcadia last week when I visited the farm to check over all the horses. He's beautiful."

She smiled, pleased. "Thank you." He'd been her sweet sixteenth birthday gift. But she'd had to work weekends at the stable to pay for his board.

"Have you ever thought of breeding him?" Ethan asked, and it felt a little too personal.

"Not really." She shook her head.

"I have clients who'd love a thoroughbred like him as a sire. If you change your mind, let me know."

"Sure."

She looked over at the grills again. Michael was talking to her uncle Cam. He was wearing dark jeans that hugged his thick thighs, and a black t-shirt that had the same attachment to his chest. Before she could look away, he turned and caught her staring. She pulled her lip between her teeth, because she'd promised to ignore him.

He lifted a single brow, and it annoyed her.

Don't mess with me, asshole. I know your secrets and you have some answering to do.

It was as though neither of them were willing to look away first. A game you'd play in kindergarten, except it never made her feel like this. Light-headed. Buzzing. A little turned on.

He parted his lips to breathe out, and she hoped he felt just as messed up.

"Your hair's turned lighter," Ethan said. "Must be something to do with the sun." He leaned forward to pick up a lock of it, sliding his fingers over her hair.

Michael's eyes narrowed. She liked that.

"It always does that in the summer," she murmured.

"It suits you. Makes you look prettier than ever." Ethan's fingertips trailed along her cheek, and she shivered – but not from pleasure. She didn't like him touching her at all.

"Thanks." She stepped back, feeling uncomfortable.

"Anytime," Ethan said, a smile warming his voice. She finally pulled her eyes away from Michael's. "Are you okay?" Ethan asked her.

"I'm fine, why?"

"I thought you were hungry or something." He chuckled. "You keep looking over at the grill."

"I forgot to eat breakfast," she told him. "And I didn't have time for lunch." At least that wasn't a lie. After riding Arcadia, then cleaning him and his stable out, she'd only just had time to shower before she came over here.

"Let me get you some food before you faint," Ethan said.

"You don't need to. I can wait." She grabbed his wrist to stop him and he looked down at it, smiling.

"Come on then, let's go sit down instead," he urged, pointing at the chairs where her cousins were now sitting, drinking their own beers and talking about the game they all went to see last night.

"Okay." She nodded, taking one last look at the older generation. Michael wasn't looking at her anymore. He was smiling at a woman she didn't recognize – one of her aunt's friends, maybe?

For a moment she imagined walking over there, sliding her arm around his waist as he carried on talking.

But she didn't. Instead, she let Ethan lead her to the chairs, helping her sit down before taking the one next to her, slinging his hand across the back of hers as though he was making a statement.

Her brother lifted a brow at her, as if to ask her what was going on. She shook her head, because it was nothing. Just Ethan doing his thing. He'd been the same when they went to prom. Proprietorial.

If she was annoyed, she'd pull her chair away, but honestly, she couldn't be bothered. And at least it would put anybody off the scent of her and Michael.

That's what they both wanted, wasn't it? For nobody to find out?

If Ethan wanted to be overeager, let him. Michael couldn't complain she wasn't holding up her side of the bargain.

CHAPTER
Seven

THE COOKOUT WAS in full swing as the sun slowly slid down toward the mountain line in the distance. Michael rubbed his face with the heel of his hands. His eyelids felt heavy. But he wasn't sure he could sleep even if his mom's backyard wasn't full of people.

Over on the other side of the yard, the cousins – his cousins if you didn't care about blood – were getting rowdier. Tequila was flowing, somebody was playing guitar, and his little sister and one of the younger cousins were dancing around the fire they'd built.

Next to him, his mom yawned and stretched her arms.

"It's late," he said softly to her. "You want me to tell them all to go home?" He glanced at the fire pit and then away again.

"I'm okay," his mom said, touching his arm with her warm palm. Someone at the firepit squealed and Michael shook his head. "They're having fun," his mom said. "Let them be. And I'm fine. I'll just disappear. No need for anybody to go home yet."

"Won't the neighbors be fed up with all the noise?" he asked her.

She laughed, shaking her still-blonde hair. "The neighbors are all here. And anyway, the closest one is a half-mile away." She slid her hand into his and squeezed it. "I'm so happy you're here."

"I'm happy, too. Now let me walk you back to the house." He was worried she was overdoing it.

She patted his hand. "It's okay, Cam will walk me in. You stay and enjoy yourself."

He wasn't sure if that was the right description. Keeping his face neutral and not reacting to Grace was more of an endurance than an enjoyment.

"And anyway, you're doing enough by taking me to the hospital on Monday." She looked happy about that. He'd done the right thing by offering to be her chauffeur for her treatment. Her outpatient appointments would be short, but the hospital was two hours away, so it was a long journey for her.

Cam walked over and offered her his arm, and Michael kissed his mom's cheek and wished her goodnight. He took a sip of his beer, but it was doing nothing for him.

And then there was another burst of laughter from the crowd of cousins by the firepit. Grace was standing on the edge of them all, a smile playing on her lips.

Her smooth face was lit orange by the fire, her glossy dark hair was tumbling down her back, the same way it was that night in New York. She'd been wearing a pair of rolled up shorts and a cropped t-shirt all day, but now she was also wearing a hoodie. It was too big for her. The sleeves were rolled up and the hem almost covered her shorts, so it looked like she was wearing nothing else.

He disliked that hoodie intensely. Mostly because he knew who it belonged to. That guy who'd been following her around all day. Touching her. Talking to her. Bringing her food.

"You doing all right?" Cam asked a few minutes later

when he got back from taking Mia to bed. He picked up a beer from the cooler.

"Yep. Mom okay?"

"She is. Just got her into bed." Cam took a long sip of beer. Michael gave him a sympathetic smile. He knew this was hard on his stepdad.

A memory flashed into Michael's mind. Of Cam patiently playing ball with Josh, who couldn't throw to save his life. But Cam had patiently worked with him every day until Josh made the junior varsity team.

He was a good guy. Michael knew they were lucky to have him in their lives.

"Thank you for taking care of her." He meant it. One of the main reasons he could pursue his career in London was because he knew his mom was happy.

Cam gave him a strange look. "What else would I do? She's my life."

"I know," Michael said. "And I know it's been hard on you, too."

Cam swallowed. "It's easier now that you're here."

They exchanged a look. "It took me long enough." Michael lifted a brow.

"You have a career. A good one. We're both proud of you." Cam nodded at him, and Michael nodded back.

"Thanks." Michael's voice was low. Cam nodded and walked off, grabbing another beer from the cooler before joining his brothers, slumping down on a chair and running his free hand through his hair.

This was why he was back. To take care of his family and make sure they were okay. Not to keep looking over at the pretty girl in shorts and a hoodie who he never should have touched.

It was old history. Finished. Forgotten.

Now he just needed to make it stay that way.

Grace wasn't really a fan of beer. And it wasn't a fine wine kind of party, so she was as sober as a judge as she watched her cousins crowd around Presley and Marley and sing *American Pie*.

It was funny, because her first boss in France had called her Miss American Pie. Back when she hadn't mastered the language, and definitely not the accent. She'd worked hard to fit in, though.

"I have to leave," Ethan said, reluctantly glancing at his watch. "I'm on call tomorrow, so I'll need to be up stupidly early."

Was it wrong that she was relieved? She'd pictured an embarrassing goodbye where he tried to get himself an invite to her house. "Good plan," she said, nodding. "Take care getting home."

"Walk me to the front of the house?" he asked.

"Oh. Um…" Grace looked around, but she couldn't grasp at a way to say no. "Okay." It would be a chance to sneak into her aunt and uncle's house and make a coffee, anyway. She was tired, but also the designated driver for Presley and Marley, so she wouldn't be leaving until they did. She ignored the knowing looks and followed Ethan through the vast lawn where everybody was sitting, to the driveway beyond.

His mom was waiting for him in the driver's seat of a station wagon. Grace tried not to find it funny that even at twenty-six his mom was picking him up, but somehow this town made you feel like you were still a kid. Still a night's sleep away from first period math and a pop quiz, you knew you were going to flunk.

Hartson's Creek was Neverland. The town where nobody grew up.

"Oh, let me give you back your hoodie," she said as Ethan nodded at his mom.

"There's no need. I'll pick it up from you later."

Ugh, she'd pass on that one. Ignoring him, she pulled the hoodie over her head, the movement dragging her t-shirt from the waistband of her shorts, exposing her stomach to the cool night air.

She gave it to Ethan and tucked herself in again.

"I had a good night. Thank you." Ethan leaned forward and kissed her cheek. He smelled of beer. It was nauseating. For the animals' sake she hoped he didn't smell like that in the morning.

"No problem." Her voice was clipped. "See you around, Ethan."

"You will."

She stepped back before he could kiss her again, wrapping her arms around her waist because the air had turned chillier now that the sun had gone down and she definitely wasn't asking for his damn hoodie back.

"Good night then." She turned around and walked down the side of the house, opening the door that led to the kitchen. It was huge, like the rest of the house, and dark, too. She flicked on the lights, ready to head for the coffee machine that Cam had told her was in the far cupboard, giving her the green light to make as much as she liked.

And then she jumped like a damn kangaroo.

Michael was sitting at the breakfast bar, a glass of what looked like water in front of him.

"Oh God." She pressed her hand against her chest. "I didn't see you there."

He gave her a wry smile. "Sorry."

"I was just going to make a coffee, but I can come back," she said, her voice hesitant. They'd promised not to be seen together after all. And the situation with Ethan was playing over in her mind. She needed to let him know she wasn't interested.

It was easy to give brush offs to people in big cities. You

never had to see them again. Or deal with their mom knowing yours, or your brother asking them for help with their car.

And ugh, them being the only vet in town if your horse got lame.

"I'm surprised you're not outside," Michael said. Oh, so now he was chatty? What happened to ignoring each other?

She was annoyed at herself for liking the fact he was talking.

"Why's that?" she asked.

He shrugged, saying nothing, but his eyes were still on her face. She felt like she was being scrutinized.

"If you have something to say, just say it," she told him. And dammit, she was getting that coffee. He could be the one to leave, thank you very much.

"You seem close to that boy."

Her mouth dropped open, but luckily, she had her back to him. She straightened her expression before she turned to look at him.

Be cool as a cucumber. Don't show him you're annoyed.

"I wasn't aware I had to get your permission to talk to a *man*," she said. "And for your information, Ethan is only a few months younger than me."

"Like I said. A boy."

She tipped her head to the side. Michael had his arms resting on the counter, his biceps tight and defined where they met the sleeves of his t-shirt. She'd always had a thing for arms. Strong, muscled ones.

Ones that knew exactly what they were doing.

Focus, dammit.

"At least he never lied to me to get me into bed," she said.

Michael blinked. "What?"

"You were married when we had sex." There. She'd got it out. But she didn't feel any better. Just more annoyed than ever.

"Who told you that?" he asked, frowning.

"My mom."

It was his turn for his mouth to drop open. "You told your mom we had sex?"

"No. She told me you got divorced last year. I worked out the rest. It just would have been nice for you to tell me you were married before you slid your dick inside of me."

He swallowed. There was an intensity to him that made her feel off-kilter. For a moment, she thought he was going to stand up and walk toward her. Cage her against the cupboard.

Did she want that? Truthfully, she wasn't sure.

But he didn't move. Just looked at her with those stupidly attractive eyes. "I got divorced almost two years ago. Long before I came to New York."

Oh.

"And I never cheated on my wife. Never would. My dad did that to my mom, and I know the devastation it could cause."

"I'm sorry." She felt terrible but couldn't find the words to tell him that. "I shouldn't have said anything."

He shook his head. "Whatever."

"I just… I don't know. I'm finding this really hard," she admitted. It was all too much. First Ethan and now Michael. Her feelings were confusing her.

He looked at her again. She couldn't read his expression at all. "Yeah. I get that."

She wanted to ask him if he felt the same. If he thought about that night every time he looked at her. If his heart hammered against his chest every time their gazes connected.

But of course he didn't. What did he call Ethan? A boy? That made her a girl. Of no interest. Inconsequential.

She hated that.

"I'm not a good liar," she told him, busying herself with the coffee machine.

"Yeah. I can see that." He lifted a brow.

He was still sitting at the breakfast bar, but he'd turned to look at her. Behind him, the wall of glass doors that led to the yard was dark, the light inside the kitchen turning them into mirrors, making two Michaels – one real, one fake.

"I have a good poker face when I'm not in Hartson's Creek," she continued. "In Paris, I could lock things out like the best of them."

Was he smiling?

"But here it's like I've gone back to being a kid. My parents reading me like a book." She hated that. She was a grown woman with a career and her own place. She could look after herself.

"Try living with them," he said, sounding amused.

"No, thank you." She pressed a button, and the coffee hissed out. Just an espresso. "I tried that for about a week before I went to Uncle Tanner and begged him to rent me a house." She pulled the little cup from the machine and lifted it to her lips.

"Won't all that caffeine keep you awake all night?" he asked.

She shook her head. "No. I could probably have three and sleep like a log."

"Sleep is wasted on the young," he said dryly.

She grinned. "Do you have trouble sleeping?"

He shrugged. "Sometimes. Mostly because of jetlag right now."

"It'll be worse the other way."

"I know." He looked at her carefully. "But I have a while before I need to worry about that."

Grace let out a long breath. This was nice. Just talking. Maybe if they hadn't messed things up by sleeping with each other, they could have done more of this. She had more in common with him than she did with any of her blood cousins, after all. They both loved Europe, good food... Wine.

And he made her laugh. It wasn't often that somebody had done that in the last year.

"I should go back outside," she told him. "Everybody thinks I have a thing going with Ethan and the longer I'm away, the more they'll think that." She wrinkled her nose. There's no way she wanted the wrong kind of gossip going around about her.

"So it wasn't just me then," he murmured.

"I'm trying to find a way to let him down gently," she admitted, saying out loud what she'd been ruminating on earlier. "It's trickier when everybody knows everybody."

"Right?" He was smiling now, and she liked that so much. She didn't want to go outside. She wanted to slip into the chair beside him and talk. Wanted to hear him laugh again.

Wanted to kiss him.

But neither of them needed World War Three to erupt in the Hartson family.

"I guess I'll see you around," she said softly, heading for the door.

"I guess you will."

She stepped outside, reaching back to pull the door closed behind her, when she heard his voice once more.

"Grace?"

"Yeah?"

"Some guys can't be let down gently. Sometimes you have to be cruel to be kind."

CHAPTER
Eight

IT HAD BEEN A LONG WEEK. Michael had taken his mom back and forth from the hospital most days, and he'd hated seeing her so exhausted as they pulled into the driveway when they got home. He'd spent every evening working, making up for the time when they were on the road. Thankfully, he'd enjoyed being busy.

Made him think less about the mess he'd made of his life.

Even though she was tired from her treatment, his mom had still insisted that they go to *Chairs* for an hour that night. And since she didn't need to be at the hospital over the weekend, he'd agreed – he could spend the next two days catching up on emails and be ready for his staff to be back in the office on Monday.

It wasn't perfect, but it would do.

Grace hadn't been at *Chairs*. And maybe that was a good thing. Michael spent an hour sitting with his mom and Cam and their friends before she got tired enough that she wanted to go home, and despite her protestations that he should stay, he was relieved to have an excuse to leave.

Cam and his mom had gone up to bed, and Mason had

gone out with his friends to a bar. Michael had agreed to pick up Sabrina from a party she'd gone to at her friend's house.

Though he hadn't heard from his baby sister all night.

"Don't let her fool you into letting her stay late," his mom had warned as she'd walked up the stairs. "She needs to be home by midnight."

He didn't bother to point out that nobody knew what time she got home when she was away at college. Nor that he'd stayed out way later at her age – and gotten into so much more trouble than Sabrina ever would. *Hopefully.*

Just after midnight he sent his sister a text because he didn't want his mom to wake up and not find her there. He waited five minutes and there was no reply.

Which was fine. Right? What self-respecting college student would be constantly checking her phone at a party?

When ten more minutes passed, he brought Sabrina's number up and pressed the call button, rubbing his hand over his face as he waited for it to connect. In another half an hour he'd be in bed, sleeping, he hoped, though the jetlag hadn't seemed to let go of him completely. Or maybe the sleepless nights were down to worry. About his mom. His staff. The stupid mistake he'd made sleeping with Grace.

"Hello?" That wasn't Sabrina. He checked the screen to make sure he'd called the right contact.

"Is Sabrina there?"

"Who's calling?"

Jesus, did she have a receptionist now? "Her brother," he said gruffly.

There was a pause. And he was trying not to get annoyed because Sabrina was an adult and she was entitled to have some fun.

"I'm afraid she's not available right now," the girl said, and his annoyance took root.

"She'd better be available. Because I'm coming to pick her up. Can you tell her that, please?"

Another moment's silence. Longer than the last. "Um, there's a slight problem."

His jaw tightened. This was one of the many reasons he hadn't had kids. He'd been a punk when he was one. Josh had been pretty good. Mason? Well, he'd smoked pot all senior year before Cam had straightened him out and gotten him into college.

And now Sabrina. If she'd gone off with somebody, he was gonna kill them.

"What kind of problem?" he growled.

"The kind where she's drunk too much," the girl told him. "Like way too much."

He pinched his nose, sighing. "Don't let her leave. I'm on my way."

————

"I'm sorry, I'm sorry." Sabrina was sobbing. And unable to stand up without his assistance. If this wasn't his little sister, it'd be a comedy sketch. Every time he put her upright, she listed to the side, threatening to hit the ground before he grabbed her.

He growled with frustration. This wasn't working. Without warning, he hoisted her into his arms. At least this way she might escape tonight without any broken bones.

The music was still pumping out of the stereo system some of her friends had rigged up. He was pretty sure there were no parents here, but that wasn't his problem. Still, he checked around for any half-comatose bodies because he wasn't that much of an asshole.

Luckily, Sabrina was the worst of the group.

"What are you doing?" she mumbled. "I'm gonna throw up on you."

"No you're not," he muttered. "Think happy thoughts."

Her hands were sticky on his neck. Her body was like a

rag doll's. He carried her to his car, a mixture of exasperated and pissed, because she was almost certainly going to throw up in it.

Sabrina full-out sobbed, and Michael grimaced. Drunk, he could deal with. Emotional? Every cell in his body wanted to run away.

"This is a rental," he warned her as he opened up the car. "If you're sick in it, I'm gonna have to pay fees."

"Just leave me here," she slurred. "I'll walk home when I'm ready."

"I'm not leaving you," he told her. She was vulnerable. Beautiful. Alone.

Yeah, she knew most of the kids here, but it only took one asshole to take advantage. He shuddered at the thought of what might have happened if he hadn't been tasked to pick her up.

"You do this a lot?" he asked, wheezing as he lifted her into the passenger seat. He reached across to slide the seatbelt buckle into the slot, then stepped away from her.

She stank of alcohol.

"I'm just sad," she muttered. "Mom's sick."

His fingers curled around her door. "I know," he said softly.

"I hate seeing her like that."

Michael swallowed. "She's doing okay. Just tired."

"I don't want to lose her. I don't know what I'd do without her." She sobbed again, then burped, and he rummaged through the pocket in the door, finding a plastic bag that at least might save him from having to pay for a full detail of the car.

"Here," he said. "Hold this."

"I'm sorry," she told him again.

He tried not to sound annoyed. "You already said that. And it's fine. Let's get you home and to bed."

Michael closed the door, walking around to the driver's side, sliding into his seat and starting the engine up.

"Oh God, that feels bad," Sabrina muttered.

"What feels bad?"

"This car."

"Just hold on. It's only a few minutes."

"I can't," she told him. "I'm gonna…"

"Hold the bag," he told her, but it was too late. She was sick everywhere. On herself, on the damn car.

Even on the bag. Not in it, though.

Shit.

"I didn't mean to," she wailed. "I feel so bad."

"It's okay. Just try to breathe." He pressed the button to open her window, hoping the fresh air would help her and the stench. "You breathing?"

"I'm trying."

Thank God. "Let's go home."

"I can't. What if mom sees me?" Sabrina asked, her words a stutter. "Please take me to Grace."

"What?"

"Her house is two minutes away. Take me there. She'll help."

Michael stared out of the windshield. "It's late. She'll be asleep."

"S'okay. She's helped me out before."

She had? It was news to him. And yet not a surprise.

"You have Grace's number in your phone?" he asked, because there was no way he was turning up without talking to her first.

"Uhuh." Sabrina sniffed and nodded at the same time. The smell wafting off of her was making his stomach turn. After three attempts, she unlocked her phone with her Face ID and passed it to him. He found Grace's contact number and pressed call.

It took five rings for her to answer and he felt like an asshole for waking her up.

Hated even more that he might not be. She could have someone there. Like the guy who was flirting with her at the cookout.

His stomach turned at the thought of it.

"Hello?" her voice was soft. It wrapped around him like a blanket. "Sabrina, is everything okay?"

"It's Michael," he said.

"Oh." She sounded confused. "I thought it was Sabrina calling."

"I'm using her phone. I need a big favor." He pinched the bridge of his nose. "Sabrina's drunk as a skunk. And she's thrown up all over herself. Can I bring her to your place?"

There wasn't a moment's hesitation from her. "Of course."

Relief washed over him. It was weird how relieved those two words made him. "Thank you. I owe you big time."

"It's okay. Just bring her here. I'll be waiting."

CHAPTER
Nine

SHE just about had time to pull on a pair of shorts and a crop t-shirt before she saw the headlights illuminate her small drive. Grace ran down the stairs and slid her bare feet into her sneakers and pulled open the door, not bothering to check herself in the mirror.

Mostly because she knew she'd look sleep ridden.

She flicked on the outside lamp as Michael climbed out of the car. For a moment, he froze in the light, his eyes connecting with hers.

She smiled at him and he smiled back. Weird how that made her heart jump.

"You need help bringing her in?" she asked, not bothering to wait for him to offer. Her nose wrinkled as soon as he opened the passenger door, the sweet cloying smell of whatever Sabrina had drunk earlier sticking to her nostrils.

"I'm sorry," Sabrina told her as soon as Michael lifted her out. "I didn't know where else to go."

It hadn't escaped her notice that Michael was carrying his sister like she was as light as a feather.

"It's okay," she told Sabrina. "Try not to worry. Let's just get you inside and cleaned up."

"Where do you want me to take her?" Michael asked. He glanced down at her legs and up again.

She liked that he noticed her. Too much.

"Let's go to my bathroom," Grace said, closing the passenger door. "You got the keys for your car?"

"Yeah, it'll lock automatically."

She led the way to her bathroom. Michael had to walk through her bedroom to get there, and she felt strangely vulnerable. The covers on her bed were thrown to the side from getting up fast.

"Okay sweetie," Grace said to Sabrina after Michael had set her gently on the tiled floor. "We're gonna get you undressed and into the shower and then you can sleep, okay?" She looked at Michael. "Could you grab a towel from the closet right outside my room for me? And maybe a long t-shirt if you can find one? There should be a few in my bedroom closet."

He nodded, walking out to her bedroom, and she turned back to Sabrina, who was half-slumped against the bathroom tiles.

"Just hang in there," she told her little cousin. "You're doing great."

"Michael must hate me," Sabrina groaned. "I'm such a mess."

"He's your brother. He loves you. He's just worried about you."

She could hear the noise of her closet door opening. Her face felt hot at the thought of him in her bedroom, rummaging through her clothes.

Not because she hated it, but because she liked it. Liked the idea of him in there.

"Have you found a towel?" she called out. Sabrina slid down further and Grace held her up. She needed to get this shower started.

"Uh, yeah. Just getting a t-shirt."

She made sure Sabrina was stable, then walked over to turn on her shower. It always took a while for the water to heat up at night. Then she reached through the spray to grab the shampoo and shower gel from the shelf. It would be easier for her to have them on this side of the shower.

"Okay, let's get this done," she muttered, then bent over to tug at Sabrina's jeans. It's only when she heard Michael clearing his throat that she realized he'd walked into the view of her own ass jutting up at him.

"You need help?" he asked, as she tugged at the denim.

She looked over her shoulder at him, her hair swaying with the movement.

"Maybe I should do this bit?" she suggested. "I don't think you want to see Sabrina half clothed."

He nodded gratefully. "Yeah. That would be good."

"You should change, too. You have vomit on your t-shirt."

He looked down. "I have nothing else to wear."

And no, neither did she. Not that would fit him, anyway. "You could put my robe on?"

He glanced at the fluffy robe hanging on her bathroom door. "I'm not putting your robe on," he growled. "If you don't mind helping Sabrina, I'll clean up the car the best I can."

"Good plan." She nodded. "I have cleaning stuff in the kitchen. In the cupboard beneath the sink. Help yourself."

"Thank you." He caught her eye. "For everything."

"You're not the one who needs to thank me."

"But I am anyway."

A smile ghosted her lips. "I'm glad you called. I'm always happy to help." And she was. Pleased they were in this together. Even though her heart hammered against her chest every time he looked at her, his eyes a mixture of dark and soft.

He glanced down at her legs again, his brow furrowing before he resolutely tore his gaze away from her. "I'll let you clean her up. I'll be outside in the car. Call me if you need me."

"I don't have your number."

"I meant shout." His lips twitched. "But yeah, I'll text you my number. What's yours?"

She reeled it off and a moment later he was tapping at his own phone, pressing the send button and making hers vibrate.

"Try not to change your number this time," he murmured.

She grinned. "Noted. Now go clean out your car."

He touched his fingers to his brow. "Yes, ma'am." She watched as he walked out of the bathroom. A moment later, she turned back to Sabrina, giving her cousin a reassuring smile.

"Ready to take a shower?" she asked, encouraging her to sit up so Grace could take her top off.

Sabrina opened her mouth to answer, then went pale. "I'm going to be sick again."

Grace got her over to the toilet before she erupted this time. Rubbing her cousin's back, she thanked god that at least there wasn't more to clean up.

"Good girl. Better out than in." She held Sabrina's hair away from her face, hearing the distant sound of the front door as Michael presumably went out to clean his car. A glance at her phone told her it was nearly one in the morning.

This was going to be a long night.

————

Michael scrubbed at the stains in his rental car as fast as he could, not wanting to leave Grace for too long. It was best that he wasn't there while Sabrina showered, but he still felt guilty for bringing this shit show to her door.

When she'd walked outside to help him with his sister, there'd still been vestiges of sleep softening Grace's face. He'd noticed her legs in those shorts. And her abdomen, or the sliver of it that was showing between her cropped t-shirt and her waistband.

God help him, he'd wanted to touch her. Even though he was here for Sabrina – and so was Grace. He'd still wanted to feel the softness of her skin.

And he knew that made him an asshole.

He'd certainly felt like one when he'd had to rifle through her closet for a t-shirt that would be appropriate for Sabrina. Mostly because his fingers had touched something silken. Not her panties, thank god, because then he might have had to cut them off. Instead, they'd curled around a tank. A white one, the fabric so soft it made his chest contract.

He finished scrubbing, putting the cloths he'd used into a trash bag. He'd buy Grace a new set of them, to thank her for her help.

Convenient how it'll give you the opportunity to see her again, huh?

Sliding the gloves off his hands and putting them into the sack too, he closed up the car and walked back to her house. Damn, he'd closed the front door. He didn't want to ring the bell, in case she was still in the middle of dealing with Sabrina. So he sat on the stoop and let out a long breath, looking out into the night. Grace lived on a quiet road, one that had a dead end, so there was no through traffic. The house across the street had some kids' bikes leaned against the wall, and the one next to it had a slide in the front yard. A family neighborhood. Nice. Safe.

"Hey."

He turned to see the front door had opened. Grace was framed by the lintel, light from the hall flooding behind her.

"What are you doing sitting there?" she asked.

"I closed the door. Didn't want to ring the bell and disturb you. How's Sabrina?" He stood, stretching his muscles because dammit, he was getting old and not used to carrying his sister.

"She's fast asleep in my bed. She still has wet hair so she'll look wild in the morning, but at least she doesn't smell anymore. I'm about to put her clothes in the washer. Want me to throw your t-shirt in there too?"

"Probably best not to. I can only imagine the look on Cam's face if he catches me walking in shirtless."

Her gaze dropped to his chest and then up again. "You could stay while it dries."

"Yeah. That would work."

"Come on in," she said. "The laundry's in the back." He followed her, this time not looking at her ass in those shorts. Not watching the way her hips rocked as she walked.

He didn't need to. It was already seared into his memory.

The laundry room was small. The washer and dryer were both front loaders, slid underneath a counter. By the time they were both inside the room, there wasn't much space left.

She took the clothes from the wash tub where she must have put them before coming to find him. They'd been soaking, and she lifted them straight into the washer, throwing in some powder before looking over at him.

"Give me your shirt."

His mouth twitched, but he did as she asked, lifting it over his head, feeling his hair getting mussed by the neckline, then rolled it into a ball and passed it to her.

Two pink discs formed on her cheeks. "Go sit down in the kitchen," she said. "I'll make us some sweet tea."

He smiled. "I haven't drunk sweet tea for years."

"It's not big in Europe, is it?" she asked, closing the washer door and twisting the dial.

He looked away again. Because looking meant wanting to touch.

"No. I think the last time I drank it I must have been sixteen. Laced with vodka, probably."

"I would've liked to see you at sixteen."

He swallowed. "I was a punk. I'm glad you didn't."

She stood. "You're not a punk now."

"Aren't I?" He turned back to look at her.

Grace shook her head. And their gazes held for a moment too long.

"You sure you don't want my robe?" she asked him, breaking the silence.

"You want me to put it on?" he asked.

"Not really." There was that smile again. Curling her pretty lips. Making her face glow. "I kind of like the view exactly how it is."

The thickness of her voice twisted around him. Made him ache. Made him hard. "You shouldn't say things like that."

"You shouldn't walk around half naked," she countered.

"That sounds like victim shaming," he shot back, but dammit, he was grinning.

"You want me to take my top off so you don't feel like a victim?" she asked him.

Yes, he did. More than anything.

"No," he replied gruffly. "For the sake of my sanity, it's best if you stay fully dressed."

She ran her tongue along her lip. His gaze followed it, desire licking at his belly. He could almost taste it. Taste her.

He wanted to.

"Come here," he said.

Without hesitating, she walked toward him. He reached out to touch her hair, her face, her skin soft as silk against his fingers.

"Christ, you're beautiful."

"Shut up."

He grinned. "You don't like compliments, do you?"

"I like them enough," she said, her voice soft as he traced her cheek, her jaw, her lips. "It's just I'm more than a face. I'm me. Not many people see that."

"I do."

She swallowed. "I know."

He slid his palm down her neck, along her shoulder, to her bare arm. Then he curled his hand around her waist and pulled her against him.

She melted into him. A willing victim. No, not a victim, not Grace. She was too strong for that. Steel wrapped in silk.

Her breasts pushed against his bare chest. Just a thin swathe of fabric between them. He could feel the tautness of her nipples. The tightness of his jeans.

She lifted her head up, her gaze on him. Her lips were pink. Slightly open. He was done fighting this, at least for tonight.

He didn't have the damn resolve. He leaned into kiss her and then...

The sound of vomiting cut through the air. Grace jumped, and the cool reality of their situation washed over him.

They'd talked about this. They both knew it was a bad idea. "I'll go help her," he said gruffly. Because Sabrina was his sister. She was his problem. And there was cold water in the bathroom.

He had a feeling he'd need a lot of it splashed against his face to get through the night.

CHAPTER

Ten

"HONEY, I'm heading out for lunch. Care to join me?"

Grace looked up from her laptop to see her mom framed in the doorway of her office.

"I can't." She grimaced, pointing at the files on her desk. "I have to get ready for this afternoon's meeting."

Her mom shrugged. "Okay then. But you know what they say about all work and no play."

"I work for you, so I wouldn't protest too much," Grace pointed out, and her mom laughed.

"That's true. Get on with it. No lunch break for you."

One reason she was throwing herself into work was so she didn't think about Friday night. Not that she could stop herself from thinking about it for long. Her face flushed as she remembered how close she and Michael came to kissing.

But then Sabrina had been sick again and Michael had gone to help her, and thank goodness they'd both come to their senses and remembered exactly why this wasn't a good idea.

What if he'd kissed her and Sabrina had seen them? The thought of it sent a shiver down her spine. Dating Pascal had complicated things for the distillery, though her parents hadn't blamed her when it ended.

But if they found out about her and Michael, things in their family would explode.

Ugh. She needed to stop thinking about this. She pulled a file toward her and opened it, then swallowed hard because it contained all the details of the partnership they'd had with Pascal's family's vineyard. She was supposed to be making some new brochures to attract another partner.

Another thing that she'd messed up. She let out a long breath and opened up her laptop. She needed to stop brooding and work.

"Hey."

She jumped at the sudden voice. Sabrina walked in, carrying a bouquet of pink and white flowers. Her eyes caught Grace's, and she gave her a sheepish smile.

"I hope I'm not disturbing you," Sabrina said. "I can leave if I am."

Grace closed the file. "You're not disturbing me at all." She stood and smiled. Yes she was overworked, but she had time to talk to her cousin. "It's good to see you upright."

Sabrina shook her head. "I'm so sorry for the other night. I spent the weekend feeling terrible, but Michael told me to wait until I was feeling better to come see you. Flowers don't really seem like enough to say thank you for all you did."

She held the flowers out to Grace, who took them.

"I'm glad you came to me," Grace told her. The flowers smelled sweet. "I'm always there for you if you're in trouble, you know that."

Michael had picked Sabrina up from Grace's house on Saturday morning, but he hadn't stopped to talk. Which was for the best. Every time their eyes made contact, her heart skipped.

He'd been right all along. They needed to keep a distance. It was the only way.

Sabrina had still looked pretty horrible when Michael took her home. Grace had messaged her to check in later that day and received an update.

But it was good to see her actually looking human now.

"I'm never drinking again," Sabrina told her.

"That's what they all say," Grace said dryly. "But maybe just don't drink so much."

Sabrina met her eye, nodding seriously. "I won't."

"Want to come get a coffee from the break room?" Grace asked her. "I can put these flowers into some water at the same time."

"Sure." Sabrina followed her down the corridor and out of the executive offices, toward the small kitchen that the office staff shared. She sat on one chair as Grace filled a glass vase with water and put the flowers in it, then grabbed two mugs and poured them out some coffee.

"It's funny to think that Mom used to work here," Sabrina said when Grace slid the coffee in front of her.

"I still come across her work occasionally," Grace said. Her job – head of sales and marketing – covered a lot of the same things that Mia did back when she was a G. Scott Carter employee.

After they had Mason and Sabrina, Mia had left her job at the distillery and her and Cam had started their own business together.

"How is she?" Grace asked.

"Still tired. That's why I hate I did this. I could have made things so much worse."

Grace's heart clenched. She leaned on the counter, looking at her cousin over the rim of her coffee cup. "But you didn't."

"Thanks to you and Michael."

Ignoring the way her heart jumped at his name, Grace took a sip of her coffee. "Michael's the one who picked you up, carried you to the car, and brought you to mine."

"He told me you were the one who cleaned me up and got

me changed." Sabrina grimaced. "Thank you for not putting him through that."

"He was busy cleaning out his car."

"Oh God." Sabrina covered her face with her hands. "He had to take it to a detailer to get it cleaned properly yesterday. Mom wanted to know why and he made up something about stepping in some dog crap."

Grace tried not to laugh. She could remember being Sabrina's age. She'd never drunk too much, but she'd made other mistakes.

"He had to do it right away," Sabrina continued. "Because he's been taking mom to the hospital for her treatment."

"He has?" Grace asked. She wanted to know more, but couldn't find a way to ask. And anyway, what kind of friend was she to Sabrina if she used her to mine information about Michael?

Information she didn't need because she shouldn't be interested in him.

And yet, here she was. Interested.

"Yeah. Dad keeps telling him he doesn't have to do it, but he says he wants to." Sabrina sighed. "Anyway, enough about Michael. There's another reason why I'm here."

"There is?"

Sabrina nodded, her hair glinting under the strip lights in the kitchen. "Are you free Saturday night?"

"I think so." Grace looked at her cousin. "Why?"

"Mom's missing having company so I thought we'd have a spa evening at our place with the aunts. Nothing big, just a way to pamper her. Your mom said she'd come."

"Is she well enough for that?" Grace asked, concerned.

"She says she is. I've made her promise not to lift a finger, though. I'll do all the organizing, and your mom and the aunts are bringing the treatments." Sabrina smiled at her. "It would be good to have you there."

"Of course I'll be there." She'd always had a lot of time for her Aunt Mia. "What can I bring or do to help?"

"Could you come over early?" Sabrina asked, wrinkling her nose. "You can help me make sure everything's ready."

"I'd love to," Grace agreed. At least this was something to look forward to. Something to concentrate on other than Michael and his stupidly handsome face.

"Thank you." Sabrina grinned at her. "You're a star."

"I wouldn't go that far."

"I would," Sabrina told her. "I'm so glad you came home. Hartson's Creek is much better now that you're here."

———

"Everything okay?" Cam asked, rapping his knuckles lightly on Michael's door.

"Uh, yeah. Just finishing a couple of emails." Michael blinked as he pulled his gaze away from his computer screen. "What time is it?"

"Seven. I'm heading into town. You coming too?"

Michael glanced at his watch. "I thought we're meeting at eight." He needed to take a shower. Change his clothes. He hadn't noticed the time passing, mostly because he'd fallen behind on work all week. Thank god he had the weekends to catch up.

Cam had told him about the plans to meet with his brothers at the Moonlight Bar earlier. An excuse to escape the house while the girls did their spa stuff. He probably should stay and work, but he knew Grace would be here.

He didn't want to risk a repeat of their almost-kiss in her laundry room.

"We are. I'm gonna grab a bite to eat in the diner. Sabrina and Grace have kind of occupied the kitchen."

Pushing his laptop screen down, he tried not to think about all the things he needed to get done by Monday morning. He had tomorrow. It would be fine. "I'll jump in the shower and follow you over in a while."

"I can wait," Cam said.

"It's fine. Go grab some food." He smiled at Cam.

"You sure?"

He met Cam's eye, nodding slightly. "Absolutely certain. I'll see you at eight." He stood as Cam left, then headed for the shower, jumping in and out before grabbing some fresh clothes from the closet and sliding them on. He had one last email to send, which he did before closing his curtains and checking himself in the mirror.

He probably should have trimmed his beard, but there wasn't time. And he couldn't be bothered, anyway. Here in Hartson's Creek, being perfectly groomed didn't seem that important.

Or at least it didn't until he bumped into Grace – *literally* – as he walked down the stairs.

"Shit!"

Grace wobbled, and he had to reach out to steady her.

"You okay?" he asked her. Thank Christ she was holding onto the handrail. With their difference in body weight, he could have sent her flying down the stairs.

"Did he just say a bad word?"

He looked down to see Delilah – Presley's daughter – standing behind Grace, peeping around her hip at him.

"He did." Grace looked at him and lifted a brow. Michael's hands were still curled around her waist. He let her go, and she looked almost disappointed.

"You should wash your mouth out with soap and water," Delilah told him, her voice serious.

Michael somehow kept a straight face. "I know. I won't do it again." He looked up at Grace. "You need something?" he asked, because they looked like they were on a mission.

"Sabrina sent us up to get some towels. She wants everybody to have a foot soak," Delilah told him. "Even me."

"That right, huh?" He smiled at the little girl.

"I'll grab you some. How many do you need?" He addressed that one to Grace, because he was pretty sure Delilah had no idea.

"Half a dozen, please."

"Can I use the bathroom while I'm up here?" Delilah asked.

"Sure. There's one over there." He pointed at the door and she skipped to it, pulling it closed behind her. "Want to come get the towels?" he asked Grace. "They're on the next floor."

"Okay."

He could hear her soft breaths behind him as he walked up the next flight of stairs. They reached the upper floor and he turned right, walking past his own room. Opening the linen closet, he found a pile of older towels that could work and turned to give them to her.

Her eyes pulled up to his almost immediately. Had she been looking at his ass?

A wry smile pulled across his lips.

"What?"

He shook his head. "Nothing."

"Good." She held out her hands for the towels.

"You need anything else?" he asked.

She shook her head. "Nope, all set. Are you going out with the others?"

"Yeah. Supposed to meet them at the bar in half an hour."

"Have fun," she told him.

"You, too."

He waited for her to turn around and walk back down the stairs. Or at least step aside so he could go past. But she didn't move, and neither did he.

"You look good," she told him.

He huffed a laugh, running his hand over his beard. "I just took a shower. I should have trimmed this, too. It's getting messy."

"I like it," she whispered. "You look dark and dangerous."

And damn if he didn't like that, too. "You don't look so bad yourself." She was wearing another pair of shorts. Cutoffs, this time. Her top was one of those tanks made of cotton with holes – the ones they called lace but weren't – that floated down to the top of her hips, and her hair was pulled back into a messy bun. She looked beautiful. Young.

Too young.

"Thank you," she said. "You'll be pleased to hear that I remembered to trim my beard."

It was a joke, he knew that. But it also made him think of that night when she apologized for not shaving – other places.

And then he was remembering how her body felt wrapped around his.

"I should go," he said hoarsely. "Have a good night, Grace."

"I will," she said, finally stepping to the side. His arm brushed hers as he walked past, their knuckles grazing.

"Don't do anything I wouldn't do," she whispered.

Their gazes connected again. He gave her the slightest of nods, then headed for the stairs before he ended up doing something they'd both regret.

CHAPTER
Eleven

"CAM TELLS me you're working yourself to the bone," Logan said to Michael, taking a sip of his beer.

"Something like that." Michael shrugged. "It's harder when we're not in the same time zone. But I have it under control. Everything's all good."

Logan nodded. As Cam's identical twin, he'd always been close to Michael. Kept in touch when Michael moved to Europe. He'd even visited him a couple of times in London when he'd been there for business.

"It runs in the family," another voice said. He turned to see Daniel standing there. Michael immediately felt guilty at the sight of Grace's dad, then shook his head. Daniel had no clue what had happened between them.

Michael'd only been here for an hour. Cam was sitting in the corner with his brothers, Gray and Tanner. Over in the other corner, Gray's sons were playing pool. Presley holding the cue as Marley took control of the table, potting one ball after the other. Michael's youngest brother, Mason, was here, too, chatting with Hendrix, the third of Gray's boys, and his friend Ethan.

Who Michael still didn't like.

He turned back to Logan.

"How's the farm?" he asked, because he didn't want to look at how his brother and Ethan were laughing. Two of their other friends were with them, too. Ones that Michael didn't know but kind of recognized from Mason's social media.

"It's good. We're looking at building an extension to the Inn next year," Logan told him.

Somebody slapped his arm. He turned to see Presley smiling at him. "Hey."

"Hi. I heard what you did for Sabrina. You're a good guy."

"What happened with Sabrina?" Logan asked, looking from Michael to Presley.

"You don't want to know," Michael told him. "But all is good."

"Does Cam know?" Logan frowned.

"He doesn't need to," Presley said, grimacing. "I spoke out of turn. It was something and nothing. Ignore me."

"Nothing to do with a guy, I hope." Logan frowned. "This is why I don't have daughters. Sons are hard enough."

"Dad says the same." Presley said, grinning. "Three boys and a head full of gray hair. And it's only getting worse now that we have Delilah to contend with."

"Gray has gone gray," Logan murmured. "I feel for him."

Michael laughed, because Gray Hartson still had it. All the Hartson brothers did.

"There are some good things about having girls," Daniel said. "Anyway, Grace has never caused us any bother."

Michael swallowed and looked back to Logan. "Sabrina's fine. We don't need to bother Cam or Mom about it."

Logan nodded. "I'm glad you're back. And I appreciate all you're doing to make things easier for Cam and Mia."

"I owe them a lot." Michael shrugged. There was a loud cheer from the pool table.

"Looks like I'm on," Presley said. "Want to come play?" he asked Michael.

At twenty-eight, Presley and Marley were the cousins closest in age to him. But they still felt young.

Like Grace.

He blinked that thought away. Weird how she somehow felt older than them all. More grown up and responsible.

But she isn't.

"A game sounds good." Michael nodded. "Count me in."

"Cool. Winner stays on, so you'll be up after me."

While he was waiting, Michael wandered to the back of the bar, heading to the bathroom to splash his face with water. It was hot in the bar, just like it was hot outside, and he felt sweaty. He'd forgotten just how humid West Virginia could be in the summer. He headed down the long, dark hallway that led to the men's room, only stopping when he heard the low rumble of laughter and talking.

"Shut up. It's all good. She's warming up to me."

"She's a fucking ice queen. Remember prom? You were the only one who didn't get any. You gotta bat at your level, man, and she's somewhere in the stratosphere."

"Doesn't matter. She'll be calling me tomorrow morning."

Was that Ethan talking? It sure sounded like him. Michael rubbed the back of his neck, feeling the dampness of sweat on his skin.

"You sound pretty certain," the other guy said.

There was a pause. Then a chuckle. "I might have loosened the shoe on her horse. It'll look hurt. She won't be going anywhere without calling me first."

"And then what? You ride in like a knight in shining fucking armor?"

"Something like that. She'll be putty in my hands by Saturday night. Every girl likes a guy who's good with animals."

"You mean pussy in your hands. She's gonna be pissed when she finds out you hurt her horse to get it, though."

"Loosening a shoe doesn't hurt a horse," Ethan replied. "And anyway, Grace doesn't have to know I did it."

Jesus Christ, these were kids dressing in men's clothes. Did Mason know what an asshole his friend was? Gritting his teeth, Michael stomped down the hallway, seeing Ethan and his friend standing by the back door that led to the lot where all the trash bins were kept. They were smoking something. Whatever it was, it smelled illegal.

He was going to ignore them, get into the bathroom, splash water on his face, and get out. Then he'd ask Logan to check Grace's horse in the morning. No need to get involved.

But then Ethan turned and caught Michael's eye. Instead of looking embarrassed, he smirked.

"What are you looking at?" Ethan asked. His words slurred, like he was trying too hard to annunciate them.

Michael shook his head. "You shouldn't talk about women like that."

The guy next to him started sniggering.

"Thanks, Grandad." Ethan rolled his eyes. "If I wanted your opinion, I'd ask."

"Don't run your mouth talking about women like you own them, and I won't ram my opinion down your fucking throat."

"Whatever." Ethan waved his hand.

"You gonna let him talk to you like that?" his friend asked.

"Nah. I'm just gonna ignore him and fuck her." His words were slurring even more. How many drinks in was he?

Michael walked toward him, his blood ice cold. Before he could think through what he was doing, his fingers curled around Ethan's shoulder.

"What are you doing?" Ethan's voice had lifted an octave.

"Keep away from her," Michael growled. "In fact, keep away from all women until you know how to treat them."

"You should hit him," Ethan's friend told him. "He can't talk to you like that."

"Whatever." Michael released his hold on Ethan's shoulder. This was stupid. He needed to walk away. So that's what he did. Turned on his heel and walked back toward the bathroom, where he should have gone all along.

Footsteps echoed behind him. Followed by a guttural roar. Glancing over his shoulder, he saw Ethan's face almost in his, saw Ethan's hand swing back, his fingers fisted.

And Michael stepped to the left.

Before he could realize what was happening, Ethan ran straight into the wall, the impact sending him to the floor, his arms flailing. He let out a high-pitched cry as his friend ran over toward them.

"My nose," Ethan shouted, squirming on the concrete floor. "He's broken my fucking nose."

"I didn't touch you," Michael said.

"You're bleeding, man," Ethan's friend said. "Oh shit, you're bleeding bad."

"Let me help you up," Michael said, reaching for Ethan. But the younger man started squealing like a damn pig, as though afraid he was going to hurt him. His friend was pawing at Michael's shoulder like he was trying to pull him away.

"What the heck is going on?" Mason asked. "I heard you all the way in the bar." He looked at Ethan, bleeding on the floor. Then up at Michael, his eyes clouding with confusion.

"He fell."

"It was your fault," Ethan groaned. His voice sounded thick. Like he had a cold. "It hurts so bad."

"Did you hit him?" Mason asked. And Michael hated the way his brother was looking at him.

"No."

"He made him fall," the other friend said. "I saw it."

Michael ignored them and looked at Ethan. "Let me at least clean you up," he said. "See what the damage is."

"Don't let him touch me." Ethan rolled onto his knees. His hands were in front of his face, warding Michael off. "Don't let him hurt me."

"Mason, can you check him over?" Michael asked, his voice low.

His brother shot him a wary glance. "Sure."

"Thank you."

And as he turned to walk back into the bar, to ask the bartender for a first aid kit, he heard Ethan whimpering like a child.

What a stupid damn night it was turning out to be. He couldn't wait for it to be over.

———

"Oh. My. God." Sabrina stared at her phone screen, her mouth falling open. "I don't believe it."

"What?" Grace asked. They were in the kitchen, loading the dishwasher while their aunts watched a movie. Mia had chosen *Steel Magnolias*, and Sabrina had made them all virgin cocktails while Grace found it on the streaming service. Then they'd put on their face masks and turned out the lights. Delilah was fast asleep next to Maddie, her grandmother, curled up against her, looking cute as a button.

"My friend's friend works in the pharmacy next door to the urgent care place. She just saw Mason and his friends come in to get a prescription filled."

"Is Mason okay?" Grace asked. The last thing Mia needed was for her son to be hurt.

"He's fine. It's Ethan. Apparently somebody broke his nose."

"What?" Grace stood, a dirty plate still in her hand. "Who? Why?"

"I don't know. She's still typing. Just a minute." Her lips curled, and she laughed. "Oh, you'll never believe this."

"Try me," Grace said dryly.

"She's talking to Mason's friend. Craig. He saw it all." Sabrina gasped. "No way."

"What?" Grace widened her eyes. She normally avoided gossip, but Ethan was a friend. Or kind of.

Whatever. She still liked him. Sort of.

"He was arguing about you."

Grace froze. "He was what?"

"No, that's not right. It can't be." Sabrina shook her head and Grace was getting annoyed now. Not with her cousin, but with the half-information she was getting.

Why the heck would Ethan argue with somebody about her? Had somebody said something?

"Oh, it gets worse. Ethan was arguing with Michael apparently," Sabrina whispered. "I can't believe it."

The plate in Grace's hands smashed to the floor, white pieces of china splintering everywhere.

"Shit." Grace dropped to her haunches, trying to pick them up. "Do you have a broom?"

"There's a small one under the sink." Sabrina pulled the cupboard open and found it, hunkering down with Grace to clean them up. For a minute they concentrated on finding every shard, putting them in the dust pan, then sliding them into the trashcan.

When the floor was clean, Grace tried to take a deep breath.

What the heck had Michael said? Did this mean people knew about them? Her hands shook as she reached for another plate.

Sabrina started stabbing at her phone with her fingers. It always amazed Grace how quickly her friend could type a message. "Apparently, Michael warned Ethan to leave you alone." Sabrina rolled her eyes. "He's such an idiot."

Grace swallowed, waiting for the inevitable. She was already trying to work out how she'd explain this all away.

"He's such a stupid older brother. He thinks we're all kids." Sabrina huffed. "You already have one dad. You don't need two."

"What?" Grace blinked.

"Does he think we're all vestal virgins or something?" Sabrina asked. "I'm sorry, he's an ass. You and Ethan can date if you want to."

"You think he hurt Ethan because he's protective?" Grace asked. This was so confusing.

And annoying.

What right did he have to hit Ethan? She hated violence. The thought of somebody hitting somebody else over her…

It made her feel sick.

"Of course. Just like he was pissed with me for getting drunk. I got a huge lecture about how vulnerable I was and that I should never put myself in that position again." Sabrina shook her head. "He shouldn't do it to you, though."

"No," Grace whispered. "He shouldn't."

———

She only half-watched the rest of the movie. As the screen flickered, she sent a message to Ethan asking if he was okay, but he hadn't responded. She assumed he was either sleeping off the pain or didn't have his phone. Speaking to him would have to wait until tomorrow.

Michael, on the other hand, she wasn't sure she wanted to talk to at all. Was he really the type of man to use his fists against somebody else? She hated violence. It made her stomach twist.

Mia had fallen asleep somewhere during the second half of the movie. They all agreed that once it was over they'd wake her up and leave – she'd protest if they left before the ending. Grace counted down the minutes, barely watching as the Magnolias – minus Julia Roberts – celebrated Easter with Shelby's baby boy.

And then the front door opened and Cam poked his head into the room, then disappeared again.

A moment later the credits started to roll and Sabrina stretched and paused the feed, as Maddie – Gray's wife – turned the lights back on. Mia woke up and whispered in Sabrina's ear.

"I'll get Dad," Sabrina said, cupping her mom's cheek.

Cam came in to help Mia to bed, followed by Grace's uncles – Logan, Tanner, and Gray, who were here to pick up their wives and Delilah, who was sleeping at Maddie and Gray's for the night.

Then Grace's dad appeared.

"Want a ride home?" he asked as her mom gathered her things up.

Grace shook her head. "I have my car here. I'll help Sabrina clean up and head home after that."

"You don't have to stay," Sabrina protested. "I can do it."

"It won't take more than a minute with both of us."

They cleared up quickly, picking up glasses and straightening cushions so Mia wouldn't have to do it in the morning. Sabrina slid a soap tablet into the dishwasher and yawned.

"I wonder where Mason is," she said. "And Michael."

"I don't know," Grace said lightly. "Well, I think we're done here. I should head home."

"Sure. Thank you for your help." Sabrina grinned at her.

"Any time. And sorry about the plate. I can buy a new one."

"It doesn't matter." Sabrina shook her head. "It was from Target. No biggie."

Taking her bag and jacket, Grace said goodbye to Sabrina and left the house, opening her car door and throwing her things onto the passenger seat. She was about to climb into the driver's side when she saw a pair of headlamps slide across the driveway, a car turning in.

Michael's car.

He pulled up beside hers and climbed out. A pulse throbbed in her neck.

"Hey." He looked tired. "Has everybody gone home?"

She nodded, her throat tight. "I'm the last one."

Michael locked his car and went to walk inside.

She took a deep breath. "Is it true?"

He turned to look at her. "What?"

"That Ethan's nose is broken."

He let out a long breath of air, like she'd just asked him to do something he hated. "Yeah, it's true."

"You did it?"

"Not like you think."

It didn't matter that she wasn't supposed to talk to him. It didn't matter that she felt as tired as he looked and just wanted to go home.

"You have no right," she told him.

"What?" His brows dipped.

"To hit somebody."

"That's what you think, is it?"

"That's what I heard. And let's get one thing straight. You don't get to hit him because of me."

"Grace, let me expl—"

"No." She shook her head vehemently. "You don't get to go all caveman because you happened to spend a single night with me. You don't get to come to town and make things difficult for me because you're jealous of another guy."

"I'm not jealous."

"No?" She folded her arms in front of her.

He stared at her impassively. "No."

"Whatever. I'm going home."

Letting out a huff she climbed into her car and slammed the door closed, starting up the engine and turning up the music. A country station came on and she jabbed at the radio button until a rock song was blasting through the speakers.

She turned it up.

"Stupid men," she muttered, putting the car into reverse and putting her foot down onto the gas.

Turning the car around, she took one last glance behind her to see Michael still standing there. He was mouthing something, and she shook her head to tell him she couldn't hear a word. Instead of getting the hint, he stormed toward the car and motioned at the window.

Reluctantly, she pressed the button to wind it down.

"What now?" she shouted over the music.

There was a twitch in his jaw. "Keep your damn eyes on the road. And drive carefully."

She gave him a glare and pressed the window button once more. "Thanks, *Dad*," she said sarcastically. "I'll try."

CHAPTER
Twelve

"WHAT?" Grace blinked, looking at Arcadia's foot, then back at her uncle. "How did you know this?"

Logan lifted a brow. "Michael told me."

"He told you that Ethan loosened Arcadia's shoe?" She'd spent most of the night tossing and turning. "When?"

"He overheard Ethan telling somebody last night." He shrugged. "He was right. I've called the farrier in. And I'll be calling the cops, too." He lifted a brow. "Not that they'll do anything."

"Don't call the cops. I'll talk to him." She walked toward Arcadia and stroked his velvety nose. "Hey, sweetie," she murmured. "No ride for us today." Dropping to her haunches, she looked at her horse's shoe. Two nails were missing, and the others were loose, just like Logan had told her.

Michael hadn't fought with Ethan about her at all. It was because he'd hurt her horse. She grimaced at the thought of the things she'd said to him last night.

"It's not a little thing, Grace," Logan said, running his hands through his hair. "Arcadia could have ended up injured. Hell, if you'd ridden him without checking, you could have ended up in an accident. He's a vet. He's supposed to take care of animals, not hurt them."

She swallowed hard. The thought of Arcadia being hurt pained her much more than thinking about her own danger. "I always check him before I ride."

"Ethan doesn't know that."

"I just don't get why he'd do this," she said. "Why would Ethan hurt my horse?"

"According to Michael, it was part of his plan to woo you. To come in and save the day, then ask you out."

She swallowed. "He hurt Arcadia because he wants to date me?"

"Yeah, that's seems about right."

"And then Michael punched him," she murmured.

Logan shook his head. "No. Ethan hurt himself."

Grace blinked and looked up at her uncle. "What?"

"You're talking about the broken nose, right?"

"Yeah." She nodded. "Michael hit Ethan." She still hated violence, but she could understand why it happened a little more now. Her stomach tightened. She was such an idiot.

"No. Ethan went to hit Michael, Michael moved out of the way and Ethan slammed into the wall and fell over. Landed awkwardly on the floor. His nose had an argument with some concrete."

Her breath caught in her throat. "He fell over?"

Logan lifted a brow. "I wouldn't have blamed Michael for hitting him, but yeah, from what I can tell, Michael didn't touch the asshole." He blinked. "Sorry for swearing."

It was nothing compared to the words she wanted to utter. All she could think about was how Michael had looked as she drove away. And he'd still warned her to drive carefully.

Dear Lord, she was the asshole. The biggest one. "I didn't know," she whispered.

"It was all a bit of a mess. And we agreed we wouldn't tell Mia, so we tried to keep things easy last night."

"I'm glad you didn't." Her hand shook as she patted Arcadia again.

"You look tired," Logan said softly. "Why don't you go home? I can wait for the farrier to come."

She shook her head. "I'll wait." She wanted to. She needed to make sure Arcadia was okay. "Thank you, though."

He nodded. "You know where I am if you need me."

"I do." She gave him the faintest of smiles.

He pressed his lips together. "I'm sorry, Grace. I trusted him."

It took her a moment to realize he was talking about Ethan. She was so fixated on Michael she had almost forgotten about him.

But not completely. The damn ass hurt her horse.

"It's not your fault. I trusted him, too." At least not to hurt Arcadia.

"We'll be changing vets, of course."

And that would cause more problems. For Ethan's sick dad. For Logan, too, because Ethan and his dad were the only vets in town. If they had to use a different company, that would mean a longer wait every time they called, and this farm was full of livestock.

She nodded, and he walked away then she turned back to Arcadia and looped her hands around his long neck. Arcadia let out a soft whinny, nuzzling into Grace.

What a mess this all was. And it wasn't just Ethan's doing, though what he'd done was bad enough.

It was her, too. She'd made assumptions. Thrown them into Michael's face.

And all the while, he'd stood up for her. Stood up for her horse.

She owed him the biggest apology.

She just didn't know if he'd accept it.

———

Michael was the only one in the house that afternoon. Cam had taken Mia out shopping, and Sabrina was at a friend's house – having promised him that no alcohol would be involved. He had no idea where Mason was. When Michael had asked about Ethan's nose earlier in the morning, Mason had rolled his eyes and shrugged.

Some things were probably best not talked about. Didn't stop Michael feeling pissed though.

At Ethan. At Grace. Mostly at himself.

He'd actually asked Sabrina to call and make sure Grace had arrived home safely last night, because damn, she was behaving like an idiot. He'd only been able to sleep once his sister had let him know all was fine.

He pushed down his laptop screen and stood, walking to the kitchen to make himself a coffee.

He'd been home a matter of weeks and was already causing problems with his family. Mason was pissed with him, Sabrina wanted all the gossip, and Cam had warned him not to say a word to his mom.

Not that he would. She didn't need this kind of hassle.

What was it he and Grace had talked about? How coming home to your family's town made you regress to feeling like a kid again?

His phone lit up with Logan's name on the screen, and Michael slid his finger to accept it, putting it on speaker.

"Hey. How's the horse?" He assumed that was why Logan was calling.

"Just being finished being re-shoed. The farrier was here."

Well, that was good at least. He'd done the right thing, even if Grace blamed him for it. "Did the cops come?"

"Grace doesn't want to press charges."

"Does she have a choice?" Michael asked, frowning. "It was your farm it happened on. Don't you get to decide if you make a report?"

"Kind of," Logan told him. "But Grace is upset, and I

didn't want to insist any more. Plus, I've had my own problems with the cops in the past."

Michael could vaguely remember something about Logan's wife being harassed by a police officer before she married Logan. A local cop, he thought. But it was before his time.

"So he's just gonna get away with it?" He hated that thought.

"I didn't say that. I've spoken to his father. And to my lawyer. Made it clear that if Ethan does anything like it again, he'll be in legal trouble. The whole town will be watching him like a hawk."

"He should face some kind of punishment."

"I know. But his dad's sick and Ethan's a kid. We all made mistakes when we were younger. It's how we grow from them that matters."

"Easy to say when you're not the one being accused of breaking his nose."

Logan chuckled. "You did good. And we all know you're not a violent man."

No, he wasn't. Not usually. But he wasn't exactly feeling peaceful now.

"Is Grace okay?" he asked, his voice thick.

"She's shaken. She loves that horse like nothing else. But she's a strong person, she'll be fine. Now the shoe is back on, she can ride to her heart's content."

He nodded. "Thanks for keeping me updated."

"Thanks for watching out for my animals," Logan said. "I owe you a beer."

"Any time."

Michael ended the call and went to grab a carton of milk from the refrigerator.

And then he saw *her*.

Standing at the back door, her hair in a high ponytail, her

face free of makeup. Grace pulled her lip between her teeth like she was trying to work out what to do.

Her skin was glowing like she'd been running or exercising. She was wearing a gray tank and a pair of black shorts. They looked washed out and old. But so, so soft.

Their gazes caught, and she swallowed before her lips curled into a smile. He walked over, flicked the lock, and opened the door.

And said nothing. Because everything he had to say happened last night.

"Can I come in?" Grace asked.

He stepped aside, and she kicked her boots off, leaving them on the back step before she walked in.

"I came straight from the stables," she said, as though in explanation.

And still he said nothing. Because talking just led to arguments.

He was so fucking tired of them.

She stepped closer, her brows knit. "Hi."

He nodded.

"I just came to talk…" She exhaled heavily. "To say I'm sorry. I messed up."

He turned to grab his coffee. Focused on it because he didn't know what else to say. He could negotiate deals worth millions of dollars. Intervene in what felt like unsolvable conflicts between sports stars and their teams.

But right now? Nothing. Just staring. And wishing things were different.

Wishing he could pull her against him and bury his face in her hair. Maybe then he'd feel better. Grounded.

Because he felt anything but that standing here.

"Can you say something?" she asked.

"Like what?" he asked, his voice rough. He took a sip of his coffee.

"Like you were a bitch, Grace. You didn't give me a chance to say what actually happened. You made assumptions, and they were the wrong ones, and now I'm pissed at you."

He swallowed. "Yeah, that."

She tipped her head to the side and the smell of hay wafted over him. "You saved my horse."

"Your horse would have been fine without me."

"We don't know that. All sorts of things could have happened. I could have been hurt."

"But they didn't. And you weren't," he said.

"You did a good thing and I shouted at you. Accused you of hurting Ethan because you were jealous." She pressed her lips together, looking regretful.

"I didn't touch him."

Her face pinked up. "I know that now. He lied. And I believed it."

"Yeah, well, I'm used to people believing the worst about me."

Her face fell. "I should have known better."

"Don't worry about it. My sister believed it, too. My brother would have if his friend hadn't told him the truth."

"But they shouldn't," Grace whispered. "They should always believe you."

"I don't care what they think."

Her lips parted as she inhaled softly. "What about me?"

"What about you?" He was confused.

"Do you care what I think?"

Yes, he did. Too much. It was a fucking mess.

"I'm not allowed to care what you think," he said carefully.

"Who says that?"

His jaw tightened. "Me. You. All of Hartson's Creek."

"Fuck them."

He'd so much rather do that to her. That was the problem.

He wanted to pull her hair, expose her neck, suck at her skin until she was calling out his name.

Wanted to bury himself inside of her until nothing else mattered. Wanted to feel her come around him like she did in New York.

"We've been so careful," he told her. "Let's not mess this up."

She ran the tip of her tongue along her bottom lip and damn if he wasn't entranced by it. "It's already messed up, isn't it? Every time I touch myself, it's your face I see."

The image of her laying in bed getting off on the thought of him was almost too much to bear. He felt himself thicken.

"Grace…"

"I assumed the worst about you because I wanted to. Maybe I wanted you to fight for me. Nobody else ever has."

She took a step closer. He didn't step away. Just watched her warily, his blood hot in his veins.

"If anybody ever found out…" His voice trailed off as she placed her hand on his chest. He could feel the warmth of her through his thin t-shirt.

She moved it down. Traced his muscles. And he stood as still as a statue.

Hard. Aching for her. Knowing this was wrong.

"I'm not scared of them finding out. I'm scared of never touching you again. Never feeling the way I do when you're around." Her voice cracked, and it killed him. "That night in New York is all I can think about."

"Grace…"

"Just kiss me. Please." She looked up at him, her eyes so wide and innocent. His gaze dipped to her lips. So sweet and so swollen.

He could remember the way they felt around him.

"I can't," he told her. "I can't kiss you and let you walk away." Not again.

"Please." She traced his pectoral muscle with her finger, her thumb grazing his nipple. "Please, Michael."

And there it was. He couldn't resist her. Maybe he'd known that all along. That's why he kept his distance. Not because he didn't want people to guess about New York, but because he knew he couldn't be trusted.

"If I kiss you, will you leave?"

She shook her head. And he liked that too much. He didn't want her to leave.

He wanted to kiss her until she forgot her name.

Reaching out, he tipped her chin up. A little sigh escaped her lips and he could feel the warmth on his wrist. Slowly, he ran the pad of his thumb along her rosy bottom lip.

And then she sucked him inside.

Her warm, velvety mouth enveloped him, her tongue fluttering against his thumb, and he turned harder than steel.

She released him with a pop. "Kiss me."

And he did. Not a soft one this time. This kiss was a clash of mouth and teeth. The hot swiping of tongues and the aching warmth of their breath as they battled to get closer. She was clawing at his t-shirt, almost certain to leave scratches, and he pushed his thigh between hers, groaning at the warmth of her.

Grace groaned right back, moving herself against him, creating a rhythm as they kissed, letting out those soft little breaths that drove him wild.

She was beautiful. She was his. That's all he could think of as he devoured her mouth.

His. His. His.

He'd fucking slay armies for her.

He slid his fingers into her hair, angling her head so he could kiss her harder. Deeper. Longer. His other hand trailed down her back, holding her tight as he moved his thigh against her.

So warm. So pliable. So perfect.

And then the front door banged open.

"Fuck." He stepped back like his ass was on fire. Grace was leaning against the counter, her eyes glazed like she was drunk.

Moments later, the kitchen door opened and Mason walked in. He looked at Grace and then at Michael. "Hey. I saw your car outside."

There was enough distance between them for it to look respectable. But Grace herself looked anything but respectable. Her hair was hanging out of her bun, her lips were swollen, her eyes darting every way they could.

She took a deep breath and transformed in front of his eyes. He couldn't quite put his finger on it, but it was like she'd grown taller. Older.

Wiser.

"Hey." Her voice was thin. "I came straight from the stables. I must look a mess."

Mason shrugged. "It's hot as hell out there. Haven't seen anybody who isn't a mess today."

"Grace came to apologize," Michael said, his voice low.

"What for?" Mason frowned.

"I kinda gave him hell last night for hitting Ethan." She glanced at him from the corner of her eye. Damn, he wanted to kiss her again.

Mason glanced at Michael, who shrugged.

"Ethan hurt himself," Mason said.

"I know that now. I just got it all wrong." She blew out a mouthful of air. "Anyway, I should go." Her eyes flickered to Michael's. "Sorry again."

"I'll walk you to your car," Michael told her.

Her eyes caught his. "No need."

"I insist."

"Okay then. Bye, Mason."

"See you around, Grace."

She shot his brother a smile and walked toward the back

door, reaching down to grab her boots. When she'd pulled them on, she looked so hot he wanted to scoop her up in his arms and take her to bed.

Short shorts. Tight top. Engineer boots.

What wouldn't he give to take her while she looked like that? Up against the stable wall, hay in her hair, head tipped back as he took her to oblivion.

When her boots were laced up, he stepped outside with her, placing his hand on the curve of her back.

"You think he suspected anything?" she asked.

He shrugged. It was Mason. He never noticed anything that wasn't right in front of his face. And from the sound of the refrigerator door opening, his mind was on other things, anyway.

"What are you doing tonight?" Michael asked as they rounded the corner toward the driveway. There really was hay in her hair. He picked out a stalk and handed it to her. She grinned.

"Washing my hair."

"I'll be there at eight."

Grace lifted a brow. "You're coming to mine?"

"That's the plan."

Her smile widened. "Good. Bring some food because I'm a terrible cook."

It was his turn to smile. "Sure. Wouldn't want you to starve."

CHAPTER
Thirteen

CALL HER SUPERFICIAL, but she spent the rest of the afternoon in her bathroom, washing her hair, shaving her legs.

Shaving *everything*.

And when she finally got out of the shower and smothered herself in moisturizer, she spent another hour trying to decide what to wear.

By the time she'd settled on a silk tank and black shorts, her bedroom looked like a hurricane had wreaked havoc in it. Clothes were scattered across her bed and floor, and picking them all up and rehanging them made her feel sweaty and as though she should take another shower.

When everything was finally tidy, she walked toward her bedroom door, glimpsing herself in the mirror. Her reflection looked exactly how she felt. Edgy. Anxious. Still completely turned on from the feel of his mouth and his body and that thick thigh between hers.

She almost embarrassed herself in the kitchen. Probably would have if Mason hadn't come in.

And thank the heavens it had been Mason. Her lovely cousin was laid back and chill to the nth degree.

Before she went downstairs to wait for him, she sprayed some perfume on her wrists and neck, the sweet aroma filling her senses.

They shouldn't be doing this. Whatever *this* turned out to be. And yet the knowledge that he'd risk everything to come see her lit her up like a damn Christmas tree.

It was wrong. Forbidden. She'd never wanted anything more.

When the doorbell rang at eight, her heart almost leapt into her throat. She wanted to run to the door, yank it open. Throw herself into his arms. But she kept it cool, fluffing her hair as she slowly walked down the hallway, taking her time to turn the knob and open the door.

And there he was. In a white shirt and dark pants. His hair was still damp from what must have been a shower. There was a smile curling at his lips as he looked down at her, taking in the silk blouse and black shorts, and hopefully her long, taut legs. Smooth from her shower, lightly tan from the summer sun. Aching to feel his thigh pressed between them.

"I brought food," he said, and her body reacted to his voice. Her nipples tightened, her thighs clenched.

She grinned. "I was kidding. I could have made you a sandwich."

He offered her the brown bag. "Actually, it is a sandwich. And an apple."

She laughed as she took it from him. "Come in. Would you like a drink?"

"Not really."

"Let me at least put this sandwich away."

Her hips swayed as she led him down the hallway to the kitchen. And she was thankful he couldn't see her grin.

"So, what changed your mind?" she asked him. "I thought we weren't supposed to talk to each other."

"That was before today. And the other night with Sabrina."

Her face flushed at the memory of his kisses.

"Where does everybody think you are?" She put the brown bag with the sandwich into the refrigerator. She was tickled that he'd made it. Following her instructions, but not really.

Weird how she liked that.

"Meeting an old friend for dinner."

"Didn't they wonder why you were making a sandwich?"

He laughed. "I'm a big man. I can eat two meals without blinking. They wouldn't think it's strange at all."

She turned to look at him. He really was glorious. Every part of him exuded masculine certainty. From the way he looked at her to the way he talked.

He knew she wanted him. The way she'd climbed him like a tree at his house was enough of a clue.

And from the way he was staring at her breasts in this tank, he also wanted her.

"I parked down the road," he told her. "So nobody will talk."

"Our little secret," she whispered.

He lifted a brow. "Something like that." He reached out, traced a line from her jaw to her clavicle. Dipped his finger beneath her silky tank to discover she wasn't wearing a bra.

"Fuck."

"That's the plan," she murmured. His touch was so sure. Every inch of her body responded to him.

He flicked one strap down her arm, then lowered his mouth to kiss her bare shoulder. Then he pushed the other strap, her tank resting on the swell of her breasts. He cupped them through the silk, his thumbs brushing her nipples and pleasure pooled deep in her belly.

He looked up at her, his eyes hazy. "You're so beautiful."

"Show me," she whispered. "Show me how beautiful."

A lazy smile pulled at his lips. Then he tugged at the silk until her breasts were exposed to him.

"I've dreamed about these," he told her. "Every night for a year."

Before she could answer, he closed his lips around her nipple. His mouth was warm, insistent, tugging at her.

His tongue devoured her and she wasn't sure how much longer she could stay upright.

"Take me to bed," she whispered. "Please."

He released her and looked up, his eyes dark as ink. "Gladly."

Michael scooped her up like she weighed nothing.

She waited for him to put her down as he reached the bottom of the stairs, because let's face it, a one-hundred-and-thirty-pound woman and a flight of steps weren't the best combination. But he didn't.

He carried her. All the way to her room. Then dipped her so she could push the door handle, and he kicked their way inside.

"Do you work out?" she asked him.

"Of course. I have to keep up with athletes."

And she had to keep up with him. Which on paper shouldn't even be a competition. She had the advantage of youth.

And yet she was the one who was breathless as he threw her on the bed and pulled off his t-shirt and exposed his bare chest.

That first time, in New York, she'd been wine-hazy. He'd kissed her everywhere, made her scream his name.

The second time? She'd woken him up with her lips around him.

And the third they'd been so sleepy it had been sensual and slow.

But now every part of her felt alive. She pulled off her tank, then unbuttoned her shorts, shimmying them down until she was left in the scantest lace panties. Little more than a triangle.

He looked at her, swallowing hard.

"Come here." She crawled across the mattress toward where he was standing. He smirked as she pushed herself up, pressing her hands on his chest, kissing him softly.

"I'm going to make you scream my name," she whispered, and he laughed.

But then she dipped, unfastened his pants, scooped out his hard, thick length, and pressed her lips against the tip.

And suddenly he wasn't laughing any more.

"Grace…"

"I said scream, not whisper." She slid her lips around him, taking as much as she could. Satisfied by the long groan that rumbled from his lungs as she flicked her tongue against him, tasting him, teasing him.

His fingers tangled in her hair. He said her name again, and she loved it. Loved doing this to him.

Loved being in control.

She was still in her panties. He was still wearing his pants and shorts, though she'd pushed them around his thighs to give her better access. She sucked him down further, winning another delicious rumble from him. She dug her fingers into his ass as he rocked against her.

"Fuck. Grace." His voice was louder this time. More ragged.

She looked up at him, still swallowing him whole. His eyes were dark, his jaw tight. His fingers dug against her scalp. She fluttered her eyelids and his cheek twitched.

He liked this. He enjoyed watching. She'd have to remember that.

His movements were getting erratic, creating a rhythm echoed by his grunts. Her caveman, motivated only by sensation and need.

And her.

"I'm too close," he told her, trying to pull away. She lifted a brow and licked him again, hollowing her cheeks to let him know she wasn't stopping without a fight.

She wanted him to explode in her. Wanted to taste him. Wanted to watch as he lost control. Looking up at him, she released him for a second. "Come in my mouth," she whispered.

His eyes narrowed. "Not yet." Pulling away from her, he shucked off his pants and boxers, kicking them to the carpet. His cock jutted out in front of him, strong and sure, and she already missed feeling it between her lips.

"Lay down," he said, and she realized that the feeling of complete control had only been an illusion. He'd let her take control, at least for a moment.

But now it was Michael's show. And she liked that. Too much.

She did as she was told, laying back on her coverlet, her hair spilling around her. There was a damp patch on her panties, and he reached out to touch it. Pleasure pulsed through her at his merest touch.

She stared up at him through wide eyes, wondering what he was going to do to her.

"You've never looked more beautiful than you do right now," he said, his voice thick.

"Then touch me."

His lip quirked. "Patience." He fisted himself once, then twice, his gaze roaming over her body. Then he walked around the bed, as though admiring a work of art.

Except she was the art. And she felt like it right now.

"Show me how you like to be touched," he told her.

Her cheeks flushed. She felt shy. Exposed. But then he touched himself again and another jolt of desire rushed through her.

Running her hands down to her breasts, she cupped them, letting each finger graze over her nipples. They were tight and aching. Needing more than her own touch. He watched her silently, his chest hitching, as she moved her palms down over her stomach, sliding one beneath her silken panties.

"What do you think of when you touch yourself?" he rasped. He was stroking himself as she slid her finger along her seam, the tip teasing the most sensitive part of herself, making every muscle in her thighs twitch.

"You. That night."

"What about that night?"

"The way you touched me. Kissed me. Fucked me."

He pumped again.

"The way you talked dirty to me in French."

She was circling herself, her breath catching as she reached a steady rhythm.

"Je veux te baiser," he told her, as her back arched from the bed.

He wanted to fuck her. "Then do it," she told him.

"Not yet."

She was on edge now. The way he had been earlier. Her breath catching, her body flushed.

"Don't come," he told her.

"But I need…"

"Don't come until I have my mouth on you." He lifted a brow, almost smirking.

She looked up, her eyes catching his. "Mange-moi," she whispered, and his smile widened.

He dropped to his knees, pushing her thighs apart as he pressed his mouth against her panties. "You only had to ask, sweetheart."

Instead of taking them off, he pushed her panties to the side, giving her a long, sweet lash of his tongue. Her eyes rolled back as he licked her again, harder this time, his fingers reaching up, curling, as he pushed them inside.

She wasn't going to last. She just wasn't. It was too good,

he was too experienced, he knew exactly what to do. Reaching for him, she put her hands on his head, whispering his name, as he ate her like he never wanted to stop.

It was almost too much. Her hips rocked in time to her moans, her fingers scraped his scalp. "Michael. I'm going to—"

"Come." He wasn't finishing her words. It was a command.

And oh God, it *was* too much. Way too much. Her senses hit overload, her back arching as she exploded into his mouth. Her body was on fire, jerking as he licked her, his lips sucking as she slowly came down.

But it wasn't enough.

"I need you inside of me, Irish," she whispered.

He smiled at the old nickname. Climbed up over her, kissed her, so she could taste herself on his tongue.

"This isn't going to be my crowning hour," he whispered against her mouth. "Or crowning five minutes. It's been a while and I'm fucking desperate for you."

"How long?" She stroked his hair.

"Since the last time."

Oh. "Me too," she said, her voice low.

And for a moment, they stared at each other. Silent. Understanding. And then he kissed her again. Softer, this time. So sweet it made her heart ache.

He reached for his pants and pulled a foil packet from the pocket. She took it from his hand and ripped it open, sliding the condom onto him. Needing him inside of her like she needed air.

He cradled her face, kissed her again, his hips sliding between her legs until he was there. Touching her. Ready for her.

And then he slid inside.

Her breath hitched. How long had she thought about this?

About feeling him like this again? It was stupid, trying to fight it. Some things were too inevitable to stop.

He was a freight train. A tsunami.

And now he was inside of her. His thickness stretching her and making every part of her feel sensitive.

He stilled, as though knowing it was almost too much. "You okay?" he asked gently, stroking her hair.

She nodded. "Don't stop."

"You feel so good," he murmured, his mouth on hers.

"Too good." He moved his hips back then surged forward. She could feel herself flutter around him, on the edge once more. His chest rubbed her nipples, his hand slid down to hitch her thigh against his hip, his fingers dug into her skin in the most delicious way.

He was being gentle. Like he was afraid to break her. But she wanted to be broken. She wanted to come apart.

She wanted this man to make his mark on her.

"Take me harder," she whispered against his cheek.

And he did. Pulled his hips back and slammed home. Again and again until she was dizzy and breathless. Her body was tight, alive, on fire.

And then she could feel the pleasure rising. Hissing and coiling in her stomach until her whole body was tingling.

"Michael!"

She contracted around him, the pleasure overwhelming her. He stilled and squeezed, his eyes shut.

"Too good. Oh fuck, Grace."

It wasn't a scream, but she'd take a grunt. Take him saying her name again as he spilled inside of her.

She'd accept him pulling out and cleaning up, then climbing back into bed beside her, holding her tight as he stroked her hair until every part of her was languid.

And she wouldn't think about how this had to stay a secret. Or that he'd have to leave soon otherwise people would notice.

No, she wouldn't think that because then everything would feel real. And she liked this little bubble with only the two of them inside of it way too much.

CHAPTER
Fourteen

"YOU REALLY HAVEN'T HAD sex since that night in New York?" Grace asked, tracing a circle on his chest with her finger. It was late. Probably too late. But he had no inclination to move right now.

He'd sneak home in a while like a damned teenager. If anybody noticed, he'd come up with some lame explanation. Being here with her like this was worth all the lies.

"You say that like you don't believe me," he said, amused at the shrug of her shoulders. "Do you think I'm some kind of sex fiend?"

"If tonight's anything to go by, yes." She grinned. "And I wouldn't have it any other way."

God, she was delicious. Her skin was so soft against his. He dipped his face into her hair, breathing her in.

"I'm too old for hookups. Sex without intimacy doesn't hold as much attraction to me anymore. If I'm going to sleep with somebody, I want to like them first."

"You slept with me the same night you met me."

He smiled. "And I liked you. Very much."

"I liked you too." She exhaled softly, putting her arm over his stomach, curling against him.

"How about you?" he asked. "You're young and beautiful. How come you haven't had sex either?"

"I've been in Hartson's Creek," she pointed out. "There's not exactly a surplus of gorgeous single men around here."

"How many relationships have you had?" he asked. He wanted to know, and he didn't. It was like pulling at a scab. Needed, but unpleasant.

"Pascal was the main one," she said. "Before that I had a few boyfriends at college, but nothing major."

"And he hurt you."

She looked up at him. She didn't look hurt right now. She looked beautiful and sleepy and pink cheeked.

"He did, but I'm over it." She kissed his chest. "I think I was over it as soon as I was under you."

He laughed. "Which time?"

"The first time."

Michael nodded. That night pretty much got him over everything, too.

"I looked for you," he told her. "On the internet, I mean. I don't think I really stopped until I saw you at *Chairs*."

"What would you have done if you'd found me?"

"The same thing I did at *Chairs*. Freak out."

She looked up at him, her eyes soft. "I'm sorry I ghosted you. I just didn't know how to handle it. I thought a clean break would be the best thing."

He nodded. "I get it. I was angry when I first got back, but mostly at the situation. I met the perfect woman and it turned out she's related to people I love."

"Wouldn't it be nice if I wasn't?" She traced a circle on his chest. It made his body heat.

"But you are."

That was the problem. What they were doing wasn't illegal. They weren't blood related. He hadn't even heard of the Hartson family until he was fifteen and moved to Hartson's Creek to finish up high school.

Yes, there was the matter of the age gap between them. But Grace didn't act like a twenty-six-year-old. She was wise. Steady. Beautiful.

And he wanted her all the damn time.

"How long were you married?" she asked, and he blinked at the sudden question.

"Not long. Less than two years from beginning to end." He winced saying it.

"Why did it end? Was it you or her?"

"A bit of both, I think." He stroked her hair again, staring up at her ceiling. There was a cobweb in the corner. He wondered if she was scared of spiders.

Either way, he'd get rid of it for her.

"We got married because we were both lonely. But we were both lonely because we weren't good at investing in relationships. So instead of being lonely on our own, we were lonely together."

"Why weren't you good at investing?" Grace asked.

"Because I'm selfish. And a workaholic." He shrugged. "A shrink would probably point to my childhood, but I'm not a big believer in all that. I'm a grownup. I'm the one who decides."

"And you decided to come to me."

He smiled. "Yeah. And in about ten minutes, once I regain my energy, I'll decide to get up, take a shower, and head home." He hated saying that to her. Hated the way she winced. But he had to keep it real.

This couldn't happen. Or at least it couldn't keep happening. Not indefinitely.

"Will you come over to see me again?" she asked him. "This week?"

He brushed his lips against her cheek. "If you want me to."

"Of course I want you to." She gave him a sappy smile.

"Then I'll be here." At least until the end of the summer.

Until it was time to head back to London. That would be a good thing, wouldn't it? Because they were playing with fire.

But he wasn't strong enough to stop it while he was here. If she asked him to come over, he'd come over. If she asked him to stay away, he'd do that too.

He'd be her slave, at least for a few months. He'd kiss her until she was breathless, eat her until she was a pool of desire, and clean the fucking cobwebs from her ceilings until she felt safe.

And then he'd walk away. And it would hurt. But not as much as finding out would hurt their families. It would hurt Grace, too, because she'd be the one who had to stay and endure the knowing looks. The gossip. The family imploding.

He'd never do that to her.

Sliding his thumb beneath her chin, he tipped his head until their lips met. She kissed him back enthusiastically, looping her arms around his neck.

And damn if that wasn't all it took to make him hard again. She must have felt it, too, because she was sliding down, her hair trailing over his stomach before her mouth enveloped him once more.

"This time you'll come down my throat," she told him when she released him with a pop. "And I definitely want to hear you scream my name."

———

"Holy hell," Ella shouted, her voice reverberating down the phone line. "Seriously? I thought you were completely against sleeping with him."

Grace sighed. She had to talk to somebody, and Ella was literally the only person in her life who knew about Michael and would understand.

Who else was she going to confide in? Sabrina? Her mom? The thought of them finding out made her shudder.

"I was. And I tried not to. Except we can't seem to resist each other." Her cheeks pinked up at the memory of the previous night.

"What was that? I can't hear you." Ella was shouting even louder. She never talked when she could scream.

Which was why Grace had ridden Arcadia out here to the foothills, where there was still a signal but no chance of being overheard. If she was going to talk about Michael, it would happen where nobody had the ability to listen in or hear.

And yes, she could have called from home, but she couldn't think straight there. Every time she looked at the stairs or her bed, she thought of him.

Twisting Arcadia's reins around her hand, Grace led him ten feet to another set of trees. The breeze was rustling through the leaves, but apart from that, there was blessed silence. "Can you hear me now?" she asked her friend.

"Yes. Perfectly. Now tell me everything."

So she did. Well, not quite *everything*. Enough for Ella to get the gist that it was good, he was amazing, and it didn't feel like a one-off.

And that when he had to sneak out of her house at three am, they'd had the world's longest kissing session as he pushed her against the door.

"Has he called you today?"

Grace's cheeks flushed. "Yes. And messaged." Like constantly. There was another message now, waiting for her to reply as soon as she got off the phone.

"And when will you see him again?"

"I don't know," Grace admitted. "It's difficult. He has to lie to get out of the house and we have to hide his car away." But it would happen. He'd made that clear.

"It's like being a teenager again. Except he knows what he's doing," Ella said. She sounded almost wistful.

Yeah, it did feel like that. The secrecy was an adrenaline

rush, but it wasn't real. Not like the softness of his touch and his sweet words when he called her this morning.

Asking her if she was okay. If she regretted it. If she wanted him to stay away.

She'd answered: yes, no, and definitely no. She wanted to see him as soon as possible.

"He insisted on cleaning some cobwebs on my ceiling," she said, smiling as she remembered him hitting the corners with a duster. "He was worried I'd be scared by spiders."

Ella laughed. "A guy who takes care of spiders and provides good sex? Sign me up. You have to see him again."

"We're talking about Tuesday, maybe," Grace admitted. It wasn't clear it could happen, though. And it felt like forever away.

"And then?" Ella asked. "When are you going to come clean and tell people?"

A bird swooped over her head. Arcadia looked up and whinnied.

"I don't think we will."

"What? Why not?" Ella sounded grouchy now. "Is he trying to keep you as his little secret?"

Grace patted Arcadia's neck, and he nuzzled against her shoulder. "It's not that simple. If anybody in our family found out, all hell would break loose." Her chest contracted at the thought. Her parents liked Michael. Heck, with the age gap, he was closer to her mom's age than hers. She couldn't even imagine her dad's face if he found out she and Michael were a thing.

"But they'll have to find out sometime, won't they? Or are you going to sneak around forever?"

Grace swallowed hard. Ella's questions were the same ones she'd been asking herself all day. But she didn't have any answers. Michael didn't want to cause any problems for his mom, especially while she was undergoing treatment, and she completely understood that. She loved Mia, too. She hated the thought of her getting upset.

There was no happy way for this to end. That was the problem. But she couldn't end it now. The thought of it created physical pain in her chest. It had been less than fourteen hours since she'd last seen Michael and she was already missing him.

"I don't know what will happen." Grace took a deep breath, her brows pulled tight. "I guess eventually he'll go back to London."

"You could go with him."

"We only reconnected last night. It's too soon to think of anything like that." She kept her voice light. "Don't worry about me. I'm always okay in the end."

"You never talked about a guy like this in all the time I've known you," Ella said, definitely sounding worried. "Not even Pascal."

"And now we know why. It's fine, honey. I just needed to talk to somebody, get it all out. That's all."

"Well, I'm here anytime you need to vent," Ella promised. "With my dry spell, it's the only excitement I get."

"What about that guy from accounts?" Grace asked.

"Turns out he was interested in my co-worker. Ryan."

"Oops."

"Yeah, well, you keep scooping up the hotties and I'll keep living my life vicariously through you."

Arcadia nudged Grace's arm. She looked over the mountains to see the sky darkening. "I'd better go. There's some rain coming in. Need to get Arcadia back." Summer storms were no joke. She wouldn't want to be caught out in one, and there was no way she'd put Arcadia through that. He was a thoroughbred, sometimes nervy. And he hated storms.

"Okay. But keep in touch." Ella sounded reluctant to let her go.

"I will."

"And ignore what everybody else thinks. You're doing nothing wrong."

Grace patted Arcadia's side and sighed. "If only that were true."

———

"What the heck is gooey butter cake?" Grace asked, laughing as Michael shook his head. It was Tuesday night, and he'd come over as planned, giving some stupid excuse about meeting another old friend. She was wearing a tank and a pair of panties, and he couldn't take his eyes off her. Couldn't stop touching her, either, even though they were both exhausted from their passionate hello.

Which had lasted an hour and a half in her bedroom, exhausting them both.

But she'd insisted on making them both a sandwich, and the growl of his empty stomach had hardened her resolve.

So here they were, in her kitchen, and he was watching as she sliced the bread, looking so damn beautiful his heart ached.

"You haven't heard of gooey butter cake?" He frowned.

"Well, I know you use butter to make a cake." Grace wrinkled her nose. Her mom was the baker in the family. She much preferred to eat than bake. "But to base the whole thing on butter? Isn't that disgusting?"

He laughed. "You need to try some. You'll never look back. It's kind of like a layer of cake with custardy butter in the middle."

She caught his eye, stilling her knife. "I thought you said a Slinger was the best thing I'd ever taste." He'd been telling her all about the food he used to love when he lived with his family in Missouri. Apparently, a slinger was a hash brown topped with chili, cheese, and a fried egg. Her stomach turned at the thought of it.

"A slinger for your meal, butter cake for dessert."

"Missouri is weird," she murmured.

He leaned on the counter, his gaze soft on her. "It just has a lot of different influences. People immigrated there and brought their food with them. French, German, African..."

"But not Irish," she pointed out. "Which is kind of ironic."

"I didn't get that nickname in Missouri."

She tipped her head to the side. "You didn't?"

He shook his head. "Nope. I got it at college. There were three Michaels on the team. They had to differentiate."

"They could have called you Devlin," she pointed out, laying slices of roasted beef onto the bread.

"That would have been too easy."

"Yeah." She smiled. "I have a soft spot for Irish."

"I've got a hard spot for you."

She laughed and threw a pickle at him. He caught it and ate it. "Let me take you out next week," he said when he'd swallowed it down.

"Where?" She widened her eyes, her lips still curled. "To the bar? Should we broadcast to the whole town that we're fucking?"

"We're not fucking."

"Then what are we doing?" she asked. Her voice was softer. The smile had gone, but she didn't look upset. Just interested.

"I don't know. Something more."

Because he wasn't just here for sex. Yes, it was good. Okay, fucking amazing. But this was perfect, too. Watching her make a sandwich for him. Knowing that another day he'd make one for her.

Laughing about slingers and butter cake and nicknames.

"We'll go to Charleston," he said. "Nobody knows us there."

"But everybody will notice that we've left town at the same time." She ran her tongue along her bottom lip. "It's not going to work."

He wanted to take her out. Wanted to feed her.

Wanted to spend the entire night with her curled in his arms. Because leaving her at night was shit. Hiding away was making him testy.

They were grown adults. They shouldn't have to do this.

"I'll have a meeting I can't miss in Charleston. A dinner meeting. I'll have to stay overnight. Nobody will blink an eye."

"How about me?"

"You'll be going to New York to meet up with your friend."

She cut the sandwiches and carried them over to where he was sitting. He reached for her, pulling her onto his lap so she was straddling him.

"Ella?"

"Yeah. Nobody will even think it's a coincidence. Seriously, who would put us together?"

"Ethan."

"No he wouldn't. Not unless throwing himself on the floor knocked any sense into him. Seriously, it's fine. Nobody will suspect a thing." He stroked her cheek. "Unless you'd rather not. I understand that."

"No, I want to. I really want to." She slid her hands onto his chest. "I just don't want this to get ruined. It's too special."

It was his turn to smile. "Yeah, I know that. And we won't."

"I'll talk to Ella. Make sure she's okay being my alibi. Plus, she kind of knows about us already." Grace's gaze met his. "I hope that's okay."

"Of course it is." It was weird, but he liked that she'd been talking to somebody about them.

It made it feel like less of a lie. More real.

She smiled and lifted a sandwich to his lips. "Eat."

He did as he was told, taking a bite and damn, it was delicious. The beef was tender, the pickles sharp, and his stomach rumbled with appreciation.

"It tastes almost as good as you."

"Let's not compare me to beef." She lifted a brow and pushed the sandwich toward him again. "Or this will end up in your face."

When they'd finished eating, Michael insisted on cleaning up.

"You've been well trained," Grace said as he slid the plates into the dishwasher.

"I've lived by myself for a while. Turns out that dishes don't magically clean themselves."

"What about when you were married?" she asked. "Did you do the dishes, then?"

"Of course I did." His brows raised. "Why wouldn't I?"

"I don't know. I just wondered..." Grace trailed off. "I guess I find it hard thinking about you being with somebody else."

"At my age, wouldn't it be weird if I hadn't been?"

"Yes. But that doesn't mean I have to like it."

He smiled. Her jealousy was soft, not angry. And he'd experienced angry before. "I don't want to be anywhere but here. With you. Now." He closed the dishwasher and wiped his hands on the towel. "So, what are tonight's plans?"

"Bed?" she asked, putting her hand on her hip. And damn, he was tempted. But between the food and the sex and the long day driving his mom to the hospital and back was taking its toll.

"Let's watch a movie."

"Now?" She blinked. "Don't you want to..."

"Yes. But I also want to spend time with you. Find out what you like. You can choose."

He watched as she walked to her living room, her hips swaying. She looked good in just a tank and panties.

She looked good in anything. That was the problem.

"This had better be a Netflix and Chill situation," she shouted out.

He grinned. "Depends on how interesting the movie is."

The sound of her TV switching on echoed through from the living room. He grabbed a soda and a beer from her refrigerator and walked in, passing the beer to Grace.

"You not drinking?"

"I have to drive."

Grace frowned. She was good at hiding it, but her natural reaction still came through. Maybe that's the other reason he wanted to watch something with her. To prove to her he wasn't here for only one thing.

She was worth more than that. So much more. But he had to go home tonight. He would not have the whole town talking about her.

"So, what movies do you like?" she asked him.

"I'm usually easy." He shrugged.

"Chick flicks? Action movies?" She twisted the cap off the beer, lifting it to her lips. "Or something arty?" There was a bead of beer on her bottom lip. She pulled her lip between her teeth, flicking the moisture away with her tongue. "Oh this is perfect. We should watch this."

"What is it?"

"*Call My Agent.* It's French. Like a mixture of you and me. You're the agent and I love France." She looked so happy and he liked that.

A lot.

"Oh. It's a series." She blinked. "There are a lot of episodes.

"Doesn't matter. We can watch it."

She turned to look at him, her tongue pressing between her teeth. "We can't watch it in one night."

"What a shame. I'll just have to come back to you night after night."

She smiled. "I don't hate the sound of that."

CHAPTER
Fifteen

"SHE'S A LITTLE TIRED TODAY," the nurse said to Michael a week later, as she helped his mom out of the treatment room the following week. "But she refuses to get into a wheelchair."

"I'm fine. I just felt a bit dizzy, that's all." Mia rolled her eyes. "Thank you, Rhona."

"You take it easy. Rest up." Rhona's eyes met Michael's. "Take care of her."

"I intend to."

He helped his mom out to the car. The fresh air seemed to waken her, and she asked if they could sit on the bench near the parking lot before they got into the car for the long drive home.

"I love days like these," she said, looking up at the blue sky. "The sun makes everything happier." She put her hand on his. "You seem happier, too."

"I do?" Michael lifted a brow.

"Yes. I'm so glad you've reconnected with your old friends. They've brought out the best in you. You should invite them over to ours. I'd love to meet them."

Guilt pulled at him. He'd been using his non-existent friends as an excuse to see Grace every moment that he could.

"For a while I wondered if you'd found a woman friend," his mom said, her voice light. Great. She was wide awake now. "Or maybe that was just wishful thinking. Hoping that you'd find somebody you cared for enough that you'd stay nearby."

"My home is in London, Mom. And there's nobody."

"There's still time." Her eyes twinkled.

"I thought we'd had this conversation."

"We have. But it didn't come to any satisfactory conclusion." She sighed. "Anyway, you're here now and that's the main thing." She smiled softly at him. "You're coming to *Chairs* this week, aren't you?"

"Yep." This weekend was the one he'd planned with Grace. In Charleston. They'd travel up late Friday night after *Chairs* – because they'd agreed it would be good to be seen there – separately. "But I have to leave early. I'm heading straight to Charleston after, remember?"

She blinked. "I'm tired, not brain dead. Of course I remember. Though I don't understand why you have to have meetings on the weekend."

It wasn't the best excuse in the world. But his job always had strange hours, thank goodness.

"It's a client. They're having a thing." He shrugged. "You know I always work weekends."

"I'm proud of you." She squeezed his hand again. "When football didn't work out, I was so scared you'd be broken. But you picked yourself up and fought back. Got a career you so obviously love."

"I learned that from my mom."

Her eyes softened.

In so many ways, she was right. He had fought back. Had found a job he loved. But now he was starting to resent it.

Getting annoyed by those middle-of-the-night calls, those early morning Zoom meetings.

The thought of having to leave to go back to London.

Yes, his mom was exhausted today, but her doctor was pleased with her progress. She was almost halfway through this course of therapy. If it went well, she wouldn't need another.

She'd be in recovery and he'd be going home.

Whatever *home* meant.

His mom's phone rang. She pulled it out of her purse and smiled. "It's Cam. Do you mind if I take this?"

"Be my guest." Michael stood, partly because the low bench was making his legs ache, but mostly to give her some privacy.

And yeah, maybe to check his own phone for messages, too.

He smiled when he saw one there. He'd stored Grace's contact as 'G'. Nothing else. He didn't want anybody to see her messages and get the wrong idea.

Or the right one.

I'm bored. Entertain me. Tell me what you used to do in the olden days before Netflix and Chill. – G

He rolled his eyes. She found their age gap amusing. He probably would too if he was the younger one.

We were too busy hunting wooly mammoths to think about Netflix. – M

. . .

I knew it! Just like I knew nobody had sex until 2015. Or booty calls. – G

He rolled his eyes. She'd been calling him her booty call ever since he'd started waiting for her to call before he left the house. Making sure the coast was clear on both of their sides.

He could hear his mom laughing softly. Fuck, he shouldn't be doing this here. And yet his whole body felt warm in a way that had nothing to do with the sunshine.

It was her. All her. And she'd sent him another message.

How did booty calls work before cellphones, anyway? Did people use carrier pigeons? Smoke signals? I'm intrigued now… – G

I have no idea. I've always had a cell phone. And be careful, or I'll show you exactly how young I can be tonight. – M

Promise? – G

"Are you messaging your friends?"

He jumped at the sound of his mom's voice.

"Ah yeah. Talking about playing some pool tonight."

"That's nice." She smiled. "Cam's insisting I go to bed as soon as we get home, especially since we're going out to the movies tomorrow."

"And *Chairs* on Friday," he said. "You'll be out two nights in a row."

"I used to love to go out every night." She sighed. "Never get old, sweetheart. It's boring."

"I'm already old." He smiled at the memory of Grace's teasing, sliding his phone into his pocket because there was no way he wanted his mom to see her messages appearing on the screen.

"That makes me ancient. And we can't have that. Come on, let's go home. I want to sit in the yard when we get there and enjoy the last of the sun."

He put his arm out for her and she took it. "I'll probably head out again tonight."

"Good. Enjoy yourself."

He swallowed. Every day, this was getting tougher. Lying to people. Hiding his feelings.

And yet he couldn't stay away from her if he tried.

———

As soon as he arrived at *Chairs* on Friday, Michael knew exactly why his mom was so insistent he should attend before leaving for Charleston.

Before she and Cam had left the house she'd asked him three times if he was still going to join them by the creek. Eventually, Cam had dragged her out and given Michael a sympathetic smile.

And now, as he walked across the grass, his mom was grinning widely at him. And next to her was a woman wearing a pretty summer dress.

Not just any woman. Rhona. The nurse who'd been taking care of his mom since she'd started treatment.

"Honey, look who's here," his mom said, her face shining with happiness. "Doesn't Rhona look pretty?"

Goddamn. He was walking straight into a set up. Which would have been funny if he wasn't heading to Charleston with Grace this evening.

"Hey Rhona." He nodded at her. He'd exchanged casual

conversation with her while his mom had her treatment, but that was it.

"Hi Michael." She smiled at him. "You look handsome."

"Isn't it lovely that Rhona could join us?" his mom asked. "Maybe you could get her a drink?"

Fuck. "Sure." He nodded. "What would you like?"

"What do you have?" Rhona asked. He'd thought she was older when she was wearing her scrubs, but in a dress she looked like she was in her mid thirties.

Older than Grace. Younger than him. Damn, he wished his mom would stop smiling like the cat that got the cream.

"Lemonade?"

"Get her a beer," his mom said. "No need to be shy."

"On it." He nodded and walked over to the drinks table. He scanned the crowd for Grace, but there was no sign of her. So he pulled his phone out and quickly sent her a text.

Are you here yet? – M

I just parked. And I thought we were radio silence until Charleston? I was enjoying pretending to be Jane Bond. – G

She sounded happy. And light-hearted. Behind him, he could hear his mom and Rhona laughing about something. His head was throbbing.

Okay. I just need you to hear me out. My mom's set me up with a friend of hers. This isn't my doing. I'm going to try to get out of here and head up to Charleston early. – M

. . .

What do you mean, set you up? As in a date? – G

I don't know. She was just really insistent on me coming tonight and now this woman is here and I'm almost certain my mom's trying to match make. It means nothing. – M

Of course it means something. – G

He let out a long breath. He couldn't tell if Grace was annoyed or not. Couldn't tell anything from her words. But there was no way he could slink away and call her without somebody noticing.

This was hell, wrapped up in a small town gathering.

He should have headed to Charleston earlier.

"Can you grab me a beer, too?" Cam asked, joining him at the table.

"There you go." Michael popped a cap on a bottle and passed it to him. "Did you know about this?" He looked over Cam's shoulder and Cam turned to follow his gaze to where Michael's mom and Rhona were standing.

"Nope. Would have warned you if I did." Cam wrinkled his nose. "Sorry."

"She's not my type."

"Who is your type?" Cam looked genuinely interested.

"Not somebody my mom chooses for me."

And then Michael saw Grace walk over to where her cousins – and his step-cousins – were sitting. She shot him a glance and then opened her chair, turning her back to him.

Yeah, she was annoyed.

He would be too, if her mom tried to set her up with a guy at *Chairs*.

"I'll talk to your mom later." Cam shifted his feet. "Can you just be nice to Rhona for tonight?"

"I wasn't going to tell her to get out of here."

Cam slapped his back. "Good. You coming back?"

"Yeah."

His phone buzzed in his pocket. "Actually, can you take the other beer back to Rhona? I'll be there in a minute." He pulled his phone out.

"Sure. Work problems?" Cam took the second bottle.

"Something like that." As soon as Cam had left the drinks table, Michael read Grace's message.

If she touches you, I'll kill her. – G x

His lips twitched. Grace had already told him how much she hated violence, but he wasn't going to lie, her jealousy touched him.

Got it. And I'm sorry. – M x

You should be. Now go talk to your new girlfriend. – G x

He rolled his eyes.

She's not my girlfriend. You are. And I can't tell you how happy that makes me. – M x

———

"You okay?" Presley asked Grace as they sat around the circle of cousins at *Chairs* on Friday. The sun was still up, and the evening warmth was still lingering. She'd slathered herself in bug spray because the insects always made a beeline for her.

"I'm fine. Why?"

"You keep looking over your shoulder at where your parents are. I wondered if you'd pissed them off or something."

Grace blinked. She wasn't looking at her parents at all, though they were standing in the same group as Michael and Rhona. No, she was watching Michael, and watching that damn woman.

She hated this. Hated the way her body tingled with jealousy. And yeah, she was trying to be cool about it because this wasn't Michael's fault, but ugh.

"When do you leave for New York?" Sabrina asked.

"First thing in the morning." Grace wrinkled her nose. "The middle of the night, really." It was scary how easily the lies ran off her tongue. But then she and Michael were lying left, right, and center.

They'd spent the week setting up their alibis. Her with her parents and cousins, him with his own parents.

"I wish I was going with you," Sabrina said.

"Why would you want that?" Marley wrinkled his nose. "It's hot as hell in New York."

"It's hot as hell here," Sabrina pointed out. "But at least there's something going on there."

"You don't have to stay here if you hate it," Mason told her. "I'll pack your bags for you if you like."

Sabrina stuck her tongue out at her brother, and he made a face back at her. And while they carried on bickering, Grace turned to see if she could see Michael again.

Rhona was still next to him, flicking her hair and laughing at something he said. She really was pretty and somehow that made Grace feel worse.

"Mom's set Michael up tonight," Sabrina whispered in her ear, following her gaze.

Ugh. Caught in the act. "She has? With who?" Grace feigned surprise and luckily Sabrina fell for it.

"The nurse who's been looking after her during her treatment."

She was one of Mia's nurses? Grace felt bad for the way she'd been thinking about the woman.

And her jealousy quadrupled. So she was pretty and caring and she and Mia had a bond.

She looked again. The setting sun caught the woman's hair, turning the blonde into a warm red. She smiled and Michael smiled back, and Grace felt dizzy.

"She's pretty, isn't she?" Sabrina whispered. "Should I go talk to her? She could end up being my sister-in-law."

"If you'd like." Grace's words were short. Sabrina shot her a confused look.

"Ah, I'll leave them to it. So, what are your plans in New York?" Sabrina asked, her brows still pinched. "Are you going to a club? Shopping? Hey, if you go to Ronnie's Deli, you need to pick me up some cannolis. Those things are to die for."

There was a peal of laughter, and Grace knew exactly where it was coming from. She couldn't help it. She had to look.

The nurse had her hand on his chest and was smiling up at him. Grace stared so hard it must have bore heat into Michael's stupid brain because he finally turned to look at her.

She widened her eyes at him, suddenly furious. She'd told him the woman couldn't touch him.

She blew out a mouthful of air. She needed to calm down. She was being stupid.

"So do you think you'll go?" Sabrina asked.

"Where?" Grace blinked. She had to pull her gaze away from Michael and the nurse, but the jealousy remained.

"To Ronnie's."

"I don't think so, hon." She shook her head. Her cheeks were flaming now. "Listen, I think I'm gonna grab a soda. You want anything?"

"A cannoli from Ronnie's," Sabrina said pointedly.

"Brat."

"I know. I'm just bored, you know?"

"Only a couple of months and you'll be going back to college," Grace told her. "You just gotta get through it."

"Come to the drive-in with me next week then," Sabrina asked, smiling at Grace. "They're showing horror movies. Should be fun."

"I'll come with you," Mason said. "I love it when you're scared."

"You're not invited." Sabrina rolled her eyes at him. "Girls only."

Their argument started up again and this time Grace couldn't stand sitting here. She needed to get up. Stretching her arms, she walked over to the drinks table and grabbed a can of soda from the ice bucket.

She popped the tab, lifting the soda to her mouth and taking a mouthful. It really was hot today. She could feel tiny curls of her hair sticking to her neck, and her t-shirt clinging to her skin. She pressed the can to her chest, closing her eyes as it cooled her, then looked up.

Her eyes meeting Michael's.

He was holding a bottle of water in one hand, the other shoved into his pocket. The nurse was next to him, her head tipped to the side as he talked to Cam, like she was listening avidly.

Grace narrowed her eyes and shook her hair, taking another sip of soda.

"Hey honey," Aunt Mia called out to her, noticing her staring in their direction. "Come talk to me."

For a minute, she considered making a run for it. Getting away from this whole scene. But everybody was watching. Including Michael. She took a deep breath and walked over to her aunt and kissed her cheek.

"How are you?" she asked Mia.

"Tired but good." Mia smiled. Then she looked over at Michael and Rhona. "What do you think?" she whispered. "I set her up with Michael. She's pretty, isn't she?"

Grace nodded. "Yep." Her voice was clipped.

"He needs some romance in his life. Goodness knows he doesn't relax enough."

Grace wanted to tell her he was completely relaxed in her bed last night. But she didn't.

"So, what do you have planned for this weekend?" Mia asked her.

Grace blew out a mouthful of air. "I'm going to New York. Meeting up with some friends." She said it loud enough that Michael could hear. "It's lovely being around my parents, and all of you," Grace said, waving her hand around. "But I need to kick back and enjoy myself."

Mia laughed. "I know what you mean. Can't be easy having your whole family surrounding you all the time."

The nurse touched Michael's chest again. She saw him subtly move back.

Okay. Breathe. It was going to be fine.

"Rhona, come meet Grace," Mia beckoned at her. "Honey, this is Rhona."

"Hi." Grace gave her a tight smile. "It's good to meet you."

"You too. Are you part of the family, too?" Rhona had a low voice. Sensual.

"She's my niece," Mia interjected. "Michael's cousin."

Grace's smile wavered.

"You look too young to be his cousin." Rhona looked over her shoulder at Michael. He was pointedly talking to Cam.

"We're step cousins." Weird how important it felt to say that out loud. "And I'm twenty-six," she told her.

Rhona laughed. "I remember those days. By the way, you're so pretty."

Why was she so nice when Grace wanted to hate her? "Thank you. So are you. I love your hair." There. She could be nice if she had to.

"Thank you." Rhona patted it. "I get so sick of having it up all day for work. So I went to the salon to give myself a treat."

Grace swallowed. "That's nice." She looked at her Aunt Mia.

"I should go," she said to her. "Sabrina and Mason were starting World War Three as I left. I think I'm gonna have to play the UN."

"Give them a shake for me," Mia said, her lips curling. "And take it from me. Never have kids."

"Wasn't planning on it." Grace lifted a brow. "Bye, Rhona. It was lovely to meet you. Have a good evening."

"Bye, Grace. It was nice to meet you, too." Rhona gave her a genuine smile. Grace tried to give one back.

And then she looked at Michael. He stared back, his expression revealing nothing.

Walking back to her cousins, she might have added a little swing to her hips. And yeah, she might have hoped that Michael watched her. Because he couldn't avoid being set up by his mom, but he could look more annoyed at it.

Maybe she should go to New York instead.

No, she knew she wouldn't. But part of her wished she had the guts to do it.

CHAPTER
Sixteen

"HONEY, can you take Rhona home for me?" Mia asked Michael, as people started leaving *Chairs*. "Cam was going to do it, but I'm so tired. I'd like to get back home and into bed."

"I have to leave for Charleston," Michael reminded her. There was no way he wanted to take Rhona home. Not when Grace was shooting daggers at him every five minutes, even though this wasn't his fault.

"Oh honey, she only lives ten minutes away. If you're worried about losing time, you could pick your bag up and take her from ours. It's on the way to Charleston, after all."

There was no way around it. Not without starting the kind of fuss that would get attention. And his mom looked so damn happy that he'd been talking to her nurse.

"Okay," he said curtly. "I'll take her on my way."

When he was back from Charleston, he'd have to talk to her about this. It was one thing to be asking him about his love life, another to be interfering with it.

"Rhona, Michael will take you home," his mom called out to her nurse.

Rhona smiled at him. "Are you sure?" she asked softly.

He nodded. "It's fine. I'm heading to Charleston, so it's on my way."

"You're going to Charleston tonight?" Rhona looked surprised. "But it's hours away. You'll be driving really late."

"I have meetings tomorrow. It's either leave late or at a stupid hour in the morning. This way at least I get some sleep."

Rhona smiled. "I can make you a sandwich for the trip if you'd like."

And damn if Grace didn't walk by at the same time with his sister. Sabrina was pulling at Grace's arm.

"You should take her up on the sandwich," Grace said, deadpan. "Somebody your age needs regular meals."

Sabrina started laughing. He cocked a brow at her and she wrinkled her nose.

But Grace just carried on walking. And he couldn't tell if she was annoyed or amused.

"Come on," he said to Rhona. "Let's get going. We'll swing by and pick up my suitcase on the way."

"Thank you." She smiled at him.

It took a while to get to his place, because everybody had left at the same time and he had to wait for a break in the cars to pull out. Still, he got home before his parents did, and before Sabrina and Mason, so he pulled into the drive and glanced over at Rhona.

"You okay staying here?" he asked. "I'm just gonna run in and out again."

"You already packed?"

"Yep." That was one good thing he'd done, at least.

"Sure, I'm happy to wait."

It took him a couple of minutes to get upstairs. He was just about to grab his overnight bag when his phone vibrated.

You're taking her home? Seriously? – Grace

. . .

Mom asked me to. It's on my way. Don't make a big deal out of it. – Michael

There was a pause that made him realize he'd said the wrong thing. Then the little icon told him Grace was typing. He picked up his duffel, sighing.

So it wouldn't be a big deal if I popped over and saw Ethan before I come to meet you? – Grace

Yeah, it would. He'd hate it.

I know you wouldn't do that because Ethan hurt your horse. Can we talk about this in Charleston, please? – Michael.

He walked down the stairs with his bag over his shoulder, sighing as he saw a pair of headlights swing into the driveway. Cam's car. Big and comfortable. Nothing like the sports car that he once drove before he became Mia's husband and Michael and Josh's stepdad.

That felt like a lifetime ago. Michael could still remember the day he and Josh threw a ball against Cam's car, damaging it and causing Cam to chase them to their brand new house in Hartson's Creek.

Where he met Mia, Michael's mom.

Cam gestured at Michael to cross the driveway in front of him, and Mia blew him a kiss through the windshield. He lifted a hand, smiling grimly. At least *she* wasn't pissed at him.

But somebody else was. He knew that when he felt his phone vibrate once more, with Grace's answer to his request.

Sure. – Grace.

Ouch. Damned by a single word. Michael had enough experience to know that *sure* didn't mean sure. It meant she was annoyed. That he was gonna get it.

And maybe he deserved that. He should have walked away the moment he saw he was being set up.

For her.

Putting his phone in his pocket, he opened the trunk, throwing his luggage in the back. Then he took a deep breath and sat down in the driver's seat, giving Rhona a tight smile.

"Sorry about that. You ready?"

"Of course."

It looked like she'd reapplied her lipstick. He couldn't work out if that was a bad thing or a good thing.

He was probably about to find out.

———

Grace sat in the hotel parking lot for ten minutes staring out at the dark night, thinking about what happened tonight. She was annoyed at herself for reacting like a child. At Michael for taking Rhona home. She was even fed up with his mom for setting him up, even though she had no idea about him and Grace.

This wasn't supposed to be how tonight was going to go. He was going to arrive first, she was going to sneak there later, and they were going to have two amazing nights wrapped in each other's arms.

No prying eyes. No escaping at dawn because somebody was going to find out.

A tap at her window made her jump. She looked out to see Michael standing there, his brows pinched like he was somewhere in between annoyance and pain.

She rolled the window down. "Hi."

"Saw you'd got here." His eyes were wary. "I was worried when you didn't come up."

Of course. They'd shared their phone locations to make it easier to sneak around. He probably thought she was an idiot for sitting here for the last ten minutes.

"I was just thinking."

"Changing your mind?" he asked.

She blew out a mouthful of air. "No. Just wondering how tonight ended up in such a mess."

He nodded, but his expression told her he didn't want to talk about it. Not here, at least. In a hotel parking lot in the middle of the balmy Charleston night.

"You want to come up?" he asked, his voice softer. That made her chest ache more.

"Yeah," she whispered. "I do."

His eyes caught hers. "Your bag in the trunk?"

She nodded, and he walked around the back of her car, popping it open, and pulling her case out. She swallowed hard as he walked back around, waiting for her to climb out and join him.

He didn't push her. Didn't grab for the door. He just waited.

It took her another minute to pull the handle and step out. The air was still warm and humid. It wrapped around her like an unwelcome blanket. "I checked us in already," Michael told her, his voice still wary. "Let's go upstairs. We can talk there."

Not have uninhibited sex, like they'd intended to. Not use every surface until both of them were seeing stars. She felt like she was letting him down. What was the point in all of this when she was just feeling like a bitch?

"I'm sorry."

He shook his head. "You don't need to be sorry about anything."

She followed him into the lobby. There was a man at the desk scrolling through his phone, but he didn't look up as they walked by. Michael pressed the elevator button, and the doors opened immediately. He gestured for her to get in and then followed behind.

He hit the tenth floor button. The highest in the hotel. She held her breath, counting the floors, neither of them saying a word as they arrived on his floor and walked to the room at the end of the corridor.

Michael pressed the card to the reader, the door clicking open as he pushed it, standing to the side so she could walk in.

Always the gentleman. Making sure she was safe before anything else.

"You want a drink?" he asked as she closed the door behind her.

She shook her head. He put her case in the hallway, and that's when she realized this wasn't just a room. It was a suite, complete with a living area and a glass wall overlooking the small city. Lights blinked in the darkness, the Kanawha River flowed like black ink. She walked over and stared out, taking in how tiny everything looked from this height.

"I didn't ask her to come tonight. I didn't ask to take her home."

She exhaled again, turning to look at him. He was five feet away, as though he needed the distance. His hand raked through his hair as he stared at her.

"I didn't like it."

"I know."

"I was jealous."

His eyes caught hers. "I know. And I made you feel that way."

"You didn't." She shook her head. "That was all me." She looked up at him. "What happened when you took her home?"

"When I dropped her off at her house, she didn't get out of the car. Just kind of shuffled around and looked at me, like she expected something to happen."

"She wanted you to kiss her," Grace said.

"Yeah. And all I could think of was you. That I needed it to be you, not her."

Grace needed that, too. So much. She nodded at the leather sofa that looked out over the city. "Sit down."

He lifted a brow. "Why?"

"Because I said so. Because I'm mad and sad and I need you to do this for me."

For a moment, he stared at her, but he did as she'd asked. Walked around in front of the sofa and sat down, his long, thick, legs bending in front of him.

She pulled her top off and his eyes almost popped out of his head.

"What…"

"You're mine," she whispered.

He lifted a brow but said nothing.

She walked over to where he was sitting and straddled his muscled thighs. He still hadn't moved. It was strange how he did that. Just watched and waited.

She liked it, though. Liked the way he wasn't a hothead like she was.

His eyes met hers, soft and understanding. "I'm yours," he told her. He slid his hands down her sides, the warmth of his palms enticing. Leaning forward, he placed a soft kiss on her collarbone.

She felt wrung out, yet more alive than she'd ever been. A cocktail of emotions spiked through her blood. Hurt, jealousy, the need to reclaim him.

And yeah, that was the strongest one of all.

Cupping his face with her palms, she felt the roughness of his beard tickle her skin. "I wanted to do this at *Chairs*. March over and kiss you. Mark you."

"I'm already marked by you." He took her hand. Placed it on his chest. She could feel the steady thrum of his heartbeat through his shirt. "Feel it?" he whispered.

She nodded.

"It's for you. It's fucking racing for you."

"I'm sorry I acted like an idiot," she whispered.

"It's not your fault. I should have said no. I should have told her to find her own way home."

"You're not that kind of guy." She kissed his jaw, his cheek, his throat. She could feel the rumble of his breath through it.

"What kind of guy am I?"

"Mine. My kind of guy."

"I like it when you say that."

She stroked his jaw. "You do?"

"Yeah." He gave her a half smile. "Probably too much."

She unbuttoned his shirt, pulling it open to reveal his chest. Dipping her head, she kissed his clavicle, his pectoral, his nipple.

"Jesus."

"Just let me do this," she told him. "Let me kiss you everywhere."

"I don't deserve it."

Her eyes flickered up to his. "Yes you do. We both do. We need this." She wriggled her hips, slithering to the floor, her knees hitting the soft rug.

She reached for his zipper, pulling it down, reaching inside his shorts. He groaned as her fingers encircled him.

He was hard for her. She liked that. She pulled him out of his boxers, the thick length of him jutting out. "You don't have to... Oh God."

Sliding her lips over his tip, she enveloped him, her warm mouth welcoming him in, her tongue reminding him whose he was.

Hers. Hers. Always hers.

She swallowed him further, eliciting another low moan, his fingers tangling in her hair. His head was tipped back, his mouth open, his eyes on her.

She loved the taste of him. The feel of him in her mouth. The way she could drive him wild with a twist of her tongue. Loved that his hips were hitching, finding a rhythm, his fingers tight against her scalp, his groans louder, his lips calling out her name.

"Stop," he rasped. "I'm not coming in your mouth."

"Yes you are." She kept her eyes on his, sliding her lips on him once more. Michael let out a low oath as she slid her tongue against him, then called out her name again. It was soft and sweet, like a prayer, as he spilled inside of her and she held him tight, taking everything he had to give.

And when he was done, she climbed back over him, and he looked up at her, his eyes hazy.

"Remind me to piss you off more often." He cupped her cheek, pressing his lips against hers. It was the sweetest kiss. The kind she wanted to remember forever.

"Do it again and I'll really show you how angry I can be."

"It won't happen again," he told her. "I'll make sure of that."

"Good." She dropped her head to his shoulder, loving the way he was touching her. It wasn't sexual now. It felt more like wonder. As though he was trying to memorize every part of her. And then a yawn overtook her and he chuckled.

"Let's go to bed," he said. "I owe you an orgasm."

"It can wait." She nestled against his chest.

"No, it can't." He stood, holding her against him, as he zipped up his pants. Then he lifted her, and she curled her legs around his waist. The smile was still playing on his lips, and she loved it.

She loved him.

Her chest contracted at the thought. At the truth of it.

She was in love with this man and she had no idea what to do with that.

Holding her close, he carried her across the living space to the bedroom on the right. Like the living area, it had a floor to ceiling glass wall overlooking the city. He pressed a button, and a blind came down with a whirr, and he placed her on the bed.

"You're so beautiful."

"You're biased," she told him.

He laughed. "Yeah, but it's still the truth." He laid beside her, cupped her face. "Now it's my turn to make you mine."

CHAPTER
Seventeen

THEY'D SLEPT past breakfast and almost into lunch. Michael had arranged for some food to be sent up, but right now they were both still in their pajamas, laying on the bed and staring out at the city.

"We really should get out and visit some places," Grace murmured, her head on his chest, where it had been most of the night. Or at least the times she wasn't under him, or over him.

Reclaiming him the way he was reclaiming her. He smiled and kissed the top of her head.

"We have the rest of today and tomorrow."

She stretched her arms out. "Yes, and I love it. Maybe we should move here and pretend Hartson's Creek doesn't exist."

"You'd hate that. I see how much you love your family," he told her, shaking his head.

She nodded. "I would. And so would you. You're here for your mom, after all."

He stroked her shoulder, her arm, then curled his fingers into hers. "You okay after last night?" he asked. All those emotions. The anger, the sadness, the desire. It made him feel like he was fifteen again.

And yet… somehow it felt right.

She tilted her head to catch his eye. "I'm fine. I'm sorry. I think I got triggered."

"Triggered?"

"By a past event. Like trauma. A trigger can take you back to that place."

He blinked, remembering how he'd felt as a teen finding out Cam and his mom had been lying to him about their relationship. How angry he'd been, the same way he'd been angry when his dad had left them.

"Yeah, I get that. What was the past event?" he asked, drawing circles on her arm. Her skin was so soft. He couldn't stop touching it.

"Pascal ended things with me because his mom chose his wife for him."

"The French guy?" Michael frowned. "Are you serious?"

She nodded.

"But that's so Victorian. What kind of guy lets his mom choose his wife?"

"One who wants to keep all the money in the family, I guess. She's rich. Enough to invest in the vineyards. Plus, she was French and his mom loved that."

"I'm sorry." He winced, because his mom had done the same thing. Not with malice – she'd done it because she wanted to see him happy – but he could see how Grace got triggered.

"Would you have stayed with him if he'd fought for you?" he asked.

Her eyes were wide. There was such an honesty in them. That was the thing with Grace. She was mature, but she was still young. She hadn't learned to hide yet.

He hoped she never would.

"I don't think so. I'm just glad he didn't, because I want to be here, with you."

"Is that right?" He smiled.

"Yep." She rolled onto him, kissing his lips. He slid his hands down her body, feeling the rise and dip of her curves. God, she was perfect. He couldn't remember the last time he'd felt this good.

This alive.

He'd spent a lifetime avoiding emotions. They were messy, people got hurt. Especially by him. And yet here she was, still with him, after a shitshow of a night.

She was prepared to fight for him, the same way he'd fight for her. It made his skin tingle.

"How long were you and Pascal together?" he asked.

She tipped her head to the side. "You're asking me that while I'm laying on top of you?"

He laughed. "I'm interested. I want to know about you."

"You pretty much know everything. I'm an open book." She widened her eyes, and he chuckled some more. "But we were together for two years. I'd ask about your dating history, but I'd like to leave this bed at some point today, Grandpa."

"I'm wounded." He grinned. "I'm not that old."

"I know." She cupped his face. "But I don't enjoy thinking about you and other women."

"There are no other women," he said gruffly. "Just you."

He slid his hands to her hips. Pulled her closer. She kissed him again, her lips soft and pliant. He was falling for her, this woman who shouldn't be his. But it felt right. Maybe for the first time in his life. Here in this room, with her, was his little slice of perfection.

He sat up, pulling her with him, and pushed her camisole down, revealing her perfect breasts. "Why would I want anybody else when I have you?" he asked her. "When I have this." He wrapped his lips around her nipple. He teased it with his tongue until she rocked against him.

He was hard. *Again.* Just like he always was with her.

She slid her hands into his hair, pulling him closer, whispering his name. He pulled down his pajama pants, then did the same to hers, reaching across the table to find another condom.

Thank fuck he'd bought a lot.

"Can we not?" she asked him.

"You sore?"

She shook her head. "Not use a condom. I have an IUD. I'm covered." She scraped her nails against his scalp and he wanted to growl like a wolf. "I want to feel you. Just you. I've never had that before."

"Christ."

"You're clean, aren't you?" she asked him. He nodded. Yeah, he'd had his annual checkup right before leaving for the states.

And he wanted it. Fuck, did he want it. Wanted to feel every part of her around him. Wanted to feel the warmth of her, the velvet softness. The way she rippled when he made her come.

"The food will be here soon," he said.

"Then we'd better make it fast."

He smiled. "If I'm inside you bareback, I can guarantee that."

———

"It's a horse," Michael said, his fingers trailing down her arm.

"It's not a horse." Grace shook her head. "Where's the mane? The body? The tail?"

"So, what do you think it is?" He turned to look at her, amused. The way his eyes caught hers sent a shiver down her spine.

They'd both agreed they had to get out of the hotel room before they ended up having sex again, and neither of them could walk for the next week. That would take some explaining. How she ended up with a stride like a cowboy from a weekend in New York, and Michael winced every time he moved after business meetings in Charleston.

"It's a rectangle."

Michael laughed. "I know that. But what's it supposed to represent?"

She leaned in closer to the painting. "I don't know," she said, her nose wrinkled. "It's called Unimaginable."

"Yeah, I can see where they came up with that title."

"Can I help you with anything?" a soft voice asked. Grace turned to see an older gentleman in a suit and bow tie standing behind them.

"We're interested in this painting," she said.

"Of course. Would you like to know the price?"

Her eyes met Michael's. She hadn't meant *that* kind of interested. And yet now she wanted to know. How much did a painting like this cost? They'd only come into this tiny art gallery to get out of the heat of the afternoon sun. And it had been fun, looking at the paintings with Michael, learning his taste.

He liked landscapes. And seascapes. Things, not people.

She loved portraits. Trying to imagine the people who sat for them. Whether they were rich or models or simply a figment of the artist's imagination.

Before they walked in here, they'd spent the last hour wandering around a flea market, hand in hand. She'd stopped to look at some jewelry and he'd bought her a cameo brooch. It was old-fashioned with a gold chain and extra pin to make doubly sure you'd never lose it. It was already the favorite thing she owned.

She loved being able to hold his hand in public. To tease him and make him smile. To feel his eyes on her as she rifled through old dusty books on a table, calling out with glee when she found a hardback copy of *Moliere*, in original French.

He'd insisted on paying for that, too. She wasn't used to that yet. She was a split-the-bill-down-the-middle kind of girl.

And now she knew he was a that's-never-happening kind of guy.

"How much?" she asked, intrigued now.

"Twenty thousand dollars. Though there's a little leeway for the right buyer. The artist is local. He wants the picture to stay nearby, since it's of the Capitol Building."

She didn't dare look at Michael, in case they both started laughing. So *that's* what it was.

"The Capitol Building is my very favorite place," she murmured, touching Michael's arm. "Can we get it, darling, can we?"

"I'm trying to work out if it'll look good next to the Van Gogh," he said with an impressively even voice. "I'm worried it will outshine it."

She slid her fingers through his. "It's so much prettier than the Van Gogh. And you can actually tell what it is, too."

"Don't forget, we just bought you a Mattise," he reminded her, kissing her brow. "You're so greedy."

She smiled up at him. "I know, but I'm worth it." She looked at the man, feeling bad now, because he was looking at them, confused. "We'll think about it."

"Don't take too long. I've had a lot of interest in it."

"I can imagine." Michael nodded. "Everybody loves the Capitol Building."

They saved their laughter until they made it outside into the heat of the Charleston afternoon. "I don't believe it," Grace said, when she'd finally got it out of her system. "Twenty thousand dollars for a rectangle. Who pays that kind of money out?"

"I just sold a football player for thirty million."

She rolled her eyes. "That's different. And you didn't sell him. You negotiated his contract."

Michael shrugged. "Doesn't matter. Price is in the eye of the beholder. How much would you pay for a horse?"

"Horses are useful. They do things."

"What things?" He put his hand on the small of her back, leading her into the shade of an old tree. She could already feel the sweat trickling down her neck. They'd have to get inside soon, or at least take a break for a drink.

"They carry things. People. Help farm the land."

"How much farming has Arcadia done?" He was still smiling, and she liked it. She'd never seen him this relaxed. This lighthearted.

"He's special. A thoroughbred. They don't work, they exist."

"Like the royalty of the horse genus."

"Something like that." She shrugged. "I still think he's worth more than a rectangle, though. It didn't even look like the Capitol Building."

They both looked over at the golden dome of the building in the distance. It was glinting in the sunlight.

"It's not even rectangular either," he murmured, kissing her again. She looped her arms around him, pressing her body against his.

"Can we go back to the hotel yet?" he asked.

"Not yet." She curled her fingers around his neck. "I want to show you my grandma's house." Not that it was her grandma's anymore. But once upon a time it had belonged to her father's family. Her grandma had died years ago, and her uncle had sold it.

"You sure there's nobody there who'll recognize you?" he asked.

"The only uncle my dad talks to lives in Tokyo. He doesn't keep in touch with his other brother and sister." She shrugged. "And anyway, even if they recognized me, they wouldn't know you."

"True."

"Come on. Let's go see it." She felt excited to show him something that was part of her. When she was a small child, she could remember playing in the yard, picking flowers and putting them in her hair. It had to have been at least seventeen years since she was last there, but when they walked around the corner, she felt it all coming back to her.

Her grandma had spoken French. As a girl she'd studied in Paris, and she'd shown Grace old yellowing photographs of her time there. The paper corners of the photographs folded and torn, as she talked about the grandeur of L'Arc De Triomphe, the dominance of the Tour Eiffel. The smell of the bakeries as she walked to college every day.

She was breathless as she told Michael about the day she'd finally landed in France itself. And somehow it had felt completely alien yet home.

For a little while, at least.

"Do you miss it?" he asked.

"Sometimes. Do you miss London?"

He blinked and looked away. "I don't think so. I'll be going back there soon, anyway."

She swallowed and smiled, because it was okay. Her heart only hurt a little. "I guess you will."

His eyes swept her face, but he said nothing. And she was glad, because she didn't want to spoil this day with thoughts of the future. Not even thoughts of next week where she'd have to pass him in the street and not be able to touch him.

It was going to be so, so hard. Because right now they couldn't stop touching each other. They were holding hands, or he was stroking her arm, or had his palm against her back.

Like he couldn't stop himself. She liked that too much.

"Here it is," she murmured, seeing the old, sprawling house. It was built in the period between the War of Independence and the Civil War. A walled yard with sculpted hedges and formal flowerbeds surrounded the imposing brownstone building. The aroma from the lilacs and lavenders invaded her senses.

"Daniel grew up here?" he asked, stopping behind her. He wrapped his arms around her waist.

She nodded.

"Wow. My dad grew up in a two-bed apartment in Cleveland. He had to share a bedroom with three brothers."

It was the first time she'd heard him talk about his dad. She knew there was bad blood there, since he'd left Michael, Josh, and Mia for another woman.

"Do you ever see him?"

"Haven't seen him since I graduated college. I hear from his wife occasionally. Mostly when they need money."

"Do you give it to them?" She turned her head to look up at him. His expression was guarded.

"Sometimes."

"You're a good man."

His lip quirked. "I'm really not. I just get sick of them asking sometimes."

Turning in his arms, she looped her own around his neck. His gaze softened. She could feel him physically relax against her.

He let down his guard when she was around, and she liked that.

"Let me take you on a horse ride some time," she said. "I think you'd love it."

He quirked an eyebrow. "Do you?"

"There's nothing more freeing than galloping through the fields. Feeling like you can run away from everything that's upsetting you. Everything that's annoying you. It's like a fresh start."

"But don't you have to turn around and run back to it?" he murmured, cupping her cheek.

"I guess. But then it doesn't seem so annoying anymore," she whispered. "Because you know it's only temporary."

"I've never ridden a horse," he confessed.

Her eyes widened. "No way."

"Seriously. Why would I ride a horse? I have a car."

Grace laughed. "Maybe I'll teach you."

"Where?" He pressed his lips to the tip of her nose. "At Logan and Courtney's farm? Don't you think they'll find out something is going on with us?"

"Maybe by then they'll know," she said carefully. "Maybe everybody will."

"Maybe." He brushed his lips against hers, sliding his hand down her side. Then he deepened the kiss, his fingers curling around her waist, pulling her closer. His lips were soft, undemanding, moving slowly against hers. Like they had all the time in the world.

And then it came to her, then. This was the first time he'd kissed her in public since they'd reconnected. The first time he'd held her so close she could feel the effect her body was having on his.

Her chest tightened. This was what she wanted. It was the two of them against the world. She felt safe in his arms. And alive, too.

And when they parted, he gave her a grin.

"Shall we go home?"

"Home?"

He shook his head, still smiling. "To the hotel, I mean."

She nodded, taking a last look at the house her family used to own. "Sure." But a building wasn't home. Nor was Hartson's Creek or a hotel.

Home was starting to feel like Michael Devlin.

CHAPTER
Eighteen

"I CAN'T BELIEVE you made me do that." Michael shook his head as he opened their hotel room door. It was almost midnight, and Grace hadn't been able to stop smiling all night.

"You were amazing. Sounded just like Springsteen."

"More like a Springer Spaniel," he grumbled, but there was still a smile on his lips.

When she'd pulled him into the karaoke bar after they'd left the restaurant, he'd been unsurprisingly resistant. And maybe that had been part of the fun of persuading him in. But she also loved karaoke.

Even if she couldn't sing, she had fun trying.

"I thought you were sexy," she told him, and he rolled his eyes again. "Seriously, you were hot. You have this graveled quality to your voice."

"Let's leave the singing to Presley and Marley, huh?" he said, kicking his shoes off.

"Sing for me now."

"Nope. You've gotten your one song for this year."

"Good thing I recorded it then," she said lightly.

He narrowed his eyes. "You didn't."

She shrugged, grinning. "I need something to keep me warm at night when we're back in Hartson's Creek."

"That's worse than taking a dick pic."

"I'll take some of those too if you'd like."

He walked toward her, his gait slow. "Take a photo of my dick and I'll show you exactly what I can do with it."

Grace stepped back, still grinning. God, he was so much fun. She loved teasing him. "That's not the threat you think it is."

"Delete the video, Grace."

"Not happening, Springsteen. It's all mine."

Her back hit the wall. He stopped in front of her, caging her with his hands on either side of her body. "You're wild."

She grinned at him. "I'm wild for you."

"The feeling's mutual. I've never sung karaoke for anybody before."

Her heart did a little flip. He hadn't meant it that way, but it felt special. Like he was pushing himself for her. Making her happy. Making her giggle.

Making her want him even more.

"I've never been sung to before."

"Not even by your ex?"

She shook her head. "He hated karaoke."

"I loved it," he said deadpan, and she laughed.

"Thank you," she whispered. "For humoring me."

"It wasn't humoring. It was…" He shook his head. "I'd do anything with you."

Oh. There was her heart again. This time hammering against her ribcage like it wanted to run out and do a victory lap.

"Let's stop hiding," she whispered.

He blinked. "What?"

"When we go back. Let's stop pretending this isn't happening. We're adults. We're single. We can do what we want."

"Grace…"

She ran her tongue along her bottom lip. "It's okay. It was just a thought."

"I want to. I do. But Mom… our family…"

"I know." She nodded.

"I don't want you to get hurt," he told her. "And you will. You said yourself it was harder for women. You'll be the one staying. I can't leave you to deal with the aftermath."

Then stay….

But she couldn't say it. Not because she didn't want it, but because she was desperate for him never to leave again. And because she knew he had to.

He lowered his head to hers. "Don't look so sad."

"I'm not sad," she lied. "I'm just thinking."

"What are you thinking about?"

She took a deep breath. "I'm thinking that I'm falling for you. And it's too late to worry about getting hurt."

"Oh, Grace." He stroked her face. "Baby."

She wouldn't cry tonight. Not after the perfect day. Last night had been hard. She was going to make this one easier for them.

She wanted a day and a night she could look back on for the rest of her life and say that she'd experienced at least twenty-four hours of perfection.

"Now *you* look sad," she whispered.

"Because I can't stand to see you hurt. If I was a better man, I'd never have put you in this position."

"You're the best man I know."

"You need to expand your repertoire," he murmured.

"I don't want anybody but you."

"Ditto," Michael whispered. "And for the record, I'm falling for you, too."

She put her hands on his shoulders, feeling the ripple of his muscles. "Let's take a bath."

"Now?"

"Yeah." She nodded. She wanted to relax with him. Cleanse the night off. Feel him holding her as the water rippled around them.

They had one last night together before they had to go home. And she wanted them both to enjoy it.

"Okay," he said, pushing himself off the wall. "You run the water, I'll grab some champagne."

———

Michael tipped his head back on the pillow, looking up at the ceiling as Grace lay sleeping on his bare chest, her arm flung across his waist.

They'd only had sex twice tonight. Which had been some kind of modesty record. First in the bath, so sweet it had made his skin tingle. Then in the bed when their skin was warm and damp. She'd looked so beautiful staring up at him.

It was almost seven in the morning, and he hadn't been able to sleep since four. Once the sex-exhaustion had worn off the over thinking had begun. He hadn't lied earlier. He hated the thought of hurting her.

She was too precious for that.

Let's stop hiding.

He wished it was that easy. That he could wave a magic wand and everything would be okay. But he'd been on this rollercoaster before. Seen his family ripped apart by lies. He couldn't be the one to do it.

It would kill him. And her.

He should let her go. Let her find somebody her own age.

Somebody like Ethan? Or do you prefer Pascal?

He pushed that thought away. Not all guys her age were assholes like them. But enough were.

But maybe he was the biggest asshole of all. Because he couldn't let her go. Not when his fucking heart beat for her. Not when everything felt perfect whenever she was around.

He was too damn selfish to be noble.

His phone started to ring and Grace turned in his arms. He grabbed it and groaned, turning it off when he saw Josh's name flashing on the screen.

His brother had a habit of calling at stupid times in the morning. He'd call him later, when he wasn't holding Grace.

When she didn't feel so good.

"What time is it?" she asked, looking up at him, her voice thick with sleep.

"Seven."

"That early?" Her eyes were only half open.

"Mmhm." He smiled softly at her.

She yawned, then stretched her arms. "Is there some water around here?"

"We finished the bottle they gave us last night." After all that singing, and ah… other stuff, they were both thirsty as hell. He grabbed the other phone – the hotel one – by the side of the bed. "I'll ask them to send up some more."

"It's okay. I'll drink from the faucet."

"No, you won't. You don't know what's in it."

She grinned. "Whatever. Call away."

He lifted the phone and murmured into it, ordering some coffee and pastries as well. When he'd put the phone down again, she'd drifted back to sleep. This time her hands were clasped under her cheek, her hair fanned out on the pillow. He leaned down to kiss her soft lips and climbed out of bed to put on a pair of shorts before room service arrived.

And then he'd check his emails and messages before Grace woke up. Maybe even call Josh back.

No. He'd save that delight for tomorrow.

When room service returned, their knock was quiet enough not to wake Grace, thankfully, and he pulled the door open and took the tray, passing a ten-dollar bill to the bellboy in return. It was only when he put the tray on the desk that he realized they'd forgotten the water. The whole point of the order. Rolling his eyes, he walked to grab the phone, but then the bellhop knocked again.

"I was just about to call you," he said, opening the door.

"Funny. I've been calling you for the last twenty minutes." Josh walked inside and Michael's heart just about stopped.

"What are you doing here?" he asked gruffly, stepping into the middle of the hallway so Josh couldn't get past him.

"Mom told me you were in Charleston. *My home town,*" His tone was pointed. "I thought we could have breakfast together."

Michael swallowed hard. "I could have been asleep."

"You have meetings all day." Josh rolled his eyes. "Come on, we hardly see each other. Let's grab something to eat before you have to work."

"Is the water here?" Grace called out from the bedroom.

Josh's eyes widened. "You've got a woman here?" He rolled onto his tiptoes, trying to look around Michael's shoulder.

"Get out of here," Michael said, pushing him down firmly. "I'll talk to you later. How did you get my room number, anyway?"

"You told mom, remember? In case of emergencies."

Shit, he had. But still…

"Michael?" Grace called out. He heard the pad of feet hitting the floor as she walked across the hotel room. She was still out of sight, at least.

Josh blinked. "Is that Grace? It sounds like her."

"No." Michael shook his head. And then she turned the corner.

"Oh." She stopped short when she saw Josh standing there.

Josh's eyes widened. Because not only was it his step cousin looking around the corner, but she was wearing nothing but a pair of panties.

———

"Dear Lord, your brother just saw me naked," Grace felt her body heat with mortification. She'd run away as soon as she'd realized Josh was standing in the vestibule of their hotel room. Why had she walked around there? She should have put some clothes on.

She should have stayed out of sight.

"Calm down, it's okay." Michael cupped her face. "I was standing between you two. And he swears he didn't see your body. Just your face."

Michael had sent Josh downstairs to the lobby café to wait for him, then walked back into the bedroom to make sure she was calm.

And she wasn't. She'd just flashed Michael's brother. And revealed their relationship in one easy, half-naked swoop.

"I can't believe I did that."

"Did what?" He was still holding her. He felt like she needed it.

"Walked out there without clothes on. There could have been a bellhop there."

"I'm glad there wasn't. I'd have had to gouge his eyes out for looking at you." He leaned forward to softly kiss her lips. "Go put a t-shirt on and eat some breakfast. I'll go down and talk to Josh."

"Do you think he'll tell your mom about us?" She swallowed hard. Yes, they'd talked about them coming out to their parents.

But not like this.

"No. I'll make sure he doesn't. This is Josh. Yeah, he's more perceptive than Mason, but he also likes a quiet life. Let me go sort this out, and then we'll get on with our day."

She blew out a mouthful of air. "Should I come talk to him, too?"

"Not yet. Let me do it."

She nodded. If it had been her brother who saw them – the horror – she'd have wanted to do the same. Talk sibling to sibling. It was only fair to let Michael do the same.

"Okay then. Go before he calls somebody."

"I'll go if you promise to calm down."

She nodded. "I will."

"And eat something. You're shaking."

"I'll try."

He looked her in the eye. "Do it. I promise it'll be okay."

It was strange how reassuring he could be. Especially in the middle of this crapshoot. "You ever think this weekend is cursed? First your date at *Chairs* and now this?"

His eyes crinkled. "No. I think this weekend is wonderful. I got to spend all of it with you."

Her heart clenched. "You're such a smooth talker."

"Just keeping it real." Their eyes connected and she felt the warmth again. How was it that this man could make her feel safe in the middle of an emotional storm? "Now go get dressed and don't open the door for any strange men."

"Does that include you?" she asked archly.

"Probably. But I've got a key." He winked.

CHAPTER
Nineteen

"ARE YOU AN IDIOT?" Josh asked, shaking his head as Michael passed him a coffee. The shop was empty, the whole concourse of the hotel was. It was too damn early for this. "What are you thinking? How long has this been going on between you two?"

"A year."

Josh's mouth dropped open. "But you've only been back in the country a couple of months."

"I met Grace in New York a year ago. I didn't know who she was. We had dinner together. We got along great. I liked her a lot."

"So, when did you find out who she was?"

"The night I arrived in Hartson's Creek. I saw her at *Chairs*." A little boy ran into the coffee shop, heading straight for the chocolate milk section, followed by a harassed man – his father – looking like he needed more than coffee to wake him up.

"You've been seeing her for a year without knowing you were related?" Josh shook his head. "Hard to believe."

"She figured out who I was after our night in New York.

Disappeared on me. I didn't see her again until I came back to Hartson's Creek."

Josh shook his head. "So you know she's your cousin and you're still sleeping with her?"

"She's not my cousin." He looked up at him. "Not *our* cousin. Not by blood."

"So why are you hiding it, then?" Josh asked, lifting a brow.

"Because we both know that everybody would react the same way you are. And we don't want to cause that kind of strife. Especially at the beginning, when things are so new."

"She's young." Josh shook his head. "Too young."

"I know that." He'd thought exactly the same thing when they first met. "But I can't help it."

"Are you in love with her?" Josh asked.

"Halfway there." That was all he was willing to admit to his brother. He hadn't told Grace how he felt about her and she deserved to hear it first. But he knew he was. Everything about her felt right. From the way she made him sing like a freaking banshee to the way they laughed every time they were together until their humor dissolved into kisses and lust.

She was perfect. And he wanted her.

"Shit." Josh sat back in his chair, staring off into the distance. "What a fucking mess."

"You could say that." Michael took a sip of his coffee.

"Do you think she knows what she's doing?" Josh asked him. "She's a kid."

"She's twenty-six. A grown woman. She has a job, a house, she's lived abroad for years. I think she's old enough to know what she wants."

"Old enough to know that this is gonna blow up in both of your faces," Josh muttered. "God, I wish I hadn't seen either of you. I should have stayed in damn bed."

"I wish you hadn't, either. But you have." Michael caught

his eye. "And I need your assurance that you won't tell anybody."

There was a moment's silence. Josh pressed his lips together, their gazes still connected.

All those times Michael had protected him when they were kids. Tried to step in the way of the harsh realities, stopping them from piercing his kid brother the way they'd hurt Michael.

And now here he was, asking for his help, to hide things from those he loved the most. He felt like a piece of shit.

"Of course I won't tell anybody. I'm not stupid, Mike. Mom's sick. This is the last thing she needs."

"I know that."

"So why are you doing this? If I found out, other people will too. Her parents…" Josh sighed heavily. "You're closer to their age than you are to Grace's. Her dad's gonna fucking kill you."

"I know that too."

"And that will kill mom. Aunt Becca's one of her best friends. They'll both choose sides."

Michael looked at him pointedly, and Josh sighed. "You're really doing this, aren't you?"

"Yep."

"So what are you gonna do about it? How will you make it work long term?" Josh folded his arms across his chest.

"That's the one thing I don't know."

"You'd better figure it out and fast. There's a girl up there who looked at you like the sun shone out of your ass. She's young. Don't hurt her."

"I'm not going to hurt her. I'm trying to protect her."

"Doesn't stop people from hurting people."

Yeah, they both knew that too well. "I'm sorry I got you involved in this."

"Not as sorry as I am." Josh squeezed his eyes shut. "Just

work it out. Don't make her unhappy. Hell, don't make yourself unhappy. And most of all, don't hurt Mom."

"I'm trying not to do any of those things," Michael said.

"I know. You're a good man. You just make really shit decisions sometimes."

"Story of my life," Michael muttered. But the decision to be with Grace didn't seem like shit. It felt like the only right choice he'd made in a long, long time. "But this thing… I don't know. I'll sort it out."

"Will you still see her after you go back to London?"

"That's what I'm going to sort out."

"Okay." Josh frowned. "Actually, that's not okay. What does that mean? You're still going to see her? Are you going to tell everyone?"

"I love you, bro, but this is a conversation for me and Grace, not you and me."

Josh shrugged. "Yeah, I get that. I just don't want to be taken by surprise again, you know? I'll cover for you, but don't mess me over."

"I'd never do that to you," Michael told him.

"I know." Josh nodded. "I do." He finished his coffee and put the cup down. "Just don't get hurt, Mike. You've been away for so long and I know you too well. Something goes wrong and you bolt."

"I'm not doing that. I'm working this out. I've learned from my mistakes."

"Okay." Josh looked sceptical.

"Are we good?" Michael asked him.

"Yeah, we're good. Now go back to your girlfriend."

Michael opened his mouth to say that Grace wasn't his girlfriend, but then he stopped. Because she was. Or something like that.

Something more.

She hadn't asked for a name to what they had going between them. She just gave and he took and that had to stop.

He needed to get control of things. Needed to work out his next steps.

He stood and so did Josh, and they threw their arms around each other. And for a minute Michael was fifteen again, and Josh was eight and they were both scared as hell.

"I love you," Josh muttered.

"I love you, too." Michael touched his brother's face, warmth enveloping him. "I'll call you later."

———

Grace had showered. Taken a bite of a croissant that turned to dust in her mouth and put it back down on the plate. Stared out of the window at Charleston as it slowly awoke from its nighttime slumber.

And waited.

It felt like a lifetime had passed before she heard the click of the door and the slow creak as it opened up. Her heart rattled against her chest as she walked into the hallway, her eyes catching Michael's.

He looked tired. But not upset.

"You okay?" he asked her. His hair was mussed, his jeans and t-shirt crumpled. He'd put on last night's clothes to run down and join Josh, and it showed.

"I'm fine. You?"

"I am now." He held out his arms for her.

She stepped into them, feeling the breath escape her lips as he folded his arms around her, pulling her close. She rested her face on his chest, and he softly stroked her hair.

"Is he going to tell anybody?" she asked.

"No. He's just worried about us both."

She looked up at him, relief flooding through her body. "That's good, right?"

"Yeah, it is."

She looped her arms around his neck, rolling to her feet

for a kiss. His mouth was soft, slow. It felt like a kiss they both needed.

"So what do we do now?" she asked him when they parted.

"Now I get in the shower, get ready, and we go out like we planned to. Then you'll drive home and I'll be back tomorrow and I guess we need to talk about what we want to do after that."

"What do you mean?"

"Josh is just the start. People are going to find out. It's a matter of when, not if." He ran his tongue along his bottom lip. "Unless you want us to stop this thing. In which case Josh has promised he'll never say a word."

"Do you want to stop?" she whispered. Her heart was racing again. The thought of walking away from him, of never feeling the way she did when she was in his arms, was like a physical pain.

"No." His voice was strong and sure. "I don't want to and I don't think I could stop if I did."

Oh. Her chest loosened. This man was killing her in all the best kinds of ways. "So we tell people?"

"When we're ready, yeah. I just want to make sure Mom is stronger first."

That made sense. The thought of dropping a bombshell when his mom was sick felt wrong. "And then what?" she asked him. "We do the long distance thing when you go back to London?"

"I don't think either of us would want to do that for long. I've been thinking about going back soon. Seeing if I can sell the business."

She looked at him. "Seriously?"

"Yeah. It's been on my mind for a while. Being back... being with my parents. With you." He gave her a half smile. "I like it here."

"You want to stay in Hartson's Creek?"

He nodded. "Yeah, but not if that's going to cause you problems."

"Why would it cause me problems?" Her heart was pounding against her chest. This was what she wanted. "You seemed set against it last night."

"I needed to think things through. And I don't want to put any pressure on you." His eyes caught hers. "You're still young."

"Shut up, old man."

He laughed. "You might not feel the same way I do."

"How do you feel?" she asked softly.

"I love you."

Oh. This time it felt like her heart was flying out of her chest. "I love you too."

He squeezed his eyes shut. "Thank God."

"And I want you here. I want you to leave London, but only if that's what you want. We can make it work long distance if we need to. Or I could move there."

"No. It makes sense for me to do the move. I have contacts here. I can set up another business in the States."

"And you'd do that for me?" she asked softly.

"I'd do that for me." He stroked her hair. "Because I want this."

So did she. So much. "Okay. So we do it. You go to London and settle everything, then when your mom's ready, we tell everyone and let all hell break loose."

He grinned. "You make it sound so romantic."

She slid her fingers into his, squeezing them tight. "Come take a shower with me." She needed to be close to him. Naked. To take away the barriers between them.

"You look like you've already showered," he said, touching her wet hair.

"I have. But I want to wash you all over. Make you dirty, then make you clean."

His eyes darkened. "Sounds like a good way to start the day."

She pulled him into the bathroom, and they both undressed.

In a few hours she'd have to go home and leave him here. But now it felt like a different kind of parting.

A softer, gentler one that felt like a blanket wrapped around her body. They were going to work this out because he didn't want to let her go.

———

Michael put her weekend bag into the trunk, then slammed it shut, walking around the car to where she was leaning against the driver's door. "The bed's going to feel way too big without you tonight."

She wanted to stay. To drive straight to work tomorrow, having spent the night curled up around him, but they both knew that was pushing things too far. She'd already asked Ella to lie for her about the last two days. She couldn't ask her to lie more.

And her brain – the only part of her that was thinking straight – knew it would look so much better if she arrived back today and Michael stayed in Charleston until tomorrow for the meetings he'd lied about.

"I'll call you when I get back," she said, smiling at him. They'd spent the day walking around Charleston hand in hand. She was getting used to it.

Getting used to being his.

She craved it, like she craved oxygen. He reached out to trace her lips with his finger, swallowing hard when she fluttered her tongue against the tip.

"We can do this for a few weeks more," he said. "Until Mom's feeling better."

And then they'd come clean. They hadn't talked specifics

yet – she'd have to work out how to deal with her parents without them exploding – but it was worth it.

She needed to be with this man.

He cupped her cheek, his eyes warm. "I can't wait until I can do this every day without worrying about who's looking." He pulled her close, stroking the hair from her face as he leaned down to kiss her. His mouth was soft, and she felt the pleasure of it all throughout her body.

He pulled away from her, but she wanted more.

"Let's go back to bed," she murmured.

He laughed. "I'd prefer that you got home before it gets dark." Reaching behind her, he grabbed the door handle. "Now get out of here before I change my mind."

"Is that an order?" She batted her eyelashes.

"Yep."

"Then yes, sir," she whispered, kissing him softly. "Whatever you say."

She stepped away, and he opened the door, holding it as she'd climbed into the driver's seat. She put her purse on the passenger seat and grabbed her phone, connecting it to her stereo so she could play some music.

Michael leaned in the opened door. "Call me as soon as you get home."

"Yes, Daddy."

He rolled his eyes, and she blew a kiss at him. She still loved teasing him.

Loved everything about him.

"And drive safely."

She grinned. "Are we going to do this every time I leave you?"

"Probably. I have a vested interest in making sure you get home safe." He leaned in to kiss her again. She sighed against his lips. There would be more times like this in the future, she knew that. But it was hard hiding this. Knowing he was hers and not being able to touch him in public, or really acknowledge his existence.

She was so happy that the lying would be over soon.

"Close the door then," she said. "Or I won't be going anywhere."

"Smartass." He closed it and she turned on the ignition, winding down her window. Then she hit play on her phone, and strings started up, followed by Lana Del Ray's voice asking if he'd be her baby tonight.

"What's this song?" he asked, almost shouting to be heard over the music.

"Lana Del Ray. *Lolita*." She laughed because she was no Lolita and he was no Humbert Humbert, but he still looked slightly annoyed.

"Bye *Daddy*."

And now he looked even more annoyed. And she couldn't help but laugh some more.

CHAPTER

Twenty

"HEY SWEETIE, HOW WAS YOUR WEEKEND?" her mom asked, closing the office door behind her and perching on the corner of Grace's desk.

"It was fun." Grace nodded, keeping her eyes on her laptop.

"And Ella? Is she okay?"

"She's fine. We drank too much on Saturday night, but all was good. Did a little exploring, a little karaoke."

"You've always loved to sing," her mom said, sounding wistful. "I remember watching you in the school choir."

"Did you have a good weekend?" Grace asked her. She wasn't in the mood for a trip down memory lane right now.

"It was fine. I went riding on Saturday and then had Mia and Cam over for lunch on Sunday. They were feeling a little lonely, I think. All their kids are away."

"Where's Sabrina at?"

"She was staying with a friend for the weekend. Josh is in Charleston, of course."

Of course. Grace said nothing.

"And I've no idea where Mason went. I forgot to ask." Her mom shrugged.

"And Michael," Grace prompted. "He wasn't there either?" She had no idea why she said that. Maybe because she hated him being left out.

Or because she needed to say his name to remind herself that he was real.

Her mom gave her a strange look. "Yeah, he was away for some meetings, I think. But he's the oldest one. I keep forgetting about him."

Grace couldn't help the feeling of protectiveness that washed over her. "Maybe you shouldn't."

Her mom blinked, surprised. "I didn't mean to."

"I know." Grace rubbed her eyes. "I guess I just didn't want to leave him out. It must be hard being the oldest of us all."

"I don't think he'd mind. He's closer to my age than all of yours." Her mom gave her a soft smile. "Anyway, tell me all about New York."

Grace swallowed. This was the part she hated. Lying. But it wouldn't be for too much longer.

"It was hot."

Her mom laughed. "Did you and Ella enjoy being together, though?"

"It was good to catch up." She let out a low breath. "We did a little sight seeing, a lot of eating, and lots of talking."

"Oh I can imagine. Although I suspect Ella did most of the talking."

Grace smiled. "She usually does. How was Mia?" She had a vested interest in that, too.

"She was wallowing over her failed attempt at match making. She'd tried to set Michael up with her nurse." Her mom grimaced. "Apparently it didn't go too well."

Grace swallowed. Okay, so she should have changed the subject completely. She'd been so jealous a few days ago, but that had all disappeared.

"Maybe he has somebody else." What was wrong with her? Why was she flying so close to the sun?

"That's what Mia thinks. He was weird with her when he told her he wasn't interested." Her mom shrugged. "Anyway, apart from that, she seemed fine. She looked brighter than I've seen her in ages."

"Sounds like she's doing good." Grace nodded.

"And she's so happy that she gets to have all her boys and Sabrina around. It's a shame it took something like this, but it's nice to see her… I don't know. Complete, I guess."

"It's always good to have family around." She sounded like an idiot. But she had no idea what else to say. This was so awkward, especially knowing it would all come out soon. Her mom would know she lied to her, and she hated the thought of hurting her.

But Michael was right. While his mom was in treatment, this was the best thing to do. Feeling uncomfortable for a little while was a small price to pay for the future. It was going to be fine.

"So, what's in the plans for this week?" her mom asked.

Grace frowned. She was planning to see Michael all week. "Um, I'm not sure. I have a lot of laundry to do."

Her mom burst out laughing. "I meant work plans. I turned into your boss without telling you."

Relief rushed through her. Talking about work was so much easier than talking about her private life. "I have a couple of calls with some vineyards. One of them would be a real catch if they want to partner up."

"Would you like me to join you?" her mom asked.

Grace shook her head. "Not yet. I'll do the initial call and if it looks favorable, I'll get you and Dad involved."

"I just like hearing you speak French." Her mom grinned. "It always fascinates me how good you are at picking up languages. I don't know where it came from."

And now she was blushing again, remembering the way

Michael whispered to her in French when they were alone. Doing things they shouldn't. It was stupid, but she wanted to tell her mom she wasn't the only one in the family good at learning different languages. She wasn't the only one who'd lived in Europe, either. And yet she got all the kudos and people seemed to forget about Michael's achievements.

But she couldn't say a word. Not yet.

"Well, I'd better go. Are you around this weekend? I'd love to take a ride with you. It feels like we haven't caught up in a while."

"I see you every day at work," Grace said, shaking her head because her mom always said this. "And we were both at *Chairs* on Friday."

"Okay, but I mean one-on-one time. Just us girls together."

"That would be nice," Grace said, because she really did like spending time with her mom. Or at least she usually did. When she didn't have to lie through her teeth every time she opened her mouth.

And anyway, Arcadia needed some exercise. She hadn't gotten to ride him last weekend, and she missed him, too.

"Perfect." Her mom stood and gave Grace a warm smile. "We can have lunch at the farm afterward." She leaned forward and kissed Grace's cheek. "I'll speak to you later."

Grace nodded. "Sure. I'll let you know how the vineyard calls go."

"You do that, honey."

———

"I'm so sorry about Friday night."

Michael put his case down on the polished wooden floor and looked at his mom. Cam had taken her to the hospital today, and the two of them were sitting in the living room, her legs curled up on Cam's lap as a movie flickered on the screen.

"What about Friday night?" he asked, confused.

"Setting you up with Rhona. Or at least trying to." She grimaced. "I realize now that it wasn't a good idea." She sighed. "Well, Cam and Josh made me realize. It was stupid. I should have talked to you in advance. I know you're not a kid anymore."

"It's okay. I've already forgotten about it," Michael told her. "Relax."

Cam grinned at him. "How was Charleston?" he asked.

"Busy." It really had been. He'd spent most of the morning on a crisis call with London. "There's a bit of an issue at work."

"Oh no. Anything major?"

"Nothing too bad." Michael shifted his feet. "But like so many things it would be a lot easier to solve if I was there in person."

He'd also made some phone calls and already had some-body interested in buying the business. The partner he'd worked with for years was ready to go at it alone if he was. But Michael didn't want to get his mom's hopes up yet.

"In London?" his mom asked. "Then you should go."

"Not if you need me here." That was fair. He'd come here to take care of her, after all. Not to rearrange his life to suit the fact he'd fallen in love.

Cam frowned. "Of course you should go. It's your busi-ness, and we've got things covered here."

"I know, but I promised I'd drive mom to the hospital."

"I can do that," Cam told him. "We have a billion volun-teers waiting to help. My brothers, my sister, their spouses. Even Sabrina can drive a car."

"That's debatable," his mom said, and the two of them chuckled. The way they looked at each other made him want to smile.

Michael sat down on the easy chair opposite them. "It would only be for a few days. A week at most. I'd fly out tomorrow night and be back by Monday at the latest. Sooner if I can smooth things over."

It would give him long enough to see if the interest was real. And to tidy things up at the office and with his client. Anything else he could fly back and do later, and any contracts could be signed from here.

"You do what you need to do," his mom told him, her expression soft. "I'm almost finished with the treatment anyway. And there's no rush to come back if you have more work to do."

"I'll definitely be back." He didn't even want to go, but he had responsibilities and he took them seriously. "I want to be here."

"I'm so happy you do." She smiled. "There's some dinner in the kitchen if you're hungry. Sabrina made chili."

His stomach rumbled at the thought. "Sounds good. You guys heading up to bed early?"

His mom tipped her head to the side. "Probably. Why? You trying to sneak out again?"

"I thought I'd go for a run. Get my head ready for London."

"Aren't you exhausted?" she asked him. "You've been working all day and driving for hours."

Yeah, he was. But tomorrow he had to fly home. Or whatever London was now. But he couldn't do it without seeing Grace. Not after the weekend they'd spent together. It felt like everything changed.

He hated leaving her. Hated leaving Hartson's Creek.

Wasn't that one for the books? He actually wanted to stay in the little town he'd run away from for the last twenty-something years.

After all this time, it was beginning to feel like home.

———

The tap on her window made her jump. She was holding a cup in her hands, empty thank goodness, because she was about to make herself a coffee. Somehow she managed not to drop it, even though her heart was hammering against her ribcage.

And then she saw Michael through the glass pane. He was in her backyard. He must have come around the back so he couldn't be seen.

And she couldn't help the huge grin that pulled at her mouth.

It had been a day and a half since she'd last seen him, and that was enough. She pulled open her back door and the warm night air rushed in.

"Hey." She blinked at the sight of him in a pair of running shorts and a sports tee.

"You should probably stand ten feet away from me. I'm sweating like a pig."

She laughed because he was definitely glowing with perspiration. "What are you doing?" she asked him. "Why did you run here?"

"It was the only excuse I could think of to get out."

"You'd better come in and cool off then." She stepped aside so he could walk into her kitchen. He leaned forward and kissed her cheek, then pulled away.

He lifted a brow. "Sorry, I must stink."

"Shut up and come here," she said, pulling him back to her. "I don't care if you're sweaty."

He felt so good in her arms. Solid. True. She lifted her head, brushing her lips against his, and he groaned, sliding his hand down her back until their bodies were close.

This was what she'd needed all day. What she'd been thinking about. After their emotional weekend, and the discussions they'd had – the tough ones and the sweet ones – she'd been wondering if he'd changed his mind.

If he'd decided this was all too much. If she was too much for him.

But he'd come for her, and it was everything.

"You want some water?" she asked him when they parted, breathless.

"Please." He nodded, watching as she put a glass beneath the sink filter, then passed it to him. He leaned his head back, swallowing it down, finishing the whole thing in less than thirty seconds.

"You were thirsty."

"Yeah. It's been a while since I've run in this heat."

"Most people prefer the gym," she said, still smiling.

"Yeah, well, if you lived at a gym, I'd run there. But you don't, so here I am."

She took his hand and led him out of the kitchen, up the stairs, and into her room. They bypassed her bed and went straight into the bathroom.

"Here," she said, passing him a fresh towel. "Shower."

"I need to get back soon." He let out a sigh. "Even I can't run for three hours."

"We can kill two birds with one stone. I'll get in with you." She was getting a taste for getting wet with him after their weekend away.

He reached out to cup her face. "How did I get so lucky to find you?"

"I've been here all along. Just waiting."

His eyes crinkled. "You didn't even know I existed."

"I knew. In here." She touched her heart. "I knew I was waiting for something. I just didn't know it was you."

"I'm glad I'm here now," he said, his voice low.

"Me too." She reached for his shirt, pulling it off. "Now get in there, handsome. All this talking is wasting time."

"Talking to you never seems like a waste." He did as he was told, stripping down and stepping into her shower. She thanked the gods that it was a double-length walk in that they both fit into easily.

By the time she'd taken her own clothes off, he was under the spray. Steam filled the cubicle, making everything look hazy. He reached for her, pulling her against him, kissing the crown of her head.

"I missed you. How is it that things only make sense when you're in my arms?" He reached for the shower gel, but she took it from him.

She needed to touch him. To reconnect.

Squeezing the gel into her palm, she lathered it onto his chest, her fingers tracing the lines of his muscles.

"I have to go to London."

Grace looked up at him. "Okay."

"Tomorrow. For business. That's why I wanted to see you tonight. It's my last chance for a week."

A week. She tried not to look sad, but she'd hardly survived a day without him.

She squeezed another dollop of gel onto her palm, rubbing his back, his hips, his ass.

"I've found somebody who might be interested in buying the business," he told her.

"Already?" She smiled. "That was fast."

"I have a guy who's a partner in the business. Only owns twenty percent right now, but he has the funds to buy the whole thing. I want to strike while the iron's hot. If we can agree on a price and I can hand things over to him, then it feels like the right thing to do."

She looked up at him, blinking.

"Are you sure? It's all happened so fast."

"I've been looking for you for a year. It feels slow." He cupped her face. "And truth be told, I've been thinking about selling for a while. I guess coming here for a few months was my way of thinking about things. Plus, my partner is my ex-wife's brother. It's been awkward as hell for a while."

"Eek." She wrinkled her nose. "I didn't know that."

"It's not a problem. We rarely mix in the same circles. But it's a tie to the past I don't need."

"What if you regret it?"

"Selling the business?"

"Yeah. What if everything goes wrong between us and you wish you could leave again?"

He took her hands in his and moved them to his lips, kissing each one.

"I won't regret it. The only things you regret are the things you don't do. I told you before that I'd be doing this for me, not you. I want to be here with my family. Spending time with them has reminded me of that. And now you..." he trailed off, pressing her hand to his chest. "Now you make everything feel right."

"I hate that you're sacrificing more than I am."

"It's not a sacrifice."

She wasn't so sure. "What will you do once you're back here for good? You talked about starting a business here."

"Yeah. I still have a lot of connections. I can stay with soccer. It's such a growing sport over here. Or I could move into football. Cam has the connections."

"You'd do that?"

"I'm excited about it."

"I can tell that," she said, hoarsely. Because she was soaping him *there*, now. Her hands curled around him, making his breath stutter. Dropping to her knees, she ran her palms down his thighs. As the water rinsed him clean she slipped her mouth over him and he groaned.

"No." He pulled back. "I didn't come here for this." He lifted her up, kissed her softly. "You don't have to do this."

"But I want to."

"I need your lips on mine," he whispered, pressing his mouth to hers. "Not there. I need to remember the way you look at me."

"Will you call me when you're away?" she asked him.

"Every damn day. And night. Once I work out the time difference." He kissed her again, harder this time, and she felt it down to her toes.

"Just let me feel you inside of me," she asked him. "Please."

He swallowed and nodded, lifting her until they were close. "Keep talking to me," he told her. "I want to hear your words."

She opened her mouth right as he pushed inside of her, and instead of words, she let out a low groan.

"Tell me what you're feeling," he asked her. "Tell me everything."

"You feel so good. So perfect. The way you move within me makes my toes curl."

He pulled back and then pushed in again, right where she wanted him.

"When I'm away, you need to remember this. Remember that this works. Us. You and me. Together."

"Yes." Her voice was tighter now. He dipped his head to kiss her throat, her shoulder, her breast. Her back was against the tiles, her legs curled around his waist. His breath was as ragged as hers.

"Tell me something in French," she asked, feeling herself tightening.

He kissed the corner of her mouth softly. "Je t'aime."

His words were a shiver down her spine. The fluttering of her body around his cock. The long, desperate tumble into pure delight. She came hard and fast, and he joined her a moment later, spilling inside of her, calling out her name as his mouth took hers.

"I love you too," she told him. "So much."

CHAPTER
Twenty-One

"I NEED A FAVOR," Sabrina said, walking into Grace's office. It had been two days since Michael had left for London and it felt like every minute was dragging. Grace couldn't help but smile at his sister.

Sabrina was a connection to him. And she needed that right now.

"If it involves underage drinking and vomit, I'm out," Grace teased and Sabrina rolled her eyes.

"No, it doesn't. Presley and Marley's band is playing on Saturday night. And I really want to watch them. But I'm too young to get into the bar but they've said I can come with the band, but only if I have you with me."

"They said I have to go?" Grace grimaced.

"They said a responsible adult." Sabrina shook her head. "It's stupid. Do you know that in Europe you can drink alcohol when you're eighteen?"

"I was aware of that fact, yes." Grace tried to hide her amusement. "But we're not in Europe, we're in America, and you have to be twenty-one to go to a bar."

"Unless my very favorite cousin is with me." Sabrina batted her eyelashes at Grace. "Please come?"

She needed to get out and do something. She was meeting her mom early on Saturday for a ride, but apart from that, she had nothing planned for the weekend.

"Okay. But you have to promise me to be good."

"I promise," Sabrina said solemnly, but there was a twinkle in her eye. "I owe you one."

"You owe me about a thousand, but we'll call it even."

Sabrina threw her arms around Grace. "I love you. You're the best."

"Hmm."

"I'll pick you up at seven," Sabrina said.

"Oh no, I'll pick you up." Sabrina's driving was famously bad. "I want to come see your mom, anyway. Check on how she's doing."

"She'd like that. She loves seeing you. And she's been a little down this week with Michael not being here."

"Is he not?" Grace feigned surprise, because this was her life now. A pretence. "Where is he?"

"He had to go to London. Some kind of business thing. She's pretending she's okay, but she's missing him."

Grace nodded. Yeah, she knew what that was like. She'd been missing him all week as well.

Her phone buzzed, and she looked down. A message from M.D. Quickly, she turned off the screen.

"I should go," Sabrina said. "I just wanted to ask you in person because you'd be less likely to say no."

"You're so devious." Grace grinned.

"I know. See you on Saturday." Sabrina winked and walked back out, a spring in her step from getting what she wanted.

Grace couldn't help but like her. She was fun and light-hearted. And Michael's sister.

Would she still love Grace when she found out the truth?

Opening her phone up, she looked at the message.

· · ·

Tu me manques. – Michael x

She ran her tongue over her lip. He missed her. But the literal translation was *you make me miss you*. It was sweet and romantic.

I miss you too. – Grace xx

She'd only just sent the message when her phone rang. "Hey," she said, accepting the call.

"Can you talk?" he asked.

"Yeah. I'm alone in the office. You just missed Sabrina, though."

It was stupid how happy she felt just to hear his voice.

"She was in your office?" He sounded surprised.

"Yeah. She wants me to take her to a gig on Saturday."

"Where is it?"

"A bar. That's why she wants me to take her. Presley told her she needs an adult chaperone if she wants to come."

Michael chuckled. "I guess Presley heard about the party fiasco."

"I think Presley just knows how uncontrollable she can be. And he'll be on stage. It's not exactly conducive to keeping an eye on her."

"I'm glad you'll be there. I owe you one."

"You don't owe me anything. I'm happy to go. It'll stop me from staying in and brooding."

"You're brooding?"

"I miss you. I already told you that."

"Yeah. I know that feeling," he said. "Only a few more days to get through and I'll be back."

"How is it over there?"

"Damp. I don't think it's stopped raining since I landed. I love London, but I hate the rain."

"And have you agreed on a price yet?"

"Still trying," he told her. "But the good news is we're getting close. If we can get this finished over the next few days, I won't have to come back to London. Anyway, more importantly, how are you doing? Have you managed to get a partnership going with a vineyard?"

"We're almost there. Dad's talking about flying out to have some face-to-face meetings."

"Won't you go?"

She cleared her throat. "It's better if it's only my dad. With everything that happened with Pascal…" She trailed off. "It doesn't matter. I don't want to travel right now, anyway." A calendar reminder flashed up on her laptop screen, reminding her that she had a board meeting in five minutes. "I'm kind of counting down the hours until you get back, if I'm being honest."

There was a pause, and she wondered if she'd said too much. But then he chuckled. "You don't know how happy I am to hear you say that. I'm already planning what I'm going to do to you."

"And what's that?"

"All the dirty things. I miss your lips. I miss your body. Most of all, I miss holding you all night."

"I miss that too," she whispered.

"When I'm back, I'm going to look for a place of my own. I'm sick of sneaking out to see you. I want to spend time with my girl without worrying about what other people think."

Her cheeks flushed. "I want that too," she whispered.

"That's good."

Her laptop flashed again. Meeting overdue. "I have to go."

He groaned. "I do, too. I'll call you tonight."

"It's already your night."

"I know."

"You need to sleep," she told him. "You've been burning the candle at both ends."

"I need to hear your voice more. I'll call you later, before I go to bed."

She smiled. "Okay. Talk later."

"We will." His voice was gruff. "Only a few days more."

Yeah, but right now, that felt like forever.

———

"Hey, wait here with me for a minute," her dad asked right as she was about to leave the boardroom. They'd just finished their strategy meeting for the vineyard partnership. She'd been the one who spoke out the most, having had on-the-ground experience.

Talking about France made her feel wistful. Not because she missed Pascal. That was so over. But because she regretted letting herself get so upset by his rejection.

And because Michael was closer to France than he was to Hartson's Creek right now.

"Sure. Is everything okay?" she asked him.

He smiled at her, his eyes crinkling. He was a handsome man. Not old enough to be distinguished yet, but he was getting there.

"Everything is fine. I just want to talk through my meetings scheduled in France with you. Do you think I should try to use the language?"

"No. They'll all speak English."

"Thank God." He smiled. "I might try a few words, though. Just to show I'm willing."

"Sounds good. I'll write some down for you. Just some greeting words will do. The French like it if you at least try to speak their language."

"Thank you, sweetheart."

Her stomach tightened. "You don't need to thank me. You wouldn't be having to do all this work if it wasn't for me." She hated that her relationship – or lack of it – with Pascal meant the distillery needed a new European partner. Her dad had worked hard for the original relationship with Pascal's family.

All she had to do was make it work in practice. And she'd completely messed that up.

"Honey, you know it's not your fault." His lips tightened. "He never should have treated you like that. I wish he hadn't."

She looked into her dad's blue eyes. "I know."

"Do you?" he asked, his voice soft. "Do you know what you're worth?"

It was funny, because conversations like this barely ever happened with her dad. Maybe once every five years or so. And yet every time they did, every time her dad stepped over that invisible line between stoicism and emotion, it hit her in the gut.

"I know what I'm worth," she told him. "That's why I walked away from Pascal."

Her dad reached for her hand. Curled his fingers around hers. "You did the right thing, honey. From the moment you were born, I knew you were special. I held you in my arms and looked into your bright blue eyes, and I knew you would change everything. You ruled our roost from the moment we brought you home from the hospital. Not because you were bossy, but because you were so damn strong. And I'm so proud of you for walking away from him when he wanted you to be anything but strong."

"Thank you," she whispered, and he pulled her into his arms, hugging her tight. She had no idea why he was doing this, but she liked it.

"Hey, look at you two," her mom said, her voice full of warmth. "Have I interrupted a moment?"

"Just telling our daughter how proud I am of her," her dad said gruffly.

Her mom beamed. "That makes two of us. Did the meeting go well? I'm sorry I couldn't make it. There was something going on with one of the stills."

Despite all the years she'd sat on the board, her mom was more at home as a distiller than anything else. It was the whiskey she loved, not the boardroom politics.

"Not too much. It looks like we'll be going to France in the next couple of months, though."

Her mom caught Grace's eye. "Won't you want to go?" she asked her.

Grace shook her head. "We agreed Dad would be the best ambassador. And I've got a lot to do here."

For a moment, her mom just looked at her. Grace could see the sympathy in her eyes. She got it. She knew Grace didn't want to go back.

And yeah, some of that was because of the break up with Pascal. But most of it was because she knew it would be best for the business. And for her.

Because Michael would be back by then and she'd much rather spend time with him.

She shook her head at how sappy she was. Hadn't she told herself she wouldn't fall for somebody again? That she wouldn't let a man come between her and her career? And yet here she was, wanting to stay here in good old Hartson's Creek rather than travel the world because of Michael Devlin.

Her Irish.

It was a good thing she trusted him. And that she was a little in love with him.

Okay, more than a little. A lot.

CHAPTER
Twenty~Two

IT WAS ALMOST SEVEN, but the heat of the day still clung to Grace's skin like a blanket. It had been humid since the time she'd gotten up before dawn. She'd taken Arcadia out for a ride before the sun had risen above the horizon, knowing that later in the day would be too hot for her thoroughbred.

Her mom had joined her, the two of them cantering across the fields to the mountains, the air lifting their hair as the sun slowly illuminated the countryside.

By the time they'd gotten back to the stables, they were sweaty and so were their horses. They'd taken their time to wash them down, to clear out the stalls, and make them comfortable.

Though the stables weren't air conditioned, they were well-ventilated and cool, and when she'd led Arcadia back to his freshly clean and straw-strewn stall, he'd seemed happy. The smell of the straw filled her nostrils, making her nose twitch as she'd petted Arcadia one last time, promising she'd be back in the morning to take him out for another run.

After they had an early lunch together, her day had been taken up with the chores she'd been putting off for weeks.

Deep cleaning her house and scrubbing down the stove, washing three loads of laundry and then getting each load dry. Before she knew it, it had been time to change out of her short overalls and take a shower, ready to pick up Sabrina so they could watch Presley and Marley entertain the town.

As soon as she knocked on the front door, Cam answered it, and she knew he must have seen her drive up on their security camera.

"Hi." He smiled, stepping aside to let her in. "Come on in. Sabrina's upstairs getting ready. She should be down soon."

She followed her uncle to the large living room that overlooked the mountains. The sun was sitting right above them, casting an orange glow on the peaks. The sky was slowly darkening to a perfect purple, making the view look almost like a picture rather than reality.

"Hey sweetie," Mia said, smiling as she walked through the door. "I hear you're Sabrina's designated driver tonight."

"It's not too late to drop out," Cam added, pointing at the chair. Grace dropped into it, smiling at her aunt. "I can tell Sabrina you came down with the plague or something."

Grace laughed. "It's not a problem. I would have been going, anyway. It's nice that Presley's band is actually playing some gigs."

Cam nodded. "Yeah, it is."

For a moment they were all silent. Presley and Delilah had been through a lot. She was so glad he was coming out of the other side of his pain.

"How are you feeling?" Grace asked Mia.

"I'm good. It's the weekend, so I don't have to go to the hospital." Mia smiled at her. "And how are you? I hear you were out riding with your mom this morning."

Another reminder that nothing was a secret in this town. Not that her going out on Arcadia was a secret, but still. How she and Michael had kept things on the down-low all this time she'd never know.

Thank goodness they wouldn't have to do it for much longer.

"We had to go super early. This heatwave is a lot to deal with," she said, just to make conversation.

"Tell me about it." Mia sighed, pulling at the collar of her sleeveless shirt to get some air onto her skin. "Even with the air conditioning on full blast, I can't get any relief."

"Let's hope they have quality AC at the bar," Cam said wryly.

She'd always liked Mia and Cam. They were a very chilled out couple. When she was little and Mia was still working at the distillery, she always used to let Grace sit on her desk and play with whatever marketing merchandise she had that week. Sometimes it was a pad with G. Scott Carter emblazoned on it, sometimes it was a stress ball that Grace would squeeze for hours.

Happy Crap, she'd heard it called. Little pieces of junk that made their customers happy because it was free.

Whatever it was, she still smiled at the memory.

Mia's phone buzzed. Before she could even pick it up, a smile was pulling at her lips. "It's Michael," she said. "What's he doing up at this time?"

Grace quickly calculated the time difference. It was just after seven in the evening in West Virginia, which made it after midnight in London. She knew from talking with Michael all week that he'd been working late every night, trying to tie up loose ends so he could sell the business.

"Hello honey, you're up late," Mia said when she'd accepted the call.

"Just checking in with you. How are you doing today?"

She'd put it on speaker phone and Grace's heart did a little leap to hear his voice. She'd spoken to him earlier, while she was getting ready to go out. He'd insisted on a video call so he could watch her.

She'd liked the look of heat in his eyes as she'd showed off her short white dress to him.

"I'm good. Just finishing up a few things at the office with Richard."

Grace knew that Richard was Michael's partner. His ex-wife's brother.

"So late?" Mia asked. "How is he?"

"Good. We're both tired. I'm looking forward to getting back for some rest."

Cam laughed. "I've never heard driving your mom back and forth to the hospital called rest before."

"It beats trying to shake off jet lag. What are you two up to?"

"Another early night for me. Sabrina's going out tonight to watch Presley and Marley's band."

"She is?" Michael's attempt to sound surprised made Grace want to laugh. He was a terrible actor.

"I thought Sabrina told you. She said you and her messaged earlier in the week," Mia said, her brow wrinkling. "Didn't you tell her to be good, and she told you she already had a dad?"

Cam coughed out a laugh. And Grace bit her own smile down because it sounded so much like Sabrina.

"Oh yeah, that's right. I forgot."

"You weren't wrong, though," Cam said, shaking his head. "She needs to be good. Did you hear that Presley insisted she have a chaperone? You should be happy that you're in London, otherwise it would have been you."

"Thank goodness for Grace," Mia said. "She's here, by the way. You should say hi."

"She's with you now?" Michael asked, sounding surprised.

"Yes."

"Hi Grace," he said softly.

"Hi Michael." It was stupid how much hearing him made her want to smile. "How's London?"

"Wet."

She already knew this. It had been raining for days.

"It's very hot here," she told him. "I think I'd prefer the rain."

It was such a pointless conversation. Words they'd already shared a few hours before. And yet her chest felt warm and achy at the same time.

"You wouldn't. Everything's gray. It's like being in a black and white movie."

"I remember." Her lips curled.

"I forgot you used to live in Europe." Mia's voice made Grace jump. She'd almost forgotten his parents were listening.

"It feels like a long time ago now," Grace said. She was about to add that she was happy to be back here when the living room door opened.

And all three of their mouths dropped. Sabrina was standing in the doorway, her body sheathed in a black dress that clung to all her curves. Her hair was up, her blonde ponytail curling down to her shoulders, and her makeup was so perfect it looked professional.

"Is that a dress or a belt?" Cam asked.

Sabrina blinked, looking down at the short hemline. "What's wrong with it?"

Mia let out a long breath. "Michael, honey, we're going to have to call you back in the morning."

"Is everything okay?" He sounded concerned.

Grace looked from Sabrina to Cam again. He was still frowning at his daughter's outfit.

She'd seen her own dad look that way, too. Back when she was in high school and had first started to dress a little older, and had started to wear makeup.

"Everything's fine," Mia said. "I just need to calm Cam down before he blows a gasket."

———

"I can't believe Dad criticized my clothes," Sabrina grumbled as they walked into the bar. "I'm twenty, for goodness' sake, not twelve." Grace tried not to smile because she remembered those days of being stuck between childhood and being an adult.

It was especially hard for Sabrina, the only daughter with three brothers. And Cam was as overprotective as Grace's dad had been when she was the same age.

At least she didn't have to deal with that anymore.

"You have to pick your battles with your parents," she told Sabrina.

"Yeah, you're right." Sabrina wrinkled her nose. The sound of rock music suffused them as their shoes hit the sticky wooden floor.

It was coming from the old-fashioned juke box in the corner. Alternate Reality – Presley and Marley's band – hadn't started yet. Grace pointed to the table by the stage. "That's the one Presley reserved for us. Go sit down and I'll get us some sodas."

"Can't we have something stronger?" Sabrina asked.

"You're underage and I'm driving, so no." Grace smiled. "Now go sit down before you get thrown out."

She'd spoken to Presley last night, and he'd told her he had to get special dispensation from the owner for Sabrina to be there. He'd told them his little cousin was part of the band. And that she wouldn't go anywhere near the bar area or drink something she shouldn't.

When Grace got to the bar, she saw Presley and Marley there, along with their bassist, Alex, and their new keyboardist and singer, a gorgeous brunette named Cassie.

Grace had met her once before and they said hello briefly, before she was enveloped in a group hug from Marley and Presley.

"How's Delilah?" she asked Presley.

"She's good. Although she's annoyed that I wouldn't let her come tonight." Presley smiled at the mention of his little girl. "Mom and Dad are babysitting. They had to promise they'd sing along to *Frozen* with her."

Grace smiled at the image of her uncle – a famous rockstar in his time – singing "Let it Go" at the top of his voice. "I bet they'll love it."

"They live for it." Marley, Presley's twin, lifted a brow. "Seriously, I think Dad prefers Disney to rock 'n' roll nowadays."

"I'm going to check the sound," Cassie said. "I'll catch you later, Grace."

"Wait up, I'll come with you." Presley reached for her, curling his fingers around her bare arm. Cassie looked up at him, then at her arm. He slowly let go.

Well, that was weird.

"What can I get you?" the bartender asked Grace.

"Two diet cokes please." She looked at Marley and Alex. "Would you guys like anything?"

Marley shook his head. "One beer and we're done. Until after the show, at least."

"We're professionals," Alex added, winking at Grace.

As soon as she'd been served, the three of them walked back to the stage, and Grace passed Sabrina a diet coke, sipping at the other one as she took the second chair, facing the stage.

Presley had hooked his guitar strap over his shoulder, plugging it into the amplifier. Alex did the same with his bass guitar, and Marley was behind the huge drum set at the back of the stage, spinning the sticks between his fingers.

Cassie was bending down next to the amp, her jeans tight

across her hips, her black top riding up to reveal a sliver of skin. Glancing at Presley, Grace noticed he was staring right at his keyboardist.

Interesting. There was something going on there. Not that it was any of Grace's business. She didn't want people prying into her own life, after all. But Presley had been alone and grieving for too long. Maybe things were looking up for him.

"Guess who just texted me," Sabrina said, as Presley strummed some chords. "*Again*."

"The President?"

Sabrina laughed. "Not quite. My brother. Telling me to behave for you."

Grace's throat turned dry. "Which brother?"

"Michael, of course. I blocked him. No wonder he and Lainey split up. She must have gotten sick of him bossing her around."

"Lainey?" Grace said. "Is that his ex-wife?"

"It's Elaine really, I think." Sabrina shrugged. "I don't know. I never met her."

"Didn't you go to their wedding?" It was like picking at a scab. And it was pointless. Michael was in London because he was cutting all ties. She trusted him. And she wasn't about to go all green-eyed monster again.

Once was enough.

"Nope. They eloped. Didn't tell anybody." Sabrina rolled her eyes. "I think Mom was upset, but she didn't tell him that. And Michael's always been private."

Grace swallowed, because she knew that. And she was the one he was keeping secrets about now.

"Anyway, they were over before they began. Apparently the divorce took longer than the time they lived together." Sabrina shrugged just as Marley hit the drums a few times. It made Grace jump.

She opened her mouth to ask a dozen more questions, but

Cassie was already leaning into the microphone fixed to her keyboard.

"Ladies and Gentlemen, we're Alternate Reality, and we'd like to play you a few songs." Her talking voice was soft and husky, exactly the way she sang.

Grace lifted her soda to her lips and decided to throw herself into the music.

———

"I think we're there," Michael said, looking at Richard. They were a similar age, though Richard looked older with his bow tie and striped shirt. Ageless, maybe.

"Yes, I think we are." Richard nodded. They'd spent three days going through everything. Getting assessments. Talking to their clients to make sure they'd be staying with the company despite Michael leaving.

He'd assured them they'd get the same attention they always did. Richard was a good agent, and without Michael, he'd be running the business with less individual client time. But their staff would remain the same, and Michael had already talked to each one of them to make sure they knew their jobs were safe.

Now all that remained was for them to sign contracts and make the announcement. That couldn't be done in the next two days, but they'd already agreed that Michael would hand everything over from the other side of the Atlantic. On Monday, they'd let the staff know they'd be reporting to Richard, and then he'd go home.

"You got plans for tomorrow?" Richard asked him.

"Just cleaning out the apartment." He'd arranged for movers to come in. Anything he wanted in the US would be shipped and arrive in a couple of months once it had gone through customs. Everything else would be donated or thrown away.

It was as though his life in London was disappearing.

"I'd invite you around to ours, but Lainey…"

"It's fine," Michael told him. "I have too much to do, anyway." He'd booked his return flight for Monday. There was no way he was missing it. And there was also no way he wanted to bump into his ex-wife. "But thank you."

"You're welcome."

There was a buzz at the front door of the office. Michael glanced at the clock. It was almost two a.m. Richard had agreed to work through the night with him if needed. This was important to them both.

But they were exhausted.

"Are you expecting somebody?" Michael asked, wondering if Richard had ordered some food.

"Nope. Let me look." He straightened his bow tie – still perfectly knotted – and walked over to the main door. "Oh shit."

"What?"

"It's Lainey."

Michael swallowed hard. He hadn't spoken to his ex-wife since he'd come back. Actually, hadn't spoken to her since their divorce. It had been fairly easy – they'd been together for such a short time and had no children – they'd both walked away with what they'd entered the marriage with.

"I'll try to get rid of her," Richard said, sighing. "I'm sorry. I told her you were here."

"No, it's fine. We were finished up and leaving anyway. If she wants to talk to me, we can do it on the way out."

Richard caught his eye. "You sure?"

Michael nodded. "Yeah." He stood and joined Richard at the door.

When it opened, his ex-wife walked in, looking like she'd been out somewhere for dinner. She was wearing a cocktail dress and a jacket, her hair immaculately swept up into a French pleat.

"I was driving past and saw the lights on," she said. "I wanted to make sure it wasn't a burglar."

"We were just leaving," Richard told her. "You don't need to worry."

She didn't answer. Just looked at Michael. He swallowed hard.

"Hello." Her voice was low.

"Hello." He gave her the smallest of smiles. "How are you?" Richard had told him that she had moved on. Was living with her boyfriend now. He was happy for her.

"I'm fine. I just wanted to talk with you for a minute."

"You want me to stay?" Richard asked.

Michael wasn't sure if he was talking to him or Lainey. They both shook their heads, though.

"In that case, I'm out of here. I'll see you on Monday," he told Michael.

"See you then."

He waited for Richard to leave before looking at his ex-wife. "I was leaving, too. Shall I walk you to your car?"

She nodded. "I just wanted to see you."

"Here I am." Michael grabbed his car keys and his wallet, sliding them into his pocket. "I hear you're doing well."

Her lips twitched. "Yes." She took a deep breath. "I heard you were moving back home. Richard told me you'd found someone, too."

Richard had a big mouth. But then again, Michael hadn't exactly tried to hide it. He'd been calling Grace daily from the office.

"That's right." He set the alarm and closed the main office door, and they walked out into the black inky night.

"Who is she?"

"Does it matter?" he asked. He didn't owe her anything, but he wasn't proud of the way they'd ended, either. He'd owed her more than he'd gave her. And he felt bad about it.

"It does to me." Lainey's eyes were soft as they met his. "I want to know what she has that I didn't."

"Lainey…"

"You told me you weren't cut out for relationships," she said. "And I understood that. Accepted it. But now you're seeing somebody else. Selling your business for her. I just want to know who she is.

His head was pounding. He really needed sleep. More than anything, he needed to get home. And he knew where that was now. Not here in London. It never had been.

"I'm sorry," he said, his voice low. "I'm sorry that it ended the way it did. I'm sorry I couldn't show you the love you needed. But we're better off apart. That's why we got divorced."

They should never have gotten married in the first place. He'd been lonely, and she'd been there, and he truly thought that was enough. But now he knew how wrong he'd been. That the affection he'd had for Lainey was nothing like the passion he had for Grace.

"Is she pretty?"

He nodded. "Yeah."

"And she probably worships the ground you walk on." Lainey's voice was soft. Sad.

"I think it's the other way around."

Her eyes caught his. "I wish it could have been us."

They'd reached her car. And he'd reached the end of his words. There was nothing more to say that they hadn't already said. But maybe this was important. A final ending. He was leaving, not looking back.

But he didn't want to leave her unhappy.

"It could never have been us. You deserved better. I hope you've found it." He watched as she opened the car door with her key fob.

She pulled the door open and stopped, looking over her shoulder.

"Do you love her?" Her voice was so low he could barely hear it. The security lights from the parking lot reflected in her eyes.

"I do."

She nodded, her lips pressed together. "Okay," she said. "Okay." Climbing into her car, she pulled the seatbelt across her, then started the ignition.

"I hope she loves you back."

A ghost of a smile pulled at his lips. "She does."

Lainey nodded again.

"Is your boyfriend waiting for you?" he asked.

"I think so." She nodded.

"Richard says he's a good man," he told her. As he went to close the door, he caught her eye. "Be happy." Then he pushed it closed and walked to his own car, intending to sit there until she was out of sight.

Although he had two more days until he'd fly home, it still felt like closure. The end of one life and the start of a new one.

And he couldn't wait for this one to begin.

———

Everybody was on the dance floor, singing along as the group performed a cover of one of Gray's old songs. Presley was loving it. She could tell from the glow on his face as he leaned into the mic and growled the words out. And the rest of the band was killing it, too.

Lapping up the adulation from the audience.

Grace's phone buzzed against her hip and she pulled it out, surprised when she saw Michael's name flash up.

Luckily, Sabrina was too busy dancing to notice.

It was nine-thirty here. Which made it two-thirty in the morning in London.

Poor Michael. He must be exhausted.

Surreptitiously, she slid the message open with her thumb, being sure to keep the screen only visible to her.

Can you talk?- M x

I'm on the dancefloor. Give me a minute and I'll call you. Is everything okay? – G x

It's fine. Or it will be once I hear your voice. – M x

Sabrina was dancing at the very front, only a few feet away from Presley. Grace was pretty sure she wouldn't do anything stupid for a few minutes, so she turned and pushed her way through the crowd, smiling in apology every time her shoulder brushed somebody else's.

Presley and Cassie were singing together, their voices making a sweet harmony. They sang of losing each other. Of never getting over the relationship they'd had.

She reached the door and pushed it, stepping out into the evening air. There were a few smokers outside – a few vapers, too – but she found somewhere quiet. The evening air was humid, curling around her body. Leaning against the brick wall at the side of the building, she pulled out her phone and hit Michael's name.

"Hi."

"Hi. You're up late."

"I just got back to my hotel room. We've agreed on a price."

Her smile widened. "You have? Congratulations."

"We still have to sign contracts, but we're almost there. And I'll be flying back on Monday."

"I can't wait." She was grinning from ear to ear.

"I also saw my ex-wife."

Her smile wavered. "Lainey?"

"Yeah." He didn't ask how she knew her name. Maybe he thought he'd told her before. "There's nothing sinister. Richard told her I was in town. We talked for about five minutes and she left."

"What did you talk about?"

"She wanted to know about you."

Oh. "What did you tell her?"

"That I'm in love with you."

She swallowed hard. "How did she take that?"

"I don't know," he said honestly. "I just wanted to tell you because I want to be honest with you."

Okay then. She took a deep breath. "Did you feel anything when you saw her?"

"No."

"Good."

He laughed softly. "I can't wait to come home and see you," he told her. "It's all I'm thinking about."

"It's all I'm thinking about, too. I wish you were here."

"So do I. More than you know. How's the concert going?"

"They sound great. Like they're really on the edge of something good." She looked at her watch. "You should go to bed. Before you fall asleep standing."

"Can I call you tomorrow?"

"Yes, please."

"I can't wait to see you. And we can stop all these damn secrets and lies."

"I can't wait either."

"Send me a message when you get home tonight. So I know you and Sabrina got back safely," he said, sounding tired.

"You'll be asleep."

"Yeah, but I'll be awake at a stupid hour. And I'll want to know you're safe."

"Okay, I'll send you a message," she promised.

"Good. I love you." His voice was gruff again. "So fucking much."

"I love you too," she said softly. "Now get some sleep."

CHAPTER
Twenty-Three

"YOU OKAY?" Presley asked Grace. The gig was over and the band was sitting at the table with Grace and Sabrina. The bar had thinned out – it was nearly closing time. Grace was waiting for Sabrina to finish her third soda of the night and then they'd head home.

"I'm good. Just tired." She bumped his shoulder with hers. "You were fabulous tonight. Reminded me of the old days."

It had been fun growing up with Marley and Presley. The twins were a few years older than her, and they'd made up all the best games. Her mom had told her she used to toddle after them, begging them to wait for her.

And they had. Every time. They'd been so patient with her as a kid. When she'd arrived at high school freshman year, they'd been seniors and usually the age difference would have meant they wouldn't be seen dead with her.

But not Marley and Presley. They'd put the word around that she was their cousin and everybody had to take care of her.

She loved them for that.

"You look happy," she told Presley. "Is it good to be back with the band?"

He nodded, a smile playing at his lips. "Yeah, it really is."

From the corner of her eye she could see Cassie and Marley laughing at something Sabrina had said. The smile on Presley's lips wavered, but it wasn't her place to say anything.

"So what's happening with you?" Presley asked.

"What do you mean?" Grace gave him a confused glance.

"I mean this guy you were talking to outside when we were playing."

"Who said I was talking to a guy?" she asked, her voice wary. She'd been alone, hadn't she?

"I saw you on the phone through the window when we took a quick break," Presley told her. "You had this stupid smile on your face. I kind of guessed the rest."

"I was talking to my mom."

Presley bit down a grin. "That confirms it."

"What?" She turned to look at him. His gaze was fond. She knew he wasn't trying to bait her. Just... interested. And maybe a little protective.

Like that time when she couldn't get a date for the spring dance freshman year and found out that he and Marley had 'spoken' to a few of the guys who'd wanted to ask her out.

"Your mom and dad went to the drive in tonight."

Oh damn, they had. She'd forgotten that.

"And I know for a fact that *Ghost* is your mom's favorite. There's no way she'd call you during that."

"Okay it wasn't my mom. Can we change the subject now?" She rolled her eyes at him.

"You can tell me who he is," Presley told her. "I won't breathe a word to anybody else."

"I can't." She shook her head. "Not yet."

His brows dipped. "Why not yet?"

"It's complicated," she told him. "Why don't we talk

about something else? Like the way you and Cassie sang together tonight."

"What about the way we sang? Was it okay?"

"It was hot. Like steaming. Is there something going on with you two?" Turning the tables on her cousin felt like the best way to protect herself.

"No." He shook his head vehemently. "There's nothing."

"She likes you," Grace told him.

"She's a bandmate. Nothing more." He looked over at her, his brows knitting. Cassie was leaning to whisper something in Alex's ear.

"Okay then. So I'm not hiding anything and you're not interested in Cassie. Got it." Grace smiled smugly, glad that she'd gotten the conversation away from her.

"Grace." He lifted a brow. But at least her telephone conversation was forgotten

She wrinkled her nose and blew him a kiss. "Good night, Presley. I'm taking Sabrina home now."

———

"Say it again," her dad asked, his brows knitting as she sat at the kitchen table with her family the next day. Her mom had invited her for Sunday lunch, and since she had nothing else to do, she'd agreed.

She was glad she had. There was no point sitting at home missing Michael. So much better to be busy.

And to be teasing her dad.

Grace's gaze met her mom's. She could see her mom was biting down a smile. Her dad was an intelligent, talented, handsome man, but he was horrible with languages.

"C'est un plaisir de faire affaire avec vous," Grace said, the words rolling off her tongue. "But honestly, Dad, they'll speak English. Just say it was a pleasure to work with them."

"I'm not speaking English when I'm in France."

"You will be," her mom said, her eyes crinkling. "Otherwise you'll starve."

"Okay. So the meetings will mostly be in English, but I'd like to start and end them with at least an attempt at their language. It's polite. If I keep practicing for the next few weeks maybe I'll pull it off."

Her brother pulled his phone out of his pocket.

"Put that away," their mom said. "No phones at the dinner table. You all know the rules."

It was Scott and Grace's turn to exchange amused looks. She'd barely seen her little brother all summer. A lot of that was her fault – she knew that. She'd spent so much of her time with Michael there hadn't been space for anybody else.

But Scott was busy, too. He'd been working as a lifeguard at the local pool during the day and in the evenings he worked at the concession stand at the local drive-in movie theater, owned by one of their uncles. And when he wasn't working he was hanging around with his friends or working on his car.

Luckily, Ethan hadn't been back again to help. According to Scott, he'd left town. She assumed he'd gone back to wherever he'd come from.

"I'm just trying to show Dad something," Scott said. "Give me a break."

The way he rolled his eyes reminded her of Sabrina. She and Scott were the same age. In a few weeks they'd both be heading back to college and the town would feel a little quieter.

They were both little punks, but she'd miss them.

"Look," Scott said, holding his phone so their dad could see the screen. "You can use this app. Type the phrase you want to use and it'll translate it."

Her dad took Scott's phone and did as he was told. His lips twitched as he typed into it.

A moment later, a digitized voice spoke out of the phone speaker.

"Ta mère est la femme la plus sexy que j'aie jamais vue."

Grace coughed out a laugh.

"What does that mean?" Scott asked.

"You don't want to know," Grace told him.

"Yeah, I do." He took his phone back and looked at the words their dad had typed in. "Oh Jesus, that's disgusting."

"Well she is." Her dad shrugged. "There's no denying it."

Her mom smiled at him softly. She'd understood the translation the same way Grace had. *Your mother is the sexiest woman I've ever met.*

It was kind of sweet. Or it would have been if it hadn't been her parents doing the flirting.

It made her feel wistful, too. Thinking about how Michael flirted with her in French. How he whispered soft words into her ears when they were together.

One more day. That's all she had to get through.

"I try to help and this is what I get," Scott said, shoving his phone back into his pocket. "You've ruined my appetite."

"That'll never happen," Grace scoffed. Pot roast was Scott's favorite, and he'd never turned down second or third helpings.

"Let's change the subject, shall we?" her mom suggested. "How did Presley and Marley do last night?"

Grace smiled. "They were so good. Reminded me of the old days. Presley sounded better than ever."

"I'm so pleased." Her mom nodded, her eyes shiny. "He deserves some happiness. Did you see anybody you knew there?"

"Only half the town," Grace said.

"She means *guys*. Did you meet any hot guys? Anybody ask for your number?" Scott rolled his eyes, though she could tell he was happy she was getting some heat, too.

"No, I didn't." Grace wrinkled her nose at him.

"She doesn't need to. I've heard she already has some-body." As soon as the words left her mom's mouth, her eyes widened. "Oh, shit."

"Mom!" Scott's mouth dropped open. Their mom never swore. Well, *almost* never. The last time Grace could remember her saying anything like that was when her mom had driven her car into a pole in the grocery store parking lot.

"You're seeing somebody?" her dad asked. "Who?"

"Sorry," her mom said to her, looking genuinely upset. "Maddie called earlier. She overheard Presley talking to Marley about it. I was going to ask you quietly."

Grace let out a long breath. Why had she ever thought they could keep a secret in Hartson's Creek?

"It's not true, is it?" her dad asked.

Grace tried not to squirm. "I don't want to talk about it."

"Why not?" Her mom frowned.

"Please tell me it isn't Ethan the asshole," Scott said.

"It isn't," she promised.

"So who is it?" Her mom wasn't letting this go.

She'd know soon enough. When Michael was back, they were going to discuss the best way to tell their parents.

"I'm not ready to talk about it yet," Grace said firmly. "But I'll tell you about him soon. When I'm ready."

Her mom groaned, looking disappointed.

"Maybe she's scared you'll feed him to the pigs," Scott said.

Her dad's first meeting with her mom's brothers was legendary in town. Grace's mom was their only sister and completely protected by them. She'd hidden the fact that she'd fallen for her boss from them for a long time.

But eventually she'd caved and come clean to them. And Logan had responded by having his pigs chase Grace's dad through a field.

"We don't even own any pigs," her dad protested.

"But we know somebody who does." Scott lifted a brow at

Grace. "Why won't you tell us more? Is he married or something?"

"No!" Grace frowned. "Why would you think that?"

Scott shrugged. "Dunno. There has to be some reason you don't want us to know."

She gave him a pointed look. "I promise I'll tell you soon, okay? There are just a few things I need to work through first."

"So it's serious then?" her dad asked. The corner of his lip pulled to the side, like he was trying not to look annoyed.

"Yes." She nodded. "It's getting there."

"So why not tell us right now?"

"Daniel, relax. She'll tell us in her own time," her mom said. "I shouldn't have said anything. Can we change the subject?"

"We already did," Scott pointed out. "To this."

Grace tried not to sigh.

"Please give me some time," she said. "That's all I ask."

Her mom cleared her throat, saving Grace from her dad. "Has everybody finished?" her mom asked. Grace looked down at her own half-full plate.

"Yes." She nodded, standing. "I'll help you clean up."

CHAPTER
Twenty~Four

GRACE LEANED on the counter and checked her clock for the fifteenth time. She'd left work early, taking some work home with her, knowing that Michael's plane was due to land at two.

He'd taken the earliest flight he could from Heathrow, which meant that he'd had to be at the airport at some stupid time early that morning. Though he'd texted her to let her know when his airplane took off, she'd been asleep and by the time she woke up and saw his message, he was somewhere over the Atlantic.

Today had felt like the longest day ever. She'd been so jittery her mom had thought she was sick and sent her home. Grace hadn't argued. She'd been planning on leaving as soon as Michael's plane landed anyway.

She was a little early was all.

Hey beautiful. We've landed. Just heading to customs. Should be with you in two hours. Can't wait to see you. – Michael xx

· · ·

His message was the warm embrace she needed right now. He was back in the US. Coming home to her. She let out a breath and finally relaxed.

Can't wait. I'm at home. Come straight here if you can. – Grace xx

There's no other place I want to be. – Michael xx

Damn, he was a sweet talker. She couldn't help the grin on her face as she finished the email she was supposed to be sending and poured herself a cup of coffee, glancing at the clock to figure out right when he'd be home.

Two more hours. She could do that. She'd waited this long, after all.

She could barely keep still as the minutes took their time ticking by. Michael called her from the baggage reclaim area, but then his luggage came fast and he'd had to go. She thought about calling him back, but she had work to do before he got here.

And she knew that as soon as he walked through the door, all thoughts of reports and emails would be forgotten.

It was almost four when she heard the rumble of an engine outside. She glanced out of the window to see him pulling up along the side of her house, where his car couldn't be seen from the road.

And then he was climbing out, running his fingers through his hair, and her heart slammed against her chest. She'd forgotten how beautiful he was to look at.

She almost ran to her back door, wrenching it open before he could reach the steps. Running out, she threw herself against him and he caught her in his arms, laughing as he kissed her.

"Never leave me again," she told him breathlessly when they finally parted.

"Not planning on it." His gaze was soft. He reached out to cup her cheek. "I've missed looking at you."

"Ditto." She grabbed his hand, pulling him inside. "How was your flight?"

"Long. I almost fell asleep, but we hit turbulence and the moment passed."

She grimaced. "I hate when that happens. I always think I'm about to die."

Michael couldn't help but laugh. "Well, somehow I made it unscathed."

"Luckily for me." She rolled onto her feet again, brushing her lips against his. "Do you want a coffee?"

He shook his head. "No."

"Something to eat?"

"Just you." His voice was husky. Curling his fingers around her waist, he pulled her closer and she could feel how hungry he was.

For her. Only for her. It sent a shot of excitement through her body.

"How was London?" she asked him.

"I'm finished with London." His eyes caught hers, and she knew he meant more than the sale of his business.

"Good." She slid her fingers into his hair, tugging him down until his lips were on hers again. "London's loss is my gain."

"*Our* gain," he said, grinning as he kissed her once again. This time, his lips were soft and teasing, sending pulses of pleasure through her body. She curled her arms around his neck as their kiss deepened.

His lips trailed down her jaw, her throat, kissing the dip at the bottom revealed by her open neck blouse. Her nipples tightened at the warmth of his mouth. At the promise it gave her.

She scratched his scalp with her fingernails and he groaned, his own hold on her tightening. His length was thick and needy against her. How had she lived for a week without this? How could she even live for a day?

"I've missed this," he muttered, unbuttoning her blouse. She was wearing her favorite lingerie. Just for him.

A celebration that they were back together.

"Are you trying to kill me?" he asked hoarsely.

"Just reminding you what you've been missing." She closed her eyes as he cupped her breast, his hands warm and strong against her sensitive skin. His thumb brushed her nipple and she let out a sigh.

His lips curled as he slid his hand inside the lace fabric, pinching her nipple until she cried out.

Then he kissed her again. "I feel like the sun just came out," she told him.

Michael blinked, still holding her tight. "Hasn't it been out for weeks?"

"Not here." She put her hand over his, moving it to the center of her chest. Her heart beat strong against his palm. "It's been dark here."

"It won't be again," he promised.

"I know." She nodded. "I know. Now take me upstairs and show me just how much you've missed me."

He grinned. "I thought you'd never ask."

———

He'd never tire of this woman. Never be anything less than amazed by how perfectly their bodies fit together. How it felt like a tiny piece of heaven was winding around them every time he slid inside of her.

She was perfect, her hair fanning out on her pillow, her

eyes wide and piercing as she gazed at his face. He'd spent the last thirty minutes teasing her, making her ready, making her beg. And now he was the one trying not to come, reciting the damn alphabet backward because it had been too long and she felt too good. She had this effect on him every time.

She tightened around him and he muttered a curse, because he was on a hair trigger here.

As soon as he and Richard told the staff that the sale would go through in the next few weeks, a feeling of peace had enveloped him. It was as though he'd been fighting an invisible enemy for all these years, but now he could finally stop and breathe.

It was only when he was on the plane, taxiing along the runway at Heathrow Airport, that he realized how true that feeling was.

And that the enemy he'd been fighting was himself.

He'd spent a lifetime thinking he wasn't good enough.

Not good enough for his dad to stay faithful to his mom. Not good enough for his mom, who deserved way more than a surly teenager for a son. Not good enough to play in the NFL and not good enough to keep a marriage going.

The stupid thing was, he damn sure wasn't good enough for Grace. And yet here she was, whispering his name, telling him she loved him, digging her fingers into his ass as he did everything to make her feel good. She was tighter still, her nipples hard like pebbles against his chest, her mouth slack as she let out a low moan.

"I love you."

The words were like a symphony cascading through his ears.

"I love you, too, beautiful." More than she could ever know. He cupped her face, his hips still rocking, the pleasure coiling in him until he could resist it no more.

"Grace." He dropped his head against hers, his gaze locking

on her eyes as he spilled inside of her. She wrapped her legs around his hips, pulling him closer, and he was still coming. Pulsing inside of her until he wasn't sure he had anything left to give. And then she was fluttering around him again, her third orgasm taking her by surprise. He slid his hands beneath her ass, holding her close as they kissed and murmured each other's names until the pleasure finally ebbed into nothing.

Or everything.

"Oh God," Grace whispered, as he slowly rolled off of her. "I don't think I'll ever walk again."

"It's okay. I'll carry you everywhere," he promised. He should get up, wash himself off, wash her. But he wasn't sure he could walk either. Instead, he brushed the hair off her face as she nestled into him.

"Monday afternoon sex," he murmured. "I could get used to this."

She laughed softly, tracing his biceps with her soft fingers. "And people say they hate Mondays."

"Not me."

"Me either." She tipped her head up, still smiling, and he had to kiss her again. Wasn't sure he'd ever get sick of it. "So I need to tell you something," she said, her voice wavering now.

"What is it?"

"I kind of need to tell my parents about us."

"Okay."

She swallowed. "I sort of hinted that there is someone. And I know they won't leave it alone until they find out."

"You don't need to sound so scared. I've been thinking the same thing. We've been sailing too close to the wind for a while. With Josh…"

"And Presley suspects something."

Michael's lips twitched. "Is there anybody in Hartson's Creek who doesn't suspect something?"

"Probably not." She sighed. "Small towns aren't the best for keeping secrets."

"How do you want to do it?"

"I don't know." She let out a long breath. "I'm scared." And then she looked at him. "Let's do it Friday."

He wanted to laugh at her sudden change in direction. "Okay."

"You sure?"

"Yeah." He nodded. "My mom's doing well and I think it's the right time. The only question is, do we do it before or after *Chairs*?" He kissed her temple. "Or do you want to do it there? Give everybody a ringside seat to the latest scandal to envelop Hartson's Creek."

"Please no." She shook her head at his teasing. "Anywhere but *Chairs*."

"You could invite them here," he suggested. "We could have dinner with them. Keep it civilized."

"You scared my dad will beat you up?"

He laughed. "Petrified." He lifted a brow, and she grinned.

"Dinner sounds like a good idea," she said. "Thank you."

"I didn't say I'd cook it."

She laughed again.

"But I will. I'll bring steaks. We can grill."

"The weather forecast says rain for Friday."

"Then we'll grill in the rain."

"Okay then." She rolled over, putting her palms on his chest, resting her chin on top of them. "What about your parents?"

"You want me to invite them too?"

She blinked. "Actually, that's not a bad idea."

"It's a terrible idea, sweetheart." He cupped her cheek. "Let's concentrate on your parents first, then we'll do mine, okay?"

"I guess." She pressed her lips together. "What if your mom hates me?"

"She loves you. Especially since you keep Sabrina under control."

"She might not think I'm good enough for you."

He chuckled. "I don't think you have to worry about that. She'll probably think you're too good for me."

"Stop it." She slapped his arm playfully.

He caught her wrist, curling his fingers around it, lifting her hand to his mouth and kissing her palm softly. "Seriously, my mom loves you. You have nothing to worry about."

"Josh was worried."

"He was worried about you. If I was treating you right."

Her brows pinched tightly together. "Well you do."

"Good."

"And maybe somebody should worry about you."

He kissed her fingertips one by one. "I'm a big boy. I can worry about myself."

"No." She shook her head. "I'll worry about you too."

His throat felt tight. Not because he hated that idea, but because he liked it. Too much. Liked that she cared.

That she loved him.

"Okay," he said gruffly. "You do that."

Pulling her hand from his, she moved across him until she was straddling him, her hands planted flat on the sheets, either side of his face. Her hair trailed down, tickling his nose, her ass wriggling on top of him until he was hard.

Again.

"You don't get it, do you?" she asked him. "I would move mountains for you. Fight lions or whatever it is."

He looked up at her. "That's my line."

"I know you'd fight them for me. We'd fight them together."

"Are you getting me ready for Friday?"

She laughed, and he pulled her down, kissing her again.

"What was that?" she asked.

"What?" He smiled at her. "You want me to kiss you again?"

"No, not the kiss. That bang? Did you hear it?"

"Probably my heart finally giving up." He trailed his lips down her throat.

"Shut up." She shook her head.

"Or the lions trying to get into the house," he murmured against her jaw.

She narrowed her eyes at him. He opened his mouth to tease her some more when the bang came again.

"You had to hear it this time." She groaned, lifting her leg to roll off of him.

Michael lifted a brow. "I did. You expecting somebody?"

"I got a grocery delivery coming this evening. The guy's probably early." She walked over to her window, her bare skin glowing in the half light as she looked out. "I can't see anybody."

Michael rolled over to grab his pants, sliding them on as he rose from the bed. "I'll get rid of them."

"Oh no you won't." She shook her head. "Stay here."

"Grace?" A loud voice made them both jump. A man. Inside the house.

Not just any man. Grace turned to Michael, her horrified eyes meeting his.

"Shit. That's my dad."

CHAPTER
Twenty-Five

THE MOMENT she heard his voice, everything froze. Everything except the fast pulse of her heart. What was her dad doing here? Why had he let himself in?

She felt sick. Like she was going to throw up at any minute.

"Oh God," she said again.

Michael caught her eye. "It's okay. We were going to tell him anyway, right?"

Yes, but not like this. What father would take finding his daughter in bed with her much older step cousin well?

She'd planned to ease him into it. Let him see them fully dressed first. Dear god, where were her clothes?

Over there. By the bed. She snatched her panties from the floor and tried to slide both feet into one hole before toppling over.

"You're white as a sheet," Michael whispered, helping her up. "Try not to panic."

"Grace? Are you here? Mom told me you came home sick." There was a thump of feet on the stairs.

She was deer-in-the-headlights panicked. "I'm okay," she shouted. "Give me a minute."

There was only drywall between her and complete devastation. It was like she was a child again, caught doing something wrong. She shot a fearful look at Michael. Why wasn't he trying to climb out of the window?

He reached for her, taking her hand. "It's okay," he murmured softly.

But it wasn't. This wasn't supposed to happen. They had it all planned out.

"Mom asked me to drop your sweater off," her dad shouted through the door. He sounded so close. "You left it at our house on Sunday. Mom forgot to give it to you at work since you went home."

Why? Why would he do that? She didn't need a damn sweater. She had an entire closet of them.

"You need to hide," she grunted at Michael.

He looked around the room. "Where?"

She followed his gaze. Her room was tiny. Even her closet was too small for this six- foot-two giant.

Why did he have to be so big?

"Get on the other side of the bed."

"Grace…" His voice was gentle.

She pushed him and somehow he actually did what she asked, hunkering down to his knees and then lying down.

She grabbed a t-shirt and padded over to the door. "Sorry," she said, pulling it open. "I have a headache. I thought I'd try to sleep it off."

Her dad was holding her blue sweater, looking confused. "Did you take something for it?"

She could hear Michael breathing. Dammit, he needed to stop.

"Something for what?" She stared cluelessly at her father.

"The headache." He smiled gently. "Want me to get you some Advil?"

"It's okay." She shook her head quickly. "I've got some."

She reached out for her sweater, taking it from her dad's grasp. "I'm just going to head back to bed."

"Whose shoes are those?" He looked over her shoulder.

"What?" She followed his gaze. Michael's huge black shoes were in the middle of her bedroom floor. He must have kicked them off there before taking her to bed.

"I don't know."

Her dad's brows tugged together. "What do you mean you don't know? There's a pair of man's shoes in the middle of your bedroom…" His eyes widened as he finally worked it out. "Oh no. I should go. Your mother…"

"Dad, it's not what you think."

His face was pale and he wouldn't catch her gaze. "You're a grownup, Grace. What you do in your own time is none of my business." It was his turn to look like he was trapped. He stepped backward, looking like he was about to be sick.

"It's okay," he muttered. "I was never here."

She took a deep breath. She was an adult. She needed to deal with this. "Michael and I…"

"Michael?"

"Yeah?" he called out.

No, no, no. Stay down. She had this.

"Michael Devlin?" her dad said, as Michael slowly rose from behind her bed. "What the hell are you doing in my daughter's bedroom?" His eyes narrowed as he looked from Michael and back to Grace again.

"No," he said, his voice shaking. "No, this isn't happening."

"Sir," Michael said, walking toward them. "This isn't Grace's fault. It's all mine."

"Just shut up for a minute." Her dad pinched the bridge of his nose. "This isn't even legal. You're cousins."

"Step-cousins," she whispered.

"And that makes it any better?" her dad asked. "Jesus Christ, Grace, you could have anybody you want."

"I want Michael."

"No, you don't." His voice was louder now. Surer. "He's too old for you. Too… related. This can't happen."

"Dad…" She wanted to explain. To tell him she loved Michael. To make him understand. But the words wouldn't come. They were locked down tight by the panic and the fear and the feeling that everything she depended on was falling apart.

She felt a warm hand on her shoulder. It was supposed to reassure her, she knew that, but all it did was make her want to shrug it off. Because her dad was staring at Michael's hand, at her shoulder.

At them both.

"Daniel…" Michael began, and her dad shook his head again.

"Don't talk to me," he told Michael, his voice low. "Don't even look at me. And get your goddamned hands off my daughter."

———

The front door slammed and a moment later an engine started up, the squeal of tires on her gravel drive making her flinch.

"Grace. What do you want to do?" Michael asked her.

She turned to look at him, and the expression of horror on her face shocked him.

"He'll calm down," he promised her. "Once he talks to your mom."

That didn't help at all. "He's gonna tell Mom," she muttered. "This can't be happening."

"We were going to tell them both on Friday," he told her.

"Don't you think I know that? But it was going to be on our terms, not like this. He practically caught us in bed together."

She must have noticed the way he flinched. "I'm sorry… I…" She inhaled sharply. "It shouldn't have happened like this."

"He shouldn't have walked into your house." Michael raked his fingers through his hair. She looked so lost. He had no idea how to make her feel better.

"He's my dad. He was worried about me."

"He could have called you. Or waited. This is his fault."

She shook her head. "No it isn't. It's mine. I'm an idiot. I have no patience. I mess everything up. And now he hates me."

He pulled her into his arms. "He doesn't hate you. He loves you. It's me he hates."

She was still trembling, and he hated it. Hated the way she was so upset. For a moment he was a fifteen-year-old kid again, watching his mom fall apart in front of his eyes as Cam walked away from her.

Because Michael demanded she choose between them.

He felt sick thinking about that. About what he'd put her through. Why was it always the women who were torn apart?

"I'll talk to your dad," he said. "Make him understand."

"No." She shook her head. "Don't do that. It'll only make things worse. I'll talk to him."

He cupped her face tenderly. But she didn't sink into him. Her eyes were misty, like she was trapped in her own thoughts.

"It's going to be okay, Grace."

"Is it?"

"Yes, it is."

"Did you get a look at his face?" she asked him. "I've never seen him so upset. I've never heard him talk like that before."

"He's your dad. He needs to think it through."

"No." She shook her head. "He's never going to accept this."

His gut twisted. He'd said that once to his mom when he found out about her and Cam.

His karma had taken almost thirty years, but it was here.

He wouldn't let it take Grace down. She was innocent. She didn't deserve this crap. "Let's go see him," he said. "It's better than sitting around here and worrying."

"I'll go," she said. "I'll explain."

"I'm not letting you go without me."

She looked up at him, her eyes shiny with tears. "I need to do it alone."

"Okay," he breathed. "Okay. You go talk to them. I should warn my mom."

"Oh no, your poor mom." Her eyes were full of tears. "She'll find out too."

Yeah, she would. The whole town would. But wasn't that the point? They were going to start telling people on Friday. They were going to be free.

No hiding, no lies. Just truth from now on.

So why did it feel like they were lying harder than ever?

———

His mom was asleep on the sofa when he let himself into the house. Cam was in the kitchen watching football, a beer in his hand. "Hey." He smiled at Michael. "How was your flight?"

"Good." Michael looked back into the living room. "Mom okay?"

"Just exhausted. A few more days and she'll be getting a break." Cam nodded his head at the refrigerator. "Want a beer?"

"No thanks."

"How about something to eat? There's some pizza left over. Even Sabrina couldn't eat it all."

"I ate on the plane," Michael told him. "My stomach still thinks it's on London time."

"It's asleep, huh?" Cam grinned. And for a second Michael wanted to hug him. Because once upon a time, he'd put this man through hell.

He'd made his mom choose between them, and his mom had chosen Michael. Cam had left town, left his family. Left everything because he couldn't bear to be in the same town as Mia Devlin without being with her.

It was only when Josh had disappeared that Michael finally called Cam to apologize. To beg for him to come back. And he had.

He hated himself for putting his mom and Cam through that.

The same way he wanted to slap himself for making Grace hurt.

His phone buzzed. He looked down to see Josh's name flashing on the screen.

"I'll take this upstairs," he said to Cam. "So I don't wake mom."

"Sure." Cam turned back to the football. "The pizza'll still be here if you want it."

"Thanks." He walked into the hallway, heading for the stairs. "Hey," he said, accepting the call. "What's up?"

"You back home?"

"In Hartson's Creek, yeah."

"Great." Josh sounded his usual sunshine self. "I tried to call you earlier. Figured you were still on the plane. Or getting strip searched. How was the trip? Did you get everything transferred over?"

"Yeah. It's all done." He walked into his room and sat down warily on the bed. He was so damn tired.

"And how's Grace?" Josh asked.

He opened his mouth to say she was good. But he was so fucking sick of all the lies. "A mess."

There was silence for a moment.

"What?" Josh finally said. "What's happened?"

Michael didn't want to tell him. He didn't want to tell anybody. But everybody was going to know soon, anyway. He slumped back on the bed, his voice low as he clued Josh in on what had happened, his little brother listening silently as he described the clusterfuck they'd just been through.

"Oh boy," Josh said. "That sounds like a major fuck up."

"Thanks," Michael said dryly. "You're a real help there."

"What did you expect?" Josh asked him. "Seriously, this was always going to be a mess. I told you that when we talked in Charleston."

"You're not helping."

"I tried. I told you to do something."

"I did. I sold my business. I cut ties with London. We agreed we'd tell our parents this weekend." If he could turn back time, he would. He'd kiss Grace and leave, and her dad never would have caught them.

They'd have let him know gently and things would be different.

"Then you would have dealt with it this weekend."

"No. We would have controlled the narrative."

Josh barked out a laugh. "You'd have what?"

"We would have told them on our terms. And her dad wouldn't have had the image of us doing the dirty in her bedroom seared into his brain."

"Of course he would. And he would have gone apeshit. Anybody would have."

"He would?" Michael frowned.

"Put yourself in his position. Or even better, imagine it was Sabrina doing the dirty with a guy twice her age."

"I'm not twice Grace's age."

"Stop splitting hairs. Imagine Sabrina was with some thirty-six-year-old guy. Our baby sister, still in college. What do you think Dad would do if he found out?"

He knew Josh was referring to Cam. Of all his siblings, Michael was the only one who didn't call him dad.

"He'd kill him."

"And if he didn't *you* would."

The image of his sister flashed through his mind. "She's just a kid."

"And Grace is Daniel's kid," Josh pointed out. "Always will be."

He opened his mouth to reply, but he couldn't think of a damn thing to say. There was a pounding in his head, reminding him he'd just spent hours flying halfway across the world. That it was something stupid o'clock in London and he should be asleep.

"I need to go," he said gruffly.

"Don't do anything stupid, Mike."

"Like what?" he asked. "Fall in love with the one woman I shouldn't?"

"Yeah, like that. But seriously, be careful. I know you like her, but she's still way younger than you. Remember all the shit we went through in our twenties?"

Yeah, he did. But he'd never thought of Grace like that. She was mature. Grounded. Beautiful.

"I'll speak to you later," Michael told his brother.

"Take care of yourself," Josh told him. "Just do that, okay?"

"Yeah. I'll try."

CHAPTER
Twenty-Six

"WHAT'S GOING ON?" Scott asked Grace when she knocked on her parents' front door. She'd spent the last ten minutes in her car at the bottom of their driveway, trying to figure out what the hell she was going to say to them.

And she still had no clue. She just wanted to make this better.

"What do you mean?" She frowned.

"Mom and Dad are having a huge fight in the kitchen. I heard your name mentioned. I tried to butt in, but then they both turned on me."

She let out a long breath. "They're fighting?"

"Like fucking bears."

"Don't swear," she said automatically, the words ingrained from when she was a teenager and Scott was learning all the ways to drive their mom up the wall.

Grace had always been the peacemaker. The one who kept things calm. She knew how to play that role, how to make everybody happy.

But this new role? The one where she ripped everybody apart? She hated it.

"I…" She shook her head. "It's about that guy. The one I told you about."

Scott blinked. "Your mystery man?"

Grace nodded.

"Dad knows who it is?"

"He found us."

Scott looked at her uncomprehendingly.

"Together," she added.

His eyes widened. "Oh, shit." He held the door open, and she stepped inside. Closing it softly, he followed her down the hallway, the echo of their parents' argument filling the air.

"Who is it then?" Scott asked. "Does dad know him? Is it someone from the distillery?"

Reaching the door to the kitchen, she turned around to look at her little brother, and shook her head. "It's Michael."

"Who's Michael?"

She would have laughed if there was any humor left in her body. Even her brother couldn't remember who Michael was.

"Michael Devlin."

Scott frowned. "Like our cousin Michael?" he asked.

"That's him." She nodded. "Mia's son."

Scott's brows raised into his hair line. "Is that even legal?"

"Yes it's legal."

"So why is dad going off about it?"

She pressed her lips together. "Because Michael's still part of the family and he's sixteen years older than me."

"Sixteen? Sheesh. I never realized that. Jesus, he's old. So you and Michael are…" Scott wrinkled his nose. "Scrap that. I don't want to know what you two are doing."

"Probably for the best," Grace muttered. A crash came from the kitchen, followed by the high pitch of their mom's voice. Panicked, she pushed the door open to see her dad standing on the other side of the room, cradling his fist with his other hand, a huge dent in the drywall next to him.

Her parents were on the other side of the huge kitchen that wrapped around the house, and clearly neither of them had heard the door open.

"You happy now?" her mom asked him. "Do you feel better?"

"No." He frowned, lifting his hand up. Uncurling his fingers, he inspected his knuckles. "I think I broke my hand."

"Good." Her mom looked furious. "What were you thinking hitting the wall? You're an old man."

Scott chuckled softly behind Grace.

"You'd rather me hit a person?" her dad asked.

Her mom rolled her eyes. "You wouldn't hit a fly, you idiot. The only person you ever hurt is yourself."

Grace cleared her throat. Her parents both turned at once, her mom pressing her hand to her chest when she saw them standing there.

"Dad?" Grace said. "I'm so sorry."

His face was red. She wasn't sure whether from anger or embarrassment. "It's not your fault," he said gruffly.

Her mom caught her eye. There was sympathy there. "He told me about you and Michael."

"Don't say his name in this house," her dad growled.

"So what? Now we're gonna pretend he doesn't exist?" her mom asked. "Or pretend that he's the big bad wolf that seduced our virginal daughter."

Scott spluttered out another laugh.

"Honey, you don't need to hear this," her mom said to him. "Why don't you go out with some friends?"

"Yeah," Scott agreed hastily, relief washing over his face. "I think I'll do that."

Grace reached for his hand and squeezed it. "Thank you," she mouthed at him.

"Good luck," he mouthed back.

They waited for him to leave, listening as he padded

down the hallway, presumably grabbing his shoes, his wallet, and his keys.

And then he was gone.

Grace turned back to her parents. Her mom was leaning on the kitchen counter, her arms crossed over her chest, her hair pulled back into a messy bun. She'd always been beautiful, the most beautiful woman Grace knew. But right now, she looked furious.

Not at her, though. At her dad. Who was still looking at his hand, frowning.

"How about you go out, too?" her mom said to him. "Get some fresh air. Knock some sense into yourself."

Grace's phone rang. She pulled it out of her pocket to see Michael's name flashed across the screen.

"Is that him?" her dad asked.

"Yes."

"Let me talk to him." He held his good hand out, as though he expected Grace to hand her phone over.

"No!" What the hell had gotten into him? He didn't usually behave like an idiot.

"Grace…"

"Dad, I'm a grown woman. Stop treating me like I'm not."

"She's right," her mom said. "Stop being an idiot."

"You'd be an idiot if you'd seen what I did. The man was half naked. Would you feel the same way if you'd walked in on Scott with a forty-year-old woman?" her dad asked.

Her mom wrinkled her nose. "Why would you ask that?"

"Think about it. This isn't just some guy. It's a grown man. He's older, he's divorced. And Grace… well, she doesn't always make the best decisions."

"Dad!" Fury washed over her. "If you keep talking like this you and I are going to have a problem. Will you just listen to me for a minute? Michael and I are in love."

"He's too old for you."

"No, he isn't." She shook her head. "You are older than

mom." Sure it was only by eight years, not sixteen, but it was still there.

"And when you're your mom's age, he's going to be drawing a pension. You'll be young and beautiful still and he'll be needing his diaper changed." Her dad grimaced.

"Oh, now I've heard it all. Is that what I'll be doing for you in ten years' time?" her mom asked him. "Because let me tell you, keep acting like this and I'll let you stew in your own crap."

Her dad sighed. "It's just not right. And let's not forget that he's family."

"You'll never think anybody is good enough for Grace," her mom said. "He could be the King of England and you'd find something to criticize."

"Christ." Her dad squeezed his eyes shut. "I need to get out of here." He reached for his keys on the counter.

"Good." Her mom nodded. "And don't come back until you're thinking straight."

Her dad stormed out of the house. It was getting to be a habit.

And then it was just her and her mom, staring at each other like they had no idea what just happened.

"Wine?" her mom asked.

"Yes please." Grace collapsed onto a stool. "Make it a big one."

———

Grace wasn't answering her phone. Michael tried five times and every time it went straight to voicemail. He left a quick message asking her to call him back and then walked back down the stairs.

He'd head to her house. And if she wasn't there, he'd head to her parents'. He couldn't stand sitting around here, waiting for something to happen.

He was a man who liked to be in control.

"Everything okay?" his mom asked as he walked into the living room. She was awake and smiling at him. And he wanted to tell her it was all fine. That he hadn't fucked up royally. That he hadn't hurt the people he loved.

Again.

Her eyes were soft as he walked over to hug her, brushing his lips against her cheek that was still warm from her sleep.

"I should ask you that," he said. "How are you?"

"Tired. But everything is looking good. I had an appointment with my doctor today. Next week should be the last one for therapy."

"That's great news." At least that was something. In all this mess, his mom was getting better. After this week, she'd be able to relax more, not sit in a car for hours and get worn out. "I have some news, too."

"You do?"

His throat tightened. He had to tell her. If he didn't, she'd find out another way. "Yeah. Can I just get Cam? I'd like to tell you together."

"Is it bad news?"

He wasn't certain how to answer that. "Not for me," was the best he came up with. "And hopefully not for you, either."

"Now I'm intrigued." She gave him a smile that reminded him of when he was young and the two of them were a team. He'd help with Josh and she'd work her fingers to the bone.

Damn, he loved her. And he hated that he'd caused problems in the family she adored so much.

"Get Cam," she said. "I can't stand the suspense."

The football game was on a break when he walked into the kitchen. Cam was sharpening knives – he loved to cook and his knives were his babies. "Hey, you ready for that beer now?" he asked.

"Can I talk to you first?" Michael said. "I want to tell you both something."

"Okay." Cam shrugged. "Now?"

"It's as good a time as any."

Cam put the knife he was holding back into the huge wooden block and ran his hands under the faucet, drying them on a towel. His phone buzzed and he checked the screen. "Wait up. Looks like we have company."

Michael's stomach dropped. He knew who it would be without even having to look.

"It's Daniel and Becca," Cam said, squinting at his phone. "No, wait, just Daniel."

Of course it was. *Shit.* It was now or never. "I need you to stall him for me."

Cam shot him a confused glance. "Why?"

"Because he knows about me and Grace."

There was a moment of silence. Cam blinked, as though taking in Michael's words. "You and Grace? As in Becca's daughter?"

"Yeah."

"You two..." Two little creases appeared above Cam's nose, like he was trying to work things out. Then he looked at Michael. "Grace? Really?"

"Daniel's not happy about it. And Mom..."

"She doesn't know?" Cam asked.

Michael shook his head. "Not yet. That's what I wanted to tell you both."

"Christ." Cam raked his fingers through his hair, pulling the strands out of his face. "Your mom's not well."

"I know. That's why I wanted to break it gently."

"This isn't fucking gentle, Michael," Cam growled.

Yeah, he knew that. And it was his fault. Daniel knew it. Cam knew it. His mom would know it soon.

"Christ," Cam said again. "What a mess."

Yeah, he'd heard that a lot recently. For a moment, the two

of them just looked at each other. And then Daniel was hammering on the front door.

"I'll deal with him," Michael said.

"It's my door he's breaking down," Cam pointed out. "Talk to your mom. She deserves to hear it from you."

Michael nodded, walking to the door that led to the living room right as Cam walked down the hallway to the front door. His mom looked up expectantly as he sat down beside her on the sofa.

"Is Cam coming?"

"We have company." Michael took a deep breath, trying to center himself because all hell was about to break loose on the woman who deserved it the least. "I'm so sorry. This isn't how I'd planned to share this, but I want you to hear it from me. Mom, I'm in a relationship with Grace."

He didn't feel any better for getting it out there. If anything, he felt worse. Like he was opening the door for the beast to run out.

And just like Cam, she didn't understand.

He could tell that from the way her mouth was open, but no words were coming out. And unlike Cam, she knew who he was talking about right away.

"We didn't mean for it to happen. We met a year ago, and…" He let out a breath. "And we liked each other. Without knowing we were step cousins."

She frowned. "I don't understand. How did you not know you were cousins?"

He didn't bother going into the technicalities of it. "I've been away for so long. The last time I'd been here, she was a kid. And I guess she didn't recognize me either."

"So you two have been in a secret relationship for a year?"

He shook his head. "No. The morning after we met she figured it out, and I didn't hear from her again. I only realized who she was when I came back to town. I saw her at *Chairs* and it all clicked."

"But you got together, anyway?" his mom asked.

"We tried to fight against it, but…"

Her hand felt so frail in his. "But you didn't." Her voice was soft.

The living room door opened. Cam looked flustered. "Michael? Daniel would like to speak with you."

"Daniel is here?" his mom asked.

Cam nodded.

"And Becca? Is she here? Do they know?"

"They know." Cam's voice betrayed no emotion at all.

Michael squeezed his mom's hand and stood, walking over to where Cam was standing. Cam put his hand on Michael's shoulder. "I'll stay with your mom."

"Thank you." Michael nodded and walked through the door to the kitchen. Daniel was standing by the breakfast bar, looking nothing like the cool, easy uncle that Michael remembered. His clothes were crumpled, his hair falling everywhere it shouldn't. But there was a haunted look on his face that made everything else fade into insignificance.

"I've come to ask you to leave her alone," Daniel said. "Before you tear the family apart."

"I can't do that." Michael shook his head. "I love her."

"If you love her, you'd leave her," Daniel said, his voice low. "You know you're no good for her. She's too young for you. And you know this town, everybody will talk. They'll say it's wrong on so many levels. That you're related, that you're taking advantage. They'll whisper behind her back until the life drains out of her."

"I won't let that happen."

"You won't have a choice. And you'll take the shine out of her, the way it disappeared when she had to leave France. Don't do that to her. If you love her, walk away."

Michael swallowed hard. He'd expected anger and fists. Not this ice cold demand. And he had no idea how to handle it. "I won't hurt her," he told Daniel. "I'll protect her. I always will."

"No." Daniel shook his head. "You couldn't even protect her from yourself."

That hit home. There was a truth to it that Michael didn't want to acknowledge. "We couldn't help falling in love."

"Of course you could. Love is a choice, not an impulse. And sometimes love means making the hardest choices. If you don't walk away, I will."

"What?"

"She's my daughter. I love her and Scott more than I've ever loved anything in my life. But I can't watch you ruin her life. You'll never be welcome in my home, ever. You think Grace will be able to deal with that?"

"You'll make her choose?" Michael asked, his voice thick.

"No. You're the one making her choose."

There it was again, that tightness that made him feel like he was suffocating. He inhaled sharply, and it hurt all the more.

"I never want to hurt her," he said again. But the fight in him was fading. He'd hurt women before. More than one.

"But you already have," Daniel told him.

And yeah, he had. She was so upset when Daniel had found them and it had been his fault. He'd hurt Grace and he'd hurt his mom and he'd hurt Lainey. His personal life had never been anything but a shitshow.

And he could tell from Daniel's eyes that the pain was in him, too.

"Daniel?" Mia said softly. Michael turned to see her standing in the doorway. "What's going on?"

Daniel's face softened as soon as he saw her. "I just needed to talk to Michael."

"About Grace?"

That made Daniel wince. "Yeah, about her."

"And is everything okay now?" she asked him. "Is everything all right?"

"I don't know? Is it?" He looked Michael straight in the eye.

Michael nodded. He knew what he had to do.

"Everything's okay then," Daniel said.

"Good." His mom beamed at them both, not understanding what was happening. "I'm so happy to hear that."

CHAPTER
Twenty-Seven

IT WAS ALMOST midnight by the time Grace got back to her house. She'd spent a couple of hours with her mom, talking about Michael and her dad's reaction, and her mom had promised her things would get better.

"I'll talk to him," her mom had promised, and she'd left with a lighter heart. She'd tried to return Michael's call when she got home, but this time he was the one not answering. Instead, she'd tapped out a message to him, telling him to come over whenever he was ready.

Because she didn't want to sleep alone tonight.

She wanted to curl up in his arms. Remind herself why they were putting themselves through this pain. Why he'd gone to London to close up his old life so they could be together.

As soon as she heard the car in her driveway, she relaxed. A smile pulled at her lips as she watched him climb out of the driver's seat and look up at the house. It wavered a little as she saw his expression.

He looked exhausted. He hadn't slept since he left London yesterday. She wanted to bundle him up and carry him to bed.

She probably would've if he didn't weigh sixty pounds more than her.

She opened the door before he knocked, pulling it wide so he could step inside.

But he didn't.

"Hey." He shifted his feet. "Can we talk?"

Her smile fell. "Is everything okay?"

He didn't nod. Just looked at her with those warm, brown eyes. "I just…" He shook his head. "I'm sorry."

Her stomach cramped. "What for?"

"This. All of it. Everything I've put you through. For you having to deal with the aftermath of my bad choices."

"We did this together," she said, not understanding. "This isn't on you."

"Yes it is. I started this. And I need to be the one to clean it up. You've done nothing wrong."

His tone was off. *Everything* was off. "Michael…" She reached for him and he shrugged her off.

It felt like a slap to her face.

And suddenly she knew where this was going. It made her heart hurt. Made everything hurt.

She'd heard this story before. But she'd never expected it from Michael.

"You want to come in?" she asked. He shook his head and that sealed it. He wasn't here to hold her. To make her feel better.

He was here to tear everything apart.

And she couldn't stand it.

"I made the choices, too." She needed him to hear that. Needed him to hear that she wasn't a little kid who didn't know what she was doing. And that's what she felt like now. A child who was getting her head patted.

"I can't do this," he told her. "Not to you."

"Do what?" she asked him. She was so, so tired. But she needed him to say it.

"I can't make you choose between me and your dad."

"My dad? He asked you to do this?" She felt sick. It was happening again. A parent asking their child to choose.

"It's not like that. I don't want to put you through this. It's not fair to you. Watching your family fall apart."

"So what, you're leaving me?" Her voice cracked. Her hands were starting to shake because this was all wrong. They were tangled in her bed only hours ago.

How could he do this to her?

"It's for the best," he said. "For your sake."

"Oh no." She shook her head. "Don't put this on me."

"What?" He blinked.

"Don't blame this on me. I'm not the one saying I can't do this. *You are.* I thought you were better than this."

"You'll thank me for this one day." He swallowed hard. "You're so young and so beautiful. You have your whole life ahead of you."

She wasn't going to cry. Not like this. She was stronger than that.

"Not beautiful enough for you to want to stay."

"Grace…" His voice cracked. "I wish there was another way."

"I would've done anything for you, you know that? Turned my back on my family, if that's what it took. But you won't do the same. And you know what? Maybe it's a good thing I'm finding this out now. Before I got too attached." What a lie. She was already so attached that every word was like a dagger piercing her heart. "So don't bother giving me this crap about it being for my own good when we both know it's for yours." She inhaled sharply. "You promised not to hurt me."

He winced. "And I'm trying to keep that promise. It's for the best. And I know you won't see that now. But one day you will." He ran his thumb over his jaw. "And maybe you'll be thankful you don't have to be with an old guy like me."

"This isn't funny."

"I know that."

They stared at each other, the night air clammy around them. And she felt the shutters come down. Pushing away the thought of his arms around her, of the way his lips would softly brush against hers.

The way he was the only man who ever understood her.

She couldn't think about them because it hurt too much. And she needed to protect herself. If he wasn't going to fight for her, then fine.

She'd fight for herself.

"You need to leave now." Her voice was thick, but there was no emotion there. Just a weariness that sleep couldn't push away.

"I'll always love you," he told her. "Always. And I'll always be here for you."

Her throat tightened. "I don't want your love if it feels like this. I don't need you to be here for me. If you can't fight for me when it matters, then I don't need you at all." She felt the tears rising, but there was no way she was going to let him see them. Instead, she closed the door softly, leaning her head against it as they finally stung against her eyes.

She half expected him to knock. To tell her he was wrong. That he'd changed his mind. But there was nothing. And she was still leaning against the door when she heard the slam of his car door and the roar of his engine.

It was only when it faded away that the tears finally fell.

———

"Are we going to talk about this?" her mom asked the following Saturday, sliding her foot into the stirrup and mounting her horse with ease. "Or are you going to avoid the subject every time his name is brought up?"

"Pretty much," Grace said, leaning forward to pat Arcadia's mane. She'd spent most of the last week here at the farm. Logan had let her be, not asking why she was there instead of at work. She assumed Cam – his twin brother – had gotten to him and told him what had happened.

Not that she really cared. Though she was planning to avoid *Chairs* for a few weeks, like she did last night, just in case the gossip was already rife. It was only a matter of time before the whole town knew that she and Michael had been together and now they were completely apart.

"Dad wanted to come here today," her mom told her. "I told him you'll come to him when you're ready."

"Probably for the best," Grace said, steering Arcadia out of the cobbled stable area and into the fields. She really didn't want to talk to her mom about this. Didn't want to talk to anybody. That's why she'd been holed up with the horses – they didn't ask questions and didn't make judgments.

The first night she'd cried until the sun pierced its way through the curtains. The next few nights she'd lain exhausted on her bed and gone through every moment they'd spent together, looking for clues.

And tonight? She hoped she'd actually get some sleep. Because she couldn't keep going on like this.

She was proud that she hadn't crumbled and called him, not even when he'd messaged a few times to check in. She'd left them unread, not just because she was afraid she'd change her mind and message him back, but because he needed to know she wasn't reading them.

Even if she really wanted to.

"Your dad's really sorry, you know?" her mom said, her horse's hooves clipping against the ground. "He shouldn't have reacted like that. Or interfered."

"It doesn't matter," Grace muttered. It wasn't his fault that Michael walked away. And she wasn't quite numb yet, but she would be. Just as soon as she could see a future without him.

They rode in silence for a while. The sun's rays were caressing their backs as they headed toward the mountains. Grace took a deep breath and tried to push Michael out of her mind, at least for a few minutes. She let her horse take the lead and they rode along the edge of the foothills.

Suddenly, Arcadia stopped dead, his ears pricking forward. Grace looked up and saw something on the ground ahead of them. A snake. A copperhead by the looks of it, with distinctive russet coloring, basking in a pool of early morning sun.

"What's going on?" her mom asked, pulling her horse to a stop next to Arcadia and Grace.

"There's a snake. Arcadia got spooked."

She leaned forward to caress her horse's mane right as the snake uncoiled. The sudden movement made her horse rear up. Grace grasped desperately at the reins, but Arcadia bucked again, throwing her to the ground, her head hitting a rock jutting out from the dry earth.

"Oh my God." Her mom jumped down, holding her own horse with one hand and reaching for Arcadia with the other. Grace blinked, pain throbbing at her temple. She reached up to her head, unsurprised when she saw her fingers coated with blood.

"Honey, are you okay?" her mom asked, her voice urgent.

Grace wasn't sure whether to laugh or cry. "I think so." What an end to a terrible week. "Is Arcadia all right?" she asked, blinking at the brightness of the sun as she looked over at her horse.

"He's fine." Her mom patted his head. "I've got him. You want me to go get help?"

She shook her head. *Ouch.* That was a bad idea. Lifting her t-shirt to the cut from the rock, she wiped away the blood. "How does it look?"

Her mom grimaced. "Like you need some good cleaning

up. You sure you're up to riding back? I can get Logan to bring the ATV over to pick you up."

"I'm sure. I just hit my head, that's all. No big deal."

Her mom pressed her lips together. "It's a big deal to me."

Slowly, Grace rolled onto her feet and stood, her head reeling from the sudden change in position. She touched her cut again – it felt stickier now. She was already clotting, that was good. She walked over to where her mom was holding Arcadia. The horse had calmed, especially since the copperhead had slithered out of sight. Patting her gently, Grace whispered calming words into her horse's ear, then slid her boot into the stirrup and hoisted herself up.

"We'll take it slow," her mom told her.

"Sure." Grace nodded, letting her mom lead the way. The horses were walking this time, not galloping the way Grace preferred, but that was okay.

Because for the first time all week, she hadn't thought about Michael. That was good, wasn't it?

Maybe she'd get over him after all.

CHAPTER
Twenty-Eight

HE'D SPENT the last few days trying – and failing – not to think of her. Which was almost impossible at the best of times, especially when you no longer had a job to distract you. He didn't even have driver duties to distract him since it was the weekend. So he was sitting in the living room, watching some re-run of a reality tv show because he couldn't stand to watch anything that involved emotions.

He should look for a house. A job. Make some kind of plans for the future. But he couldn't find the energy to do anything at all. Which explained why he was sitting in his mom and stepdad's house on a Saturday evening when he was in his forties and should be anywhere fucking else.

With her.

"Hey." Cam sat down on the chair opposite him, scowling, and Michael knew there was only one reason for that scowl. Michael's mom had sent him to have a 'talk.' Which was pretty funny because Michael was almost middle-aged and Cam definitely was.

Or at least it would be funny if it wasn't so sad.

"Hi." Michael picked the remote up and shut off the tv. No

point in doing this to the soundtrack of New Yorkers screaming at each other.

"Your mom…" Cam trailed off, running his fingers through his hair. "Well, I… yeah. How are you doing?"

"I'm good."

"Uh huh."

There was silence. The two grown men looked at each other, and it felt like there was understanding there. Neither of them was exactly excited about having this conversation.

"You want to tell her you tried, and I wasn't forthcoming?" Michael asked.

Relief flooded Cam's face. "Yeah, I'd like that a lot."

Yeah, that's what he'd like, too. To be left alone. "I'll be okay," he reassured his stepdad. On Monday I'll look for somewhere to live. And then I'll work out what I want to do with my life."

"You're still going to stay around here, right?" Cam asked. "I know your mom's treatment has finished but there's no need to up and leave."

"For a while." Until his mom was feeling completely right, at least. He wasn't sure he could stand to live in this small town after that. Not when *she* was here.

Not when he knew he'd broken her heart.

"Okay." Cam nodded again. "You hear about her accident?"

"Mom's?" Michael frowned.

Cam grinned. "Nah, I meant Grace. She fell off her horse."

It was like somebody had hit him in the chest. The air rushed out of him. "What? Is she okay? What happened?"

"There was a lot of blood, according to Logan. He wanted to take her to the doc to get her checked out, but she refused."

Michael stood without thinking. Started pacing the room. "Logan should have made her. Where is she now? Is somebody with her?"

"I don't know." Cam gave him a strange look. "I didn't ask. I was just making conversation."

"Somebody should know. She might be hurt." Pulling his phone from his pocket, Michael pulled up her contact, pressing the little phone symbol next to her name. He needed to talk to her. Needed to make sure she was okay. He felt sick at the thought of her being in pain.

It rang twelve times before he accepted she wasn't picking up. It didn't go to voicemail either. So he tapped a message out, asking her to call him when she got the chance.

"She's not answering," he said, more to himself than to Cam.

"Are you surprised?" Cam asked him. "Didn't you break it off with her?"

"Yeah. But…" He blew out a mouthful of air. "Doesn't mean I don't care."

"You think she knows that?"

"Where's Mom?" Michael asked, ignoring Cam's question.

"In the kitchen."

Michael nodded and strode toward the kitchen door, pushing it open to find his mom sitting at the breakfast bar, a book in her hand.

She looked up and smiled at him. "You moved off the sofa."

"Yeah. Ah, look. Did you know about Grace's accident?"

His mom nodded. "I think it looked worse than it was. Becca said there was blood everywhere."

"Becca was with her?" Michael asked. At least that was something.

His mom nodded.

"And is she with her now?"

It was his mom's turn to give him a strange look. "I've no idea."

He leaned on the table, catching her eye. "Can you call her and ask?"

Tipping her head to the side, his mom frowned at him. "Why would I do that?"

"Because Grace isn't answering my calls. I need to know that she's okay."

His mom pulled her lip between her teeth like she was trying to decide how to respond.

Then Sabrina walked through the back door. "Hi," she called out, warm air rushing in behind her. "What's going on?"

"Grace got hurt. I want to make sure she's doing all right." He turned his attention to Sabrina. "Can you call her?"

"She's fine. I saw her a while ago." Sabrina looked unperturbed.

"How bad is she hurt? Does she have a concussion? Is somebody with her?"

Sabrina looked like she was trying not to laugh at the volley of questions. "What's it got to do with you?"

He opened his mouth, then closed it again. She was right. What did it have to do with him?

He was supposed to not care, right? Supposed to walk away emotionless because he ended things. But damn it, he needed to know she was okay.

"If you're that worried, why don't you ask her at church tomorrow?" Sabrina asked, smiling because she knew he wouldn't go.

"She's going to church?"

"Duh." Sabrina rolled her eyes. "Of course. Delilah's singing in the choir. We're all going."

"Okay." He nodded. "I'll go to church."

His mom narrowed her eyes. "You never go to church."

He shrugged. "Maybe I've changed my mind."

Sabrina crossed her arms over her chest. Her expression could only be described as sassy. "Don't you say anything to hurt her. You've already hurt her enough."

His mom tried to stifle a snigger. And failed miserably.

"I don't expect you to understand why I did what I did," he told her. "But there were good reasons."

"Like what? You're a jerk?" Sabrina asked.

"Honey, don't say that." Their mom frowned at her.

"Well he is. He hurt her. Told her he didn't want to be part of her life. And now he's being all concerned ex and it just isn't right. He doesn't get to be the good guy when he's the asshole."

"Sabrina!" Their mom's voice rose an octave.

"Whatever." She stomped over to the refrigerator, pulling it open and grabbing a soda. "I'm going up to my room. I guess I'll see you at church."

"I guess you will." Michael lifted a brow at her.

"I'll believe it when I see it." She popped the key of her can and lifted it to her mouth. "And if you say anything to hurt her there, I'll join the line of people waiting to slap some sense into you."

"I won't say anything to hurt her."

Sabrina huffed. "Whatever. I'm going to watch a movie in bed. Night, Mom."

Their mom smiled softly. "Night, honey."

His little sister turned her gaze to Michael. "Night, idiot."

He shook his head at her. One day, when she was older, she'd understand. That he was doing the right thing. Not making her choose between him and her family because he knew it would break her.

The same way it had almost broken his mom.

"I guess I'll head up, too," he said, even though it was barely eight o'clock. He'd watch that stupid reality show on his laptop. Or just sleep. Whatever. Though he'd probably just stew about Grace's injury.

And that's why he'd go to church tomorrow, even if it meant facing everybody that was angry with him.

To check for himself that she was okay. Then maybe he'd finally find some peace in his life.

———

Grace had done her best to hide the gash on her temple, but even with her hair down there was no covering up the bandage she'd put on it this morning, replacing last night's attempt at covering up the sticky sutures.

When she and her mom had gotten back to the farmhouse, her mom was freaking out at the blood still streaming down Grace's face. Even when she pointed out that it was mixed with perspiration, she still hadn't calmed down.

In the end, Logan had taken her into the farmhouse and helped clean her up, patiently sticking sutures onto her skin, while murmuring to Becca to chill the hell out before she worked herself into a frenzy.

And then she'd faced the second battle, when her mom wanted Grace to go home with her, so she could keep an eye on her in case of concussion.

But Grace still hadn't talked to her dad yet. And there was no way she wanted to spend the night in the house with him. So she'd stubbornly refused and driven herself home despite her mom's protests, promising she'd see her at church.

That was one reason she was sitting in their family pew right now. The other reason was Delilah. Presley's little girl was making her debut in the church choir, and the whole family had turned up to support her. She looked angelic in a white dress, her hair pulled back into a French braid Grace knew for certain Presley hadn't done. That man could play a guitar like an artist, but he knew nothing about hair.

Still, seeing her cousin's little girl look so happy at the corner of the church warmed Grace's heart.

She was glad she came, even if she knew the whole family was muttering about her.

The Hartson family – and extended members – took up most of the five front pews.

More than one of them was shooting her an interested look right now.

So the story was out. They knew about her and Michael. She caught her cousin Marley's eye, and he smiled at her, sympathy softening his features.

Yeah, they knew but they also loved her. Somehow that felt warming.

More people were still coming into church, even though it was only a few seconds until the service was about to start. Any minute now Reverend Maitland would come out and they'd all stand up. Not that they'd have to do it quickly. The old reverend walked like a snail nowadays.

"Oh," her mom whispered. Then she took Grace's hand in her own. The sound of chatter behind her increased and Grace turned around, frowning to see what the issue was.

And that's when she saw *him*. Looking devastating in a dark suit and tie. Freshly shaven, his hair short and neat, his face impassive as he stood at the back of the church.

It hurt to even look at him. But she wasn't going to show it. Not when everybody was watching them like a hawk.

There was no way she'd give him the satisfaction of thinking that she was upset by him being here. Even if he never came to church before.

Jutting her chin out, she watched as he followed his mom and Cam down the aisle of the church. Sabrina was behind him, and when she looked at Grace, she rolled her eyes.

That was so Sabrina.

It was only when he was closer that she finally let her gaze rest on Michael. From here she could see the dark circles beneath his eyes. And there was a small cut on his lip, like he'd cut it shaving.

That gave her a grim sense of satisfaction.

Lifting her gaze, her eyes met his. A jolt of electricity rushed through her. His expression didn't betray a thing. His jaw was tight and his mouth thin as he glanced at her temple.

Then she saw the twitch. Was he annoyed at her for not returning his call? Good.

The organ started and then the choir sang and she was so relieved at not having to look at him anymore. She'd been an idiot to think she was getting over him.

Because his rejection hurt more than any cut could. And she wasn't sure how to make it stop.

———

"You okay?" Presley murmured to her as they walked out of the church.

"I'm fine." She smiled at him, even though it took some effort. "Delilah was fabulous. I guess good voices run in your family."

"And in yours," he pointed out. "You're family, too."

That made her think of the night she and Michael sang karaoke and then laughed until dawn in Charleston.

Her chest tightened.

There was a thick feeling in the air as they walked down the steps. Though the sun was beating down, there were dark clouds in the distance, and the thought of a storm coming almost felt like a relief. Everybody was milling about in the lawn in front of the church, talking like they hadn't just seen each other at *Chairs* two days ago, or at church the previous week.

It always amazed her how much the townsfolk of Hartson's Creek had to say.

"Grace."

Her heart skipped a beat at his voice. She took a deep breath and looked up at him. "Michael."

"How are you?"

"I'm fine." She kept her voice icily polite. "And you?"

"I heard about your accident. I tried to call."

"I saw." She wasn't going to lie. Not to him.

"Why didn't you pick up?"

"Because I didn't want to talk to you," she told him. He winced at her words and it felt almost satisfying.

"I just needed to know you were okay."

Was he being serious right now? Her eyes widened because yes, he looked deadly serious.

"You lost the right to know that," she told him. "Or anything about me."

"Don't be childish," he said. "I still care about you."

He was calling her childish? Seriously? She wasn't sure whether to laugh or cry.

Luckily the anger washed over her. "You think I'm behaving like a child?" she asked him, her voice low. She looked over to see Presley watching them, and he inclined his head as though he were asking if she needed help.

She shook her head. She was a big girl, even if Michael called her otherwise. She could eat him for breakfast if she wanted.

"I didn't mean it like that," Michael told her. "I just wanted to check on you."

"That's funny, because that's how it sounded. And it's weird, too," she told him. "Because I'm not the one running away like a scared little boy. Not the one who walked away at the first sign of trouble. If anybody's acting like a kid around here, Michael, it's you."

He winced again. *Good*. She wasn't here to make things easy for him. Sure, she cared about him. Okay, she was still stupidly in love with him. But he was the one who caused this devastation, so he had nobody to blame but himself.

"Can't we be friends?" he asked.

She shook her head. Part of her wanted to say yes. To cling on to anything he offered. To fill the hole he'd created by walking away. But she was too proud for that, even if she wanted to cry right now. "I have a lot of friends. I'm selective about them." She took a deep breath. "In fact, we're heading to the diner now." And I really hope you're not coming. "I guess I'll see you around."

She didn't wait for an answer. Just turned and walked over to where Presley and Marley were standing with Delilah. And with her back to Michael, she finally let out a breath.

"All right?" Marley murmured, out of Delilah's earshot.

"No." Grace tried to stem the tears that were threatening to flow. "Can we get out of here?"

"Sure." Marley flung his arm around her shoulder and pulled her close. "Want me to beat him up?"

"No. I just want to forget he exists."

Marley chuckled. "I can't help you with that, but I can buy you your body weight in pancakes and syrup."

She nodded. "That sounds good."

He squeezed her shoulder. "Come on then. Let's go."

CHAPTER
Twenty-Nine

"HERE YOU GO," Josh said, popping the lids off two bottles of beer and handing one to Michael.

"Thanks." Michael lifted it to his lips, taking a long, cool sip. He'd come home from the mess at church to find his brother sitting in the living room, waiting for him. His mom must have called him, disappointed that Cam had gotten nowhere the other day.

His kid brother had a determined look on his face, the same one he used to have when they played ball together. That he wanted to be as good as Michael. His equal.

"Okay then, let's do this," Michael said. "Want to just shout at me?" He was tired of fighting his family. They were the only ones talking to him now.

"Nope. I want to listen to you," Josh said. "Let you do some talking for once."

"There's not much to say." Michael shrugged. Josh knew he and Grace had split up. Knew that it was Michael's choice. The only thing he didn't know was about today. "I tried to talk to her at church, but Grace doesn't want to know me anymore. Doesn't want to be friends."

"Can you blame her? You broke her heart."

Michael's gut twisted. "But I did it for a good reason."

"What reason was that?"

Michael let out a long breath. Surely their mom had filled Josh in on that. "Her dad wanted her to choose between us. And I wouldn't let her do that."

"Because you were scared she'd choose him?" Josh frowned, as though he didn't understand.

"No." Michael shook his head. "Because I asked Mom to choose between Cam and me all those years ago and we saw what it did to her. She cried for a fucking week, if you remember. And I was the one who did that to her. I can't do it to Grace as well."

Josh blinked, not speaking. He lifted his beer to his lips and swallowed a mouthful.

Christ, Michael was tired of this. Of being the asshole. It didn't matter what he did or what he didn't do. He always ended up in the same place.

The bottom rung.

"We were just kids," Josh finally said. "I understood why you did what you did."

He met his brother's gaze.

"And Cam always maintains it was his fault. He's the one who walked away when you demanded it. He said he should have stayed and fought for her."

Michael blinked. "He said that?"

"Yeah. Don't you remember?"

Michael shook his head. He remembered little about that time. Maybe because he didn't want to. It was a mess, and he was no better.

"Cam said she cried because he walked away, not because you asked her to choose. You would have gotten used to him if he'd stayed, wouldn't you?"

"I guess…"

"Did you two never talk about this?"

"I don't know. We tried, but you know how things were

like back then. I was a punk and Cam was walking on eggshells around me."

Somebody cleared their throat. Cam walked into the living room. "I should have talked to you," he said.

Michael got the feeling he was being ambushed. But in a loving way.

Cam gave him the smallest of smiles. "When I walked away, I was thinking of me. Of how I couldn't be in the same town as your mom without breaking down. But I didn't think of her. If I had, I would never have walked away."

Michael's stomach twisted. "I don't get this."

"We should have talked about it back then," Cam told him. "But things got better between us. And then you left for college and then London. It felt too late, but it never was."

And he'd left for London after his injury because he never felt he was good enough. Michael loosened his tie, wrapping it around his hand. "I thought you were all better off without me."

"We're always better when you're here," Josh said. "I don't know if you noticed, but Mom's over the damn moon you came back. All of us, we feel complete when you're here."

Michael looked at Cam. He was nodding.

Fuck, his eyes were stinging. He couldn't remember the last time they had. When he was a kid? He knew for sure he'd never cried as an adult.

Mostly because he'd learned to block his emotions.

"And Daniel telling you she needed to choose was an asshole move," Cam said. "But I'm pretty sure he knows that by now. Give it a few more days and he'll be on his knees begging her to talk to him. And he should because that woman deserves so much more than she's been given."

His mouth felt as dry as the desert. "Grace isn't talking to Daniel either?"

Cam shrugged. "That's what I've heard. But it doesn't

matter about him. What matters is you and Grace. Do you love her?"

Michael nodded. "So much."

"Then why the hell are you walking away?" Josh asked.

He opened his mouth to answer, but all the words were stuck. He'd thought he was doing the right thing. Sacrificing his own happiness for Grace's.

But he wasn't. He was being an idiot. Walking away the same way Cam had.

"Fuck." He dropped his face into his hands.

Josh chuckled. "Yeah. So now what are you going to do about it?"

He closed his eyes for a moment, but all he could see was her. The way she'd looked the day they'd met, soaked by the rainstorm, her eyes fiery as they argued over a cab.

And then that night, the way she'd felt so soft in his arms, yet she'd always been the strong one. Until he'd told her it was over and he walked away.

He'd broken the one thing that made sense in his life.

People would talk. He knew that. But they would have moved on just as soon as a new topic came along. He should have been man enough to ride out the wave. To protect her from it. To face their families and tell them they could hurt him all they wanted, but he loved her and would never let anybody cause her pain.

Instead, *he'd* caused her pain. And then she'd hurt herself yesterday and he wasn't there to help. That's what got him most of all. He wanted to be the one she called when she fell off her horse. Or won a contract at work. The one she turned to with a smile when somebody said something stupid.

"Fuck," he said again, because he had no idea how to make this better.

All he knew was it was time to fight. For her. For him. For the future.

And the person he needed to fight hardest against was himself.

————

The diner was full to bursting, every seat, booth, and stool taken up by a member of the Hartson family or their friends. And in the center of it all was Delilah. She'd changed out of the little dress she'd worn to sing in the choir, mostly because she was almost certain to get ketchup on it, and was wearing a pair of shorts and a t-shirt with a unicorn printed across the front.

She was talking excitedly to Cassie, sitting next to her on a stool, and Cassie was nodding with a smile at whatever Delilah was saying.

Grace's mom was sitting with her aunts, all of whom were fussing around Mia, who looked like she wasn't enjoying being the center of attention. As though she knew Grace was watching her, Mia turned around and caught her eye.

She gave her a soft smile that reminded Grace so much of Michael that it hurt. The same eyes, the same crinkles beside them.

Somehow, she managed to smile back.

And yeah, it wasn't real yet. But it would be. She'd make sure of that. She'd gotten over heartbreak before, even though it had never felt physically painful like this.

Surely she could do it again.

"I think I'm going to head home," she murmured to Presley, pushing her half-eaten plate of pancakes away.

He shot her a concerned look. "You okay? Is your head hurting?"

She touched the bandage. She'd forgotten it was even there. "I'm just tired." That was the truth. She hadn't gotten a lot of sleep this week. "Thank you for letting me watch Delilah make her debut. You must be proud of her."

He nodded, his gaze landing on his daughter. "I am."

"And Marianne would be too."

Presley swallowed. "Yeah. She would."

Squeezing her cousin's shoulder, she stood and flicked some bills on the table. Enough to cover five meals rather than just her one, but she knew how these things went. There was no way Presley should have to fork out for their family's enormous appetite.

She didn't go over to say goodbye to her mom, mostly because she wasn't ready for the inquisition. She'd send her a text once she was home. Instead, she smiled at her family and friends as she wove her way through the tables and finally made it out of the door.

Her head was still too full from her conversation with Michael to really look at where she was going. And she walked straight into her dad, who gave a little oof.

"Hey sweetheart. Can we talk?"

She lifted a brow. She hadn't seen him since last week's epic clusterfuck. He'd sent messages and tried to call, but she hadn't been ready. Not when he was as much to blame for this as Michael.

Well, almost.

"I was just heading home," she told him.

"Did it get to be a bit much in there?" he asked, nodding at the diner.

"Something like that."

His face softened. And she tried to harden her heart because she really was angry with him. But it wouldn't listen.

"Grace, I'm so sorry that I hurt you. Those things I said, the way I reacted." He grimaced, gritting his teeth together. "It was so, so wrong of me."

"Yes, it was." Her voice was thin. "You hurt me," she told him.

This time, there was pain in his eyes. "I know. And I hate

myself for it. I wish I'd walked away and taken a breath. But the red mist descended, and I acted like a fool."

"You treated me like a kid. I'm a grown woman, I deserve to be treated like that."

He blew out a long breath. "I know. I'm a damn idiot for interfering where I'm not wanted." He caught her eye. "I know you love him."

"Loved," she corrected. "We aren't together anymore."

His mouth twitched. "Yeah, and I also know you can't turn love on and off like a faucet. You love too hard for that."

Yes, she did. Loved so hard it hurt. "I'm still turning, but it'll go off eventually."

"Maybe it won't," he said. "Maybe he's the one. I know I'd never stop loving your mom even if she walked away for years."

Yeah, and that's what she was afraid of. That this time she wouldn't get over it. "That's not exactly a comforting thought."

He reached out, his hand hanging in the air while he waited for her reaction. And she knew he was asking a silent question.

Did she forgive him? Could she?

She'd never been one to hold a grudge. People made mistakes. They did stupid things. And her dad had done the ultimate.

But he was still her father. She still loved him. And she knew he loved her.

She took his hand in hers and his face crumpled before he pulled her close, her face resting on his chest, his arms enveloping her like they had when she was a child.

"I'm so sorry," he whispered. "So sorry.

"I know," she murmured against his chest. "I'll get over it."

"You shouldn't have to. Nobody should treat you like this. Least of all your father."

She lifted her head up, her eyes shining. His were too. "I'll expect you to grovel for the next month."

He smiled. "Done." Then his face turned serious again. "You and Michael…"

"Are over. I wasn't lying about that."

"Is that what you want?"

She swallowed hard. "It doesn't matter what I want. He made that decision, not me."

"I could talk to him…"

"No." That was the last thing she wanted. "Please don't."

"He left you because of me."

She took a deep breath, her chest aching with the movement. "He left because of his own stupid reasons. Because he wasn't willing to fight for me. Maybe he didn't think I was worth all the problems this caused."

He cupped her cheek. "You're worth everything."

The ghost of a smile passed her lips. "Thank you." And yeah, she was trying to think that too.

"Thank *you*," he said. "For listening to me. For letting me apologize."

"Don't do it again."

He smiled. "I won't."

She stepped back from their embrace, shading her eyes from the midday sun. "I'm going to head home now."

"Want me to walk you to your car?"

"It's okay. I've got it." She pulled her keys from her purse. "I guess I'll see you at work tomorrow."

"Only if you're feeling better." He looked at her temple and she almost laughed, because she'd forgotten about her cut again.

It would heal. Probably in a few days. She had young skin, and she was resilient.

"I'll be fine." She nodded and walked over to her car, pressing the button on her keys to unlock it.

It was only when she climbed inside that she realized she

was facing the area where she and Michael had spoken only hours earlier.

Where she'd told him she didn't want to be his friend. That she was selective about who she hung around with.

And the memory of his expression hurt more than any gash on her head ever could.

She'd hurt him in return. And it only made her feel worse.

CHAPTER
Thirty

MICHAEL PULLED up outside the house and waited for a moment, his gaze hazing over as he remembered the last time they spoke.

But he needed to do this. It was the first step. The move forward. Time to stop feeling sorry for himself and attempt to make everything better.

When he knocked on the door, she opened it almost right away, her eyes betraying no surprise that he was standing on her doorstep.

"Aunt Becca," he said, his voice firm. "I'm here to talk to you and Daniel."

She stepped to one side, giving him a rueful smile. "Then you'd better come in."

Daniel must have heard his voice, because he was standing in the hallway when Michael walked in. There was no anger in his expression like the last time they spoke. He, too, gave Michael a smile.

"I'm glad you came. I wanted to talk to you but…" He shrugged. "Grace asked me not to."

The mention of her name made Michael's chest contract. "How is she?"

"Her head is getting better," Becca said. "Her heart is still a work in progress."

He nodded, knowing that it was his fault. "I'm in love with her."

Becca laughed. "I would hope so. She's easy to love."

"Yeah, she is. And I wanted to tell you before I tell her. Not because I'm looking for your blessing, but because you need to know that this is all my fault."

"I think I can take some of the blame," Daniel said, pressing his lips together.

"Yes you can." Becca put her arm around Daniel's waist. "I should have just smashed your heads together. So why are you still here? Why aren't you going to Grace's already?"

"I don't like loose ends. And this felt like one." He looked at Daniel. "I understand why you were upset. But I need you to know that your opinion shouldn't have mattered to me. I should have ignored you. Fought for her."

"And I shouldn't have asked you to walk away."

Becca rolled her eyes. "No, you shouldn't have. You're both idiots who seem to have forgotten that Grace is old enough to make her own decisions."

Ouch. That hurt. But it was true. "I hate that I hurt her," he told them. "I'm trying to work out how I can make it right."

"Then go do what you need to." Daniel held his hand out and Michael took it, folding his fingers around Daniel's strong knuckles. "I know you don't want my blessing, but you have it anyway."

"Thank you." Michael nodded, releasing their handshake. "That means a lot."

He turned and made his way back outside, hearing the front door click behind him, and let out the long breath he'd been holding.

The first step was done. There were so many more to come. But at least he was moving forward.

And it felt good.

———

Grace spent the afternoon tidying her house, even though there really wasn't anything out of place. Moving photographs from one table to another, pulling out clothes in her closet that she hadn't worn in more than a year, though the one piece of clothing she should have thrown away she couldn't bring herself to.

She'd stolen Michael's t-shirt from him when he'd gone to London to close up his business, claiming she wanted something of his to keep her warm at night. She hadn't worn it, just cuddled up to it, the soft overwashed cotton pressed against her cheek. Like a child who needed to be comforted with a lovie.

And when she found it in her drawer, she had every intention of throwing it away. She'd crumpled it in her hand and stomped down to her kitchen, opening the trash can. But instead of dropping it in, she'd lifted it to her face and inhaled.

The smell of him had overwhelmed her. A mixture of laundry soap and Michael, it was an intoxicating combination.

She should be better at this by now. Maybe she needed to harden her heart. Be the ice queen. The thought of it made her want to laugh, because if there was anything she wasn't, it was icy.

She didn't have it in her.

Putting his t-shirt on the kitchen counter – because let's face it, she was taking it back upstairs – Grace walked into her living room and slumped down on the chair.

Had she been wrong to tell him they couldn't be friends? For a moment, she tried to imagine it. Waving hi to him at *Chairs*, nodding to him when they filed into church. Sending him a message about a bad day she was having and him commiserating but never holding her.

No, she couldn't do it. As much as she missed him, she couldn't settle for the friend zone. Couldn't watch him date other women. The thought of it was like a knife to her heart.

Ugh, she couldn't sit still. It gave her mind too much space to think dark thoughts. Her bedroom closet was rearranged, the kitchen was sparkling, and there was no more laundry to do.

Her brows lifted. She'd do some yard work. Sure, it was almost evening, and her yard was mostly deck and paving, but she could find some weeds if she looked hard enough. It'd give her satisfaction to yank them out. Pushing up from her chair, she rolled her shoulders and started walking to the kitchen.

And she didn't stomp this time. That was progress, wasn't it?

The shrill ring of her doorbell stopped her in her tracks. She turned and walked to the front door, pulling it open to see Michael standing there.

And her stupid heart did a loop-de-damn-loop.

He was still wearing the clothes she'd seen him in at church, though his tie was gone and his top two shirt buttons were unfastened, revealing the slightest smattering of chest hair. The hair on his head was mussed, like he'd run his hands through it too many times.

It reminded her of all the times she'd mussed it up in bed.

"Can we talk?" he asked, his dark eyes capturing hers.

Grace swallowed. "I thought we already said everything we needed to. I told you, I don't want to be friends."

He didn't move an inch. "I don't want to be your friend."

And damn if that didn't hurt. She wouldn't flinch, though, not this time. "Good." She went to close the door, but he put his foot in the way.

"Please," he asked, his voice soft. "Just two minutes of your time."

"You're not coming in."

"I don't want to. I can say it all right here on your doorstep." He ran his tongue along his bottom lip and she didn't follow it with her eyes at all.

Okay, she did. But hell, what else was she supposed to look at? The dip in his throat where it met his chest?

"You want to put on a timer?" he asked, a smile ghosting his lips.

"This isn't funny," she told him, because it wasn't. It was sad. Because all the love she felt for him wouldn't vanish, no matter how much she wanted it to.

His smile disappeared. "I know. None of this is funny. And it's all my fault."

She said nothing. But damn right it was.

"So maybe I can try to explain. And apologize."

She let out a short breath. "For what? Why? Haven't we done this enough? Haven't you hurt me enough already?"

He winced. "Yes. Too much. Way too much. And I can't tell you how much I hate that."

A wave of exhaustion washed over her. Being hard-hearted had taken it out of her. She wasn't sure how much longer she could keep it up. "Okay, then go. Two minutes."

He nodded, running his hands through his hair. "I was wrong, so wrong, not to fight for you. I thought I was doing a good thing in walking away. Making sure you didn't have to choose between me and your family—"

"I didn't ask you to do that," she interjected.

"I know. And when I finally got my head out of my ass, I realized that. I took away your choice because I thought I knew best." He tipped his head to the side, his brows crunched tight together. "But I didn't. I made the wrong decision. I should never have walked away."

"But you did."

"Yeah, I did. Sweetheart, I'm so sorry for hurting you."

"I'm not your sweetheart."

He winced again. "I know. But I want you to be."

Grace felt her throat tighten. "I can't. I can't let you do this to me again. It hurt too much." She let out a mouthful of air. "I have things to do. You can go now."

"What things?"

She straightened her shoulders. "Yard work."

"It's getting dark."

"And cool. The best time to do it."

He reached out for her hand. And her stupid treacherous fingers curled around his. The mere touch of his skin was enough to send a bolt of need through her.

"Grace," he said softly. "Let me show you how much I care for you."

"I can't…" Her eyes filled with tears. "It's too much."

He nodded, his gaze soft on hers. "I get it. I do. I understand the pain. Let me help you get over it. Just give me a chance. Two weeks. If you still feel the same after that, tell me."

"What will you do for two weeks?"

He smiled. "I'll fight."

She hadn't realized how much she needed to hear that until her whole body flushed at his words. He wanted to fight for her. Nobody had done that before. They'd used her. Discarded her. Run away at the first sign of problems.

He'd done that, too. And it had hurt the most of all.

But he was here now. Standing in front of her, his eyes shining and true. She wanted to believe him. But she couldn't.

What she could do was give him two weeks.

"Your two minutes are up," she told him.

"Okay." He nodded. "I'll go." He slid his hand away from hers and it immediately hurt. "Thank you for listening to me." He glanced at her temple. "Does it hurt?"

"My head? No." She attempted a smile.

"Good." He nodded. "By the way, you look beautiful. You always do, but today you look… amazing."

She was wearing yoga pants and an old t-shirt. And yet

his voice sounded true. "You can fight," she said, her voice thin.

His eyes lit up. "Thank you."

"I can't promise you'll win."

"That's not the point of a fight," he told her. "You don't know if you'll win or lose, but you do it, anyway. Because the thing you're fighting for is so precious. It's worth fighting for."

She nodded and curled her fingers around the door. If she wasn't careful, she'd drag him inside. And she couldn't do that and stay true to herself. Not after everything that had happened.

Instead, she gave him the softest of smiles and slowly closed the door.

"I hope you win," she whispered.

"I hope I do too."

CHAPTER
Thirty~One

THE GIFTS STARTED COMING the next day. A loud knock on the front door woke her up and when she got downstairs, there was a surly teenager on her doorstep.

He was holding a cardboard coffee cup and a bag. "Delivery from the diner. Coffee and pastries."

"I didn't know you did deliveries," she said, smiling because the coffee smelled so good it was making her stomach dance with delight.

"We don't," he muttered. "But the guy paid triple and my boss made me do it."

"Well thank you." She took the delivery from him and smiled wider when she saw Michael's name written on the cup. "I appreciate it."

When she got into work, she sent Michael a quick message to say thank you. His reply came back less than a minute later.

This isn't me fighting yet. I'm just warming up. Have a good day. – Michael x

. . .

At lunchtime she was in her office, working on a marketing plan for the international blend that G. Scott Carter Whiskey was famous for when she heard a tap on the door. Not looking up from her laptop, she called for whoever it was to come in, only to smell the delicious aroma of food wafting into her office.

"Miss Carter?" a voice asked.

She looked up to see one of the servers from her Uncle Logan's restaurant walk in. "May I set up your room?" he asked her.

"For what?" she questioned.

He didn't answer. Just put the tray he'd been carrying down and pulled his backpack off, taking out a white tablecloth, which he spread out on the empty corner of her desk.

"I'll move my laptop," she said hastily, pulling it away to give him more room. He laid out silverware, then placed a white porcelain plate between the knife and fork before grabbing the tray of food and slowly portioning it out.

"Grace Carter?" another voice asked.

"Um, yes." She was still half-watching the server lay out the food on her desk. Ravioli in a light foaming sauce. There was a smaller plate of salad to the side.

"I have flowers for you." The woman carried them in, placing a huge bouquet on the white tablecloth.

"Thank you," Grace murmured. "I have some money somewhere for a tip."

"Don't worry, everything has been taken care of." The florist winked at her. "Your guy is the best. You're a lucky woman."

Her guy. Weird how much she liked the sound of that.

"Please enjoy," the server said. "Your lunch is served."

"What's going on here?" her mom walked in. "Hey Darren," she said to the server. "Is that from Logan's place?"

"Yep. Got the order in an hour ago."

Grace's mom lifted a brow. "I can guess who gave the order."

"My lips are sealed." Darren placed a bowl on the table-cloth. "This is your dessert. Black chocolate mousse with a cherry compote."

"Thank you," Grace said. "Has Michael tipped you, too?"

"Very well." Darren smiled. "Enjoy your meal."

He left with the florist, and Grace looked at her mom from her chair. "So this is happening."

Her mom grinned. "Michael came to see me and your dad last night."

"He did? Why?" Grace lifted a ravioli to her mouth with her fork. Damn, it was good.

"Because he wanted us to know he was wrong. And that he planned to fight for you."

"Oh." Grace swallowed the pasta. "What did Dad say?"

"That Michael had his blessing. Not that he needed it. I don't think anybody could change his mind." Her mom looked at Grace's desk and sighed. "That's so romantic."

"Yes, it is." Grace nodded. He was fighting a good fight.

"I'll leave you to it." Her mom winked. "Enjoy."

Once her mom was gone and Grace had finished the pasta and salad, she lifted her phone up and sent Michael a message.

This can't still be a warmup. And thank you – lunch was delicious. – Grace

Just pulling on my gloves. Getting ready for the first round. Working my way up to the knockout. – Michael x

. . .

She didn't ask who was getting knocked out, her or him. Instead, she spooned the mousse into her mouth, groaning at the sweet delicious taste of the chocolate mixing with the cherries.

It was hard to work that afternoon. She kept waiting for somebody else to knock on her door, carrying a sweet tea or an afternoon snack. It was a good thing they didn't. She wasn't sure she could fit anything else in her after that lunch.

On the way home from work, she stopped in at the farm to check on Arcadia. After her fall last weekend, she'd given him as much love as she could daily. It was almost five when she pulled up into the dirt-and-gravel parking area, and her brows knitted as she saw a familiar car pull out and drive past her.

What was Michael doing here?

Uncle Logan was walking out of the stables as she crossed the yard. "Hey, how's the head?"

"Much better, thanks." She only had a Band-Aid over it now. Hopefully, she'd be able to keep it uncovered later in the week. "Was that Michael I just saw leaving?"

Logan smirked. "Yep."

"What was he doing here?"

Logan tapped his nose. "Can't tell you. Sorry."

"Was he ordering me some more food?" She really wanted to know. Damn her curiosity. It was always getting the better of her.

"Nope. Something else." Logan grinned. "And it's funny as hell."

She rolled her eyes at him. "If I beg, will you tell me? You've always been my favorite uncle."

He chuckled at her lame attempt at flattery. "Nope. You gotta be patient and wait for the big reveal."

As soon as she walked into the paddock, Arcadia ran over to her, nuzzling against her as she patted his mane. "Hey sweetie. Did you see Michael? Want to tell me what he's up to?"

Arcadia whinnied and she wished he could talk. Grabbing the carrot she'd brought with her, she fed him and petted him some more, before he walked back to the shade of the tree to take a rest. She spent the next hour clearing out his stall and replacing the hay, then waved goodbye to her uncle before heading back home to take a well-earned shower.

As soon as she pulled into her driveway, she could see that somebody had been in her yard. The grass was short, there were no weeds to be seen, and there were pots of fresh flowers leading up to her porch.

"What the hell?" She opened the door and looked out the back. The grass out there was freshly mowed as well. It had been hot today, way too hot to be doing yard work.

And there was only one person she knew who was foolish enough to do that in the heat of the West Virginian sun.

This time she called him, and he picked up right away.

"Grace." The sound of his warm voice sent a shiver down her spine.

"What does yard work count as?" she asked him. "The first round?"

"Sure." She could hear the smile in his voice. "Just the start of the first round, though."

"I can't wait to see the knockout."

"You'll have to. It's not happening until Friday."

That was four days away. She wasn't sure she could stand the anticipation. "That long?"

"I asked for two weeks. It's less than one."

"You kind of had me at the coffee and pastries this morning," she admitted.

Michael laughed, and it warmed her. "You don't know how good it is to hear you say that. But don't sell yourself short. You're worth the fight. And I'm enjoying doing it."

"I saw you drive out of Uncle Logan's earlier."

"Yeah, I saw you too."

"Why didn't you stop and say hello?" she asked him.

"Because you were there to see your horse, not me. And I had things to do."

"What things?"

He laughed again. "Things you'll find out about on Friday."

"Can't you tell me now?" she asked, her voice sweet. She really needed to know.

"Where's the fun in that? A few more days and all will be revealed. I promised you a knockout. I intend to give it to you."

"All this effort," she breathed. "I hope I'm worth it."

"You are, sweetheart. There's no doubt in my mind."

———

On Tuesday, the love letters started to arrive. She found the first one on her doorstep as she walked outside to head to work. Next to it was another coffee and a pastry, and she couldn't help but smile as she picked them up. She slid her finger under the flap to loosen the envelope and pulled the notepaper out, unfolding it.

Dear Grace,

I've never been good at writing letters. I'm more of an in-the-moment kind of man. A face-to-face guy. But since I'm trying to give you space I thought I'd put into words how I feel about you.

The first time we met in the rain, I thought you were the most beautiful woman I'd ever seen. Your hair was sticking to your face, your jacket was plastered to your skin, and you looked mad as hell.

And I think I knew even then that you'd change my life forever.

We argued. You took my cab. I thought I'd never see you again. But then I did, and it felt like fate.

It still does. And I've stopped trying to fight it. Instead, I'm fighting for you.

I love you.

Michael xx

She stared at his words, her breath ragged. It was only eight-thirty in the morning and she already felt emotional. Folding the note carefully, she slid it back into the envelope, grabbed her coffee and pastry, and walked to her car.

This man was going to kill her if she didn't get the knockout soon.

The next letter came by courier at lunchtime.

Dear Grace,

The second time I saw you I was lost for words. I stood at the bar trying to figure out how to get you away from your friends and talk to you. You had a smile that lit up the room, and every guy in that bar noticed.

I wanted to tell them that I had dibs. That I'd given you my cab. That it wasn't just physical attraction that drew me to you. It was more.

It still is.

I'd been on edge that day. A bad meeting, a damn rainstorm, and then I'd had to wait almost an hour to get another cab. But as soon as you walked over to me, your eyes rolling, your smile tight, that all disappeared.

And then you disappeared. I never realized a soul could ache until I couldn't find you after that night.

And when I saw you at *Chairs* and realized who you were? It felt like fate was laughing at me.

What I didn't know was that she was giving me a gift. You.

And I want it back. I want you back. I want to spend the rest of my life showing you how much you are worth fighting for.

Have a good lunch. I love you.

Michael xx

This time she cried. Not sad tears, but emotional ones. They felt cleansing as they poured down her cheeks. And yes, he'd sent her lunch again, but this time she couldn't eat it.

She was pining too much for him.

You can stop fighting. It's a knockout already. Please come see me tonight. – Grace xx

And of course he called her instead of replying. A man of words, not letters. She picked it up, breathing out a hello, her face still damp with tears.

"Friday. I'll see you Friday. We'll make it one week not two."

"Why not now?" she asked. "I need you."

He let out a soft breath. "I'll always be here when you need me. If you want me to come over, I will. I'm done making decisions for you. I know you can make them perfectly fine by yourself. Say the word and I'll be there."

She pulled her lip between her teeth. Three days. It felt like forever, but she knew it would pass quickly. And maybe part of her was enjoying this attention from him.

Even if she was aching for him to hold her all night.

"Friday," she said. "Where?"

"You'll find out. And Grace?"

"Yes?"

"Friday isn't the end. It's only the beginning."

She smiled through her tears. "I like the sound of that."

———

The next two days passed in a whirlwind of notes and gifts, and with each one, the wound in her chest closed a little more. Grace had spoken to Michael so many times, but she hadn't seen him once.

Her heart was yearning. She hoped his was, too.

By Friday afternoon, she was getting jittery. He hadn't told her where to meet him or what to wear. She was closing up her laptop, ready to go home, when her mom walked into her office with a huge smirk on her face.

"What's so funny?" Grace asked, smiling too, because somehow she'd made it to Friday without cracking and rushing to see Michael.

"Nothing." Her mom shook her head. "Just a funny video Uncle Logan sent me."

"Show me." Anything to take her mind off the fact it was Friday.

"I can't. It's…" Her mom widened her eyes, as though trying to think of a good excuse. "It's rude."

"Why is your brother sending you rude videos?"

Her mom blushed. "Okay, it's not rude. It's just personal. Anyway, stop changing the subject."

"I'm not. We didn't start on a subject." Grace wanted to laugh at her mom's expression. Whatever was on that video was obviously distracting her. And if it hadn't been Friday – knockout day – maybe she would have cared more.

"We didn't? Oh. Okay then. I just wanted to let you know I'll pick you up at seven for *Chairs*."

"I'm not going to *Chairs*." She was waiting for Michael. And the last thing she needed was for the whole town to be asking her questions.

"Of course you are. Don't forget to bring a sweater."

"It's a hundred degrees out there right now." Grace frowned. Her mom really was distracted.

"Bug spray then. Seven." Her mom lifted her hand. "I gotta go."

"What if I get a better offer?" Grace called out after her.

"You won't."

Wasn't that nice? Grace grabbed her bag and fluffed her hair, then checked her phone for a message from Michael.

But there was nothing.

There was still nothing from him at seven when her mom picked her up. She tried to hide her disappointment as she walked over to her mom's car, sliding into the passenger seat. The day was ending and he hadn't given her the knockout he'd promised.

"Dad not coming?" she asked.

"He's finishing some work." Her mom pulled out of her driveway. It was only a few minutes to get to the green field that bordered the creek the town was named after.

Despite the warm, muggy heat of the evening, there were people – and chairs – everywhere. She carried her mom's chair to where her aunts were sitting. Mia smiled softly at Grace. "I'm so glad you came."

She wanted to ask if Michael was there. But what if he wasn't? The waiting was killing her. It was Friday, dammit, where was her knockout? Maybe he was going to make her wait for two weeks after all. "Thank you," she said to Mia. "How are you?"

"Just fine, honey."

"I'll grab some lemonade," she told them, mostly because she couldn't stand around doing nothing right now. "Can I get you anything?"

They all shook their heads, then her aunt Van said something, and they all laughed. "Oh, I need to tell him she's here," Mia whispered as Grace walked away.

And she would have turned back, but she really was thirsty, and her aunts were all laughing again. It was aggravating. Trying not to stomp this time – because she wasn't a kid – she walked over to the table where the town had piled their food and drinks, and helped herself to a glass of lemonade.

She was just finishing her drink when she heard the giggles start. Then she heard hooves. What was going on?

It was only when she turned to look behind her that she realized the crowd had parted.

Michael was riding into the field on the back of a horse, his brows dipped with concentration, his knuckles clenched as he clung onto the reins. Grace recognized the horse he was on. Arabella, her uncle's gentlest mare.

Somehow, he got Arabella to stop. She tried not to laugh at the intensity of his expression. His eyes caught hers and she wasn't sure whether to laugh or cry.

"What are you doing?" she asked him, walking over to pat Arabella's mane. It was only up close that she saw how white Michael's knuckles were as they gripped the leather reins.

"Trying to woo you."

She looked up at him. Apart from the death grip, he was showing no fear. And if you liked that sort of thing he looked amazing in his jeans, black t-shirt, and boots.

And yes, she liked that sort of thing.

"Well, you're doing a terrible job of it. You look like you're about to fall off that poor horse."

Michael grinned.

"I've been throwing myself to the ground all week. I've got the bruises to prove it."

"You've been riding all week?"

"Logan's been teaching me. The knockout had to be something to remember. What better way to do it than to be a knight riding in on shining armor?"

She couldn't help but laugh. "I'm not sure you're ready for a jousting tournament yet."

He shrugged. "I'm thinking more rodeo. But whatever." He took a deep breath and held his hand out to her. "Can you climb on if I help?"

"Oh boy," she muttered. Of course, she could climb on any horse, especially one as docile as Arabella. But Michael added a little bit of danger to the mix. "Give me a second."

She didn't climb in front of him, though that would be the normal way to ride two on a horse. Instead she hoisted herself behind him, like he was on a motorcycle and she was riding shotgun, sliding her arms around his waist.

"Hello," she whispered against his back.

"Hello." There was so much warmth in his voice that it touched her heart. "You ready to head off into the sunset?"

She chuckled. "I've been ready since Monday. You had me at a coffee and pastry."

"Noted. My girl's a cheap date."

She ignored the way her heart hammered at his words and cuddled against him tightly, feeling his muscles ripple as he moved the reins and encouraged Arabella to move.

Everybody was watching them. And she couldn't give a

damn. Let them talk, let them gossip, let them stare. She was with Michael, and that was all that mattered. The breeze ruffled their hair, as they left the field behind them, heading toward the center of town. They passed the diner, the church, Arabella clip clopping into the square itself.

"Logan?" Michael called out as they rode onto the grass.

Her uncle was sitting on a bench. When he saw them, his mouth split into a grin. "You managed it without falling," he said. "Never thought I'd see the day. Everybody's gonna be sad there are no more videos to share."

"Videos?" Grace asked.

"It was one of the conditions of him teaching me to ride," Michael told her. "He got to record me and share it with his brothers."

So that's what her mom had been smirking at. She'd seen Michael learning to ride a horse.

It made her heart feel like it was bursting.

"You learned to ride for me?" she asked.

He nodded. "I wanted to be able to go riding with you. Share your hobbies. It's important to me."

"And be my knight in shining armor."

His eyes were soft. "I don't think you need one."

"I still like it."

"You want me to take this horse or what?" Logan asked. "There's a beer at home with my name on it."

The next minute wasn't pretty. Grace dismounted easily, taking the reins to steady the horse. Then Michael attempted to do the same, but his foot got caught and he kind of slid slowly to the ground, his ass landing in the grass.

From the corner of her eye she could see Logan trying not to laugh. He took the reins from her and winked at Michael.

"Be good, kids. See you later." Then he climbed onto Arabella and rode away with ease.

"So what now?" Grace asked Michael. She was still grinning. Wasn't sure she'd ever stop.

"Now we start the rest of our lives together." He cupped her face, his palms warm on her cheeks as he leaned down to kiss her softly, his lips brushing against hers. She curled her fingers around his neck, rolling onto her tiptoes, her heart hammering against her chest as he kissed her into oblivion.

He was right. She didn't need a knight in shining armor.

But she was so happy she had one anyway.

Epilogue

A FEW MONTHS LATER...

Grace couldn't believe how quickly the weeks were passing. Apart from the past week, that was. She was so ready to see Michael after being apart from him for the last five days.

He'd moved in with her almost as soon as they'd reconciled. And then when all his things arrived from London there hadn't been much space left in her little house, so they'd bought a piece of land at the edge of the farm.

Their new home was already under construction, a large ranch house that would have enough space for them and maybe a few others.

Because they'd talked long and hard and agreed they wanted children and sooner rather than later. Michael was adamant he didn't want to be drawing a social security check and sitting on the PTA at the same time.

And in the middle of it all, he and Cam had set up an advisory agency for college football players. That's where Michael had been this week – at a college in New York, working with freshmen who needed some guidance.

And now it was Labor Day, and Cam and Mia were holding a party to celebrate her being back to full health. Grace smiled at her family as she walked into their backyard. The party was already in full swing – it looked like half the town was there. Everybody wanted to celebrate with Mia.

Things were finally going the Hartson family's way.

"Auntie Grace." Delilah ran over to her, grabbing Grace's hand. "I'm doing my first solo tomorrow."

"You are?" Grace grinned. Delilah looked so much like Presley, it was scary. "Can I come watch?"

"Yes please." Delilah nodded happily. "I'm singing 'Ava Maria'." Delilah tugged her over to where Presley and Marley were standing.

"Hi." Grace hugged them both, despite only seeing them yesterday when they played another gig. This time at a concert venue. "You two were great yesterday."

Presley nodded, his face tight. "Thanks. Want a beer?"

"Sure." Grace gave him a confused smile. He looked pissed about something. He turned and walked across the yard to where the cooler was. "What's up with him?" she asked.

Marley shrugged. "We've had some interest from a record company."

"You did?" Grace grinned. "That's amazing."

"Tell that to Pres." It was Marley's turn to frown.

"Why? Isn't he happy about it?"

"He refuses to talk to them. Says he can't play professionally and be a dad." Marley shrugged. "So that's that."

Oh. Grace gave her cousin a sympathetic look. "How does the rest of the band feel about that?"

"They're pissed." Marley shrugged. "Understandably. It's a shot at the big time and he's stopping us all from taking it."

"Maybe he'll change his mind," Grace said, looking over at him. Presley was leaning down, Delilah whispering in his ear. He reached out and hugged her.

And Grace's heart melted.

"He won't." Marley shook his head.

She opened her mouth to respond, but then Sabrina joined them. "Hey!" She threw her arms around Grace. "Have you heard from Michael?"

"His plane landed an hour ago. He should be here soon," Grace told her.

"Thank God. You two can take the parental heat off me." Sabrina let out a sigh.

"Why? What have you done?"

Sabrina widened her eyes. "Um, I might have stayed out all night."

"Where were you?" Grace asked her. No wonder Mia and Cam were annoyed. Sabrina was their wild child, for sure.

"Just at a friend's. I go back to college next week and we had a farewell party. It got late. I fell asleep." Sabrina shrugged. "Mom and Dad need to chill."

"Or maybe you could message them next time?" Grace suggested.

Presley passed her a bottle of beer right as she noticed movement from the corner of her eye. And then *he* was there.

Michael Devlin. Her Irish. Looking better than ever as he glanced around the crowd.

Then his eyes caught hers and it felt like everything was okay again. She exhaled and smiled and he smiled back. Without taking his eyes off of her, he stalked toward her and her heart hammered against her ribcage.

Maybe she should have played it cool, but she had no idea how to do that when it came to him. Instead she ran toward him, straight into his arms, smiling widely as he cupped her face with his hands and kissed her like he meant it.

Like it was the only thing he wanted in life.

And right now it was all she wanted, too.

"I missed you," she breathed when they parted.

His eyes crinkled. "I missed you, too."

"Then stop going away."

He laughed. "I've got a few weeks before the next trip. And it's only for two days."

"Good." She slid her arm around his waist. "Come see your mom. She's missed you, too."

"I will." He kissed her temple. "But first I need to show you something."

"What?"

He pulled his phone from his pocket and unlocked it, then showed her the screen.

"That's a horse."

"My horse."

Her mouth dropped open. "You bought a horse?"

"Yeah. I figured it's the only way to keep up with you. Plus we have a ranch with stables, we need horses."

She looked at the picture again. "How old is she?"

"Ten. Pretty docile but she sure can run."

Grace took in the horse's tawny coloring. "She's beautiful. What's her name?"

"Hera."

She smiled. "Arcadia and Hera. I think they're going to love each other."

"Yeah." He nodded. "I think they are."

"Now let's go talk to people. Before they start talking about us."

"You still worried about that?" he asked, his brows dipping.

"Not really." She shook her head. They'd been the talk of the town for a week or two, but the gossip soon moved on. They were happy, they were settled, there wasn't much to gossip about.

She loved that a little too much.

"Michael!" Mia called out, her face beaming as she saw her oldest son. She was fully recovered and it showed. "Come over. We want a family picture. You too, Grace. We all need to be in it."

"Duty calls," Michael murmured, sliding his arm around her shoulder. "Come on, let's get this over with."

And so they did. It took five minutes to corral the whole family in, there were so many of them. Aunt Gina was at the center – the matriarch of the family. Surrounded by Grace's mom and her uncles, and their spouses. Then there were the cousins and their partners. And Delilah at the front.

Sabrina and Josh were having a heated debate about something – probably her non-arrival home last night. And Presley's face looked like a thunderstorm until Marley elbowed him and told him to smile.

"Okay then. Let's try a couple more," the photographer said.

Michael pulled her close. And she didn't have to pretend to smile. Because she couldn't be any happier than she was in that moment.

———

A few hours later it started to rain. The sudden downpour caused them all to rush to get the tables and chairs underneath the canopy. Michael watched as Grace laughed with her cousins as the torrential rain plastered her hair to her face and for a moment it was like that first time he saw her.

She was the pretty drenched girl trying to steal his cab.

He was so in love with this woman it hurt in the sweetest of ways. And he had the ring in his pocket to prove it. He'd thought long and hard about how to ask her to be his.

Thought about doing it when his horse arrived and they rode together. Because she never looked more beautiful than when she was riding fast and free.

He'd thought about doing it in bed, but she deserved more, so much more. Even if it was their happy place.

And also their dirty place.

Grace turned around and caught him looking at her. Her dress clung to her skin, revealing the curves he loved to touch. Her eyes were bright, her smile still pulling at her lips. He loved her so much.

There was no good time to ask. And no bad time.

Just time. And the time was now.

He dropped to one knee and Grace blinked, her brows crunching together for a second, as though she was worried he was hurt. He could feel the damp from the grass soaking into his pants. Then everybody stopped moving. Started staring at him.

"Grace Carter, you look beautiful in the rain," he called out.

"What are you doing?" she asked.

He pulled the box out of his pocket. He'd bought the ring last week while he was away. Asked Sabrina for advice because she was an annoying little sister but she had great taste.

"Oh this is fabulous." Sabrina clapped her hands together. "He's doing it."

"Michael?" Grace looked at him. "What's happening?"

He opened the box, the rain dampening the diamond, but taking away none of its luster. "Will you do me the absolute honor of becoming my wife?" he asked.

His mom gasped. A few others did too.

Grace put her hand on her chest, where her heart was, her eyes wide with shock. He liked that he'd surprised her. He'd been almost certain that Sabrina would give it away.

Another reason to do it sooner rather than later, if there weren't enough already.

"Are you going to answer him?" Sabrina whispered, and everybody laughed.

"Yes. Of course." Grace was breathless.

"Yes, you're going to answer him, or yes, you're going to

marry him?" Sabrina rolled her eyes. "We're getting soaked here."

"Yes, I'll marry you." Grace only had eyes for Michael. "Was there ever any doubt?"

"Thank God," Sabrina muttered. "Now, can we go inside?"

Michael stood and walked over to where Grace was standing, still shocked, taking her hand and sliding the ring onto her slender finger. People were milling around them, congratulating them, but she was still staring straight into his eyes.

"I love you," he told her.

A fat tear ran down her cheek.

"Come here." He pulled her close. She was soaked through. So was he. But then he kissed her and the rain was forgotten.

At least until a crash of thunder filled the air.

"Come on, let's go inside," he told her. And it was like he'd waved a magic wand because everybody moved. He held Grace's hand. The one with his ring on it. The one that showed everybody how much she was loved.

"You okay?" he asked.

She nodded.

"Can you say something? Because I'm getting freaked out here."

"Je t'aime," she whispered.

"Moi aussi," he told her, because it was true. He loved her so much and he needed her to know it. "Now, let's get inside and dry off before I have to argue with you over a cab."

The End

Author's Note

I'm so grateful to those who took the time to talk through their experiences of Ductal Carcinoma In Situ (DCIS) with me, including two friends and a doctor who tried to answer my questions as best they could And I had a lot of them. What's the best way of treating it, how would Mia feel going through the radiotherapy? Could she still work, be close to children? How quickly would she recover?

The answer to many of these questions was 'it depends'. But one thing that everybody I spoke to agreed on was the important of regular mammograms. DCIS is usually only detected by mammogram. It's a stage 0 cancer, which often has no external signs and symptoms. But if caught correctly and treated properly it has over a 98% five-year survival rate.

Treatment can range from the lumpectomy followed by radiotherapy that Mia underwent, to mastectomies, hormone therapy and (currently under trial) monitoring without surgery.

As always, the experts provided me with the information I needed, and any mistakes are my own. In one case (the length of her radiation course of therapy) I extended it by one more week to fit the timeline of the book.

For more information and support regarding DCIS you can visit the following websites:

UK: https://www.cancerresearchuk.org/about-cancer/breast-cancer/types/ductal-carcinoma-in-situ-dcis

US: https://www.cancer.org/cancer/types/breast-cancer/about/types-of-breast-cancer/dcis.html

And please, if you're eligible for one, make sure you get regular mammogram checks!

With love, Carrie x

Dear Reader

Thank you so much for reading THAT ONE REGRET. If you enjoyed it and you get a chance, I'd be so grateful if you can leave a review. And don't forget to check out my free bonus epilogue which you can download by putting this address into your web browser: https://BookHip.com/ZCKTLZG

The next book in the series is Presley's story - find out what happens when he falls for Cassie in THAT ONE TOUCH

WANT TO KEEP UP TO DATE ON ALL MY NEWS?

Join me on my exclusive mailing list, where you'll be the first to hear about new releases, sales, and other book-related news.

To sign up just put the following address into your phone browser:
https://www.subscribepage.com/carrieelksas

I can't wait to share more stories with you.

Yours,

Carrie xx

Also by Carrie Elks

THE HEARTBREAK BROTHERS NEXT GENERATION SERIES

That One Regret

That One Touch (Releases 2024)

THE HEARTBREAK BROTHERS SERIES

A gorgeous small town series about four brothers and the women
who capture their hearts.

Take Me Home

Still The One

A Better Man

Somebody Like You

When We Touch

THE SALINGER BROTHERS SERIES

A swoony romantic comedy series featuring six brothers and the
strong and smart women who tame them.

Strictly Business

Strictly Pleasure

Strictly For Now

Strictly Not Yours (available for pre-order)

THE WINTERVILLE SERIES

A gorgeously wintery small town romance series, featuring six
cousins who fight to save the town their grandmother built.

Welcome to Winterville

Hearts In Winter

Leave Me Breathless

Memories Of Mistletoe

Every Shade Of Winter

Mine For The Winter (available for pre-order)

ANGEL SANDS SERIES

A heartwarming small town beach series, full of best friends, hot guys and happily-ever-afters.

Let Me Burn

She's Like the Wind

Sweet Little Lies

Just A Kiss

Baby I'm Yours

Pieces Of Us

Chasing The Sun

Heart And Soul

Lost In Him

THE SHAKESPEARE SISTERS SERIES

An epic series about four strong yet vulnerable sisters, and the alpha men who steal their hearts.

Summer's Lease

A Winter's Tale

Absent in the Spring

By Virtue Fall

THE LOVE IN LONDON SERIES

Three books about strong and sassy women finding love in the big city.

Coming Down

Broken Chords

Canada Square

STANDALONE

Fix You

An epic romance that spans the decades. Breathtaking and angsty and all the things in between.

If you'd like to get an email when I release a new book, please sign up here:

CARRIE ELKS' NEWSLETTER

About the Author

Carrie Elks writes contemporary romance with a sizzling edge. Her first book, *Fix You*, has been translated into eight languages and made a surprise appearance on *Big Brother* in Brazil. Luckily for her, it wasn't voted out.

Carrie lives with her husband, two lovely children and a larger-than-life black pug called Plato. When she isn't writing or reading, she can be found baking, drinking an occasional (!) glass of wine, or chatting on social media.

You can find Carrie in all these places
www.carrieelks.com
Carrie@carrielks.com